THE DOGS OF CHERNOBYL

ANIMAL EYES, #1

JUSTIN MORGAN

Although inspired by real events, this book is a work of fiction. Any resemblance to actual events, places or persons, living or dead, is entirely coincidental.

Dog Illustration by Viktorija Čeliković

ISBN (paperback): 978-1-7399570-0-1
ISBN (digital): 978-1-7399570-1-8

Published by Paws On Publishing

For Lots,
who's never had a pup of her own.

THE DOGS OF CHERNOBYL

1. Hurt Dogs	1
2. The Assembly	12
3. Sunrise at Midnight	22
4. The Shimmer	33
5. The Sickness Creeps	43
6. The Dog Face Men	53
7. Ghost Town	63
8. Fairytale	75
9. Ball Boy and Red Cross Girl	85
10. Bloodshed at Creche	96
11. The Dragon of Chernobyl	106
12. House of Beds	117
13. False Peaks	127
14. Enemies Old and New	138
15. Collecting the Canaries	148
16. Breath of the Beast	158
17. Zone of Alienation	168
18. Forest of Death	179
19. Miners' Best Friend	189
20. Into the Lair	201
21. Leap of Faith	212
22. Call of a Leader	225
23. Hurt People	234
Historical Note	239
Acknowledgments	243
About the Author	245
The ANIMAL EYES Anthology Series	247

1

HURT DOGS

Soviet Ukraine
April, 1986

Now wasn't the time for pain.

On the crest of a riverbank, a lone stray stood calculating his next move. His wounded flank heaved in and out, but his pursuers would appear from the pines any moment, and if they caught him, he was dead. Hurting would just have to wait.

Opting for the mudflats, he took a single step down the bank before changing his mind. The murky water waiting below was a barrier. As soon as he grew hungry enough, he'd be driven up again, into their fangs.

The stray threw a glance back at the western horizon, where tall tubes, like strange limbless trees, were towering from the roofs of Plant. How very unappealing that vast site was. The smoke it belched gave it the impression of an enormous sleeping creature, and it thronged with industry at all hours – yet it seemed now to be his best option. Human folk wouldn't stand for a scrap on their turf, after all.

Turning back on himself, he dashed toward the forest, his paws a blur of white and his bright coat aquiver as spring air rushed across his torso. A dog with fewer smarts would have paid for a mistake like that, but not Ony. His enemies had nothing on him.

Enemies. It jarred as it went through his mind. How had relations with this pack become so very strained? Until today, those boys were little more than troublesome acquaintances. But when Han and Starla cornered him behind the vegetable stands this morning, it was clear a new phase of animosity was about to begin.

'Meet us by the river later, bony Ony,' Starla had growled, pleased with his rhyme. 'We want to discuss your behaviour.' But when the time came, all they offered was abuse, which wasn't the same as chat. Acquaintances didn't hurl threats and insults. Foes did.

As he rushed into the maze of pines, Ony went over their riverside meeting in his mind. It was Han who'd set the tone. 'Ever since you gave the butcher that nip, he's been lashing out at the rest of us. And we don't appreciate it.' The half-dozen other ruffians snarled in agreement, emboldening Han. 'Do you hear us, Ony-all-alone-y? You're to keep your mangy muzzle away from the butcher's shop.'

Ony considered the instruction carefully. 'Who's telling me? You, or your alpha?'

Feliks, the biggest of the six, stepped forward with a scowl. 'We're telling you, Ony. My father's not concerned with a little cur dog like you.'

'Why do you keep trying to attack the old man, anyway?' asked Han. 'That business happened ages ago.' But the answer was so obvious Ony gave no reply.

Glancing at his pack mates, Starla let a smirk spread across his face. 'It's not like the butcher forced your mother to eat that meat. If she hadn't been so stupid in the first place, she'd still be alive.'

And for saying that, Ony ended the meeting early by taking Starla's life.

The sole pup of Levka's first litter, Ony emerged into a moonlit world the summer before last. His fur was the same hue of orange as his father's, but unlike Pyotr, a strip of white ran from his chest down under his belly. The doting mothers of Creche likened him to a fox, and as a nimble wit began to develop it was a comparison made ever more frequently.

The summer litters lived together in the fields bordering the factories in the south. Throughout the hot first months of his life, Ony seldom left Levka's side, staying close by even after he'd weaned. Few pups looked as adoringly at their mothers as Ony did Levka. His friends teased him for it, and sweet Belka – with whom, even then, he shared a special bond – expected every playtime to finish the instant his beloved mother called.

But Levka knew that such dependence would do her son more harm than good. So, when summer neared its end and the air grew fresh and sweet with apples, she sent him off to the orchards to get his first glimpse of people.

Much encouragement was needed to coax the pups out of Creche's sheds. Yet once they ventured into the fun-filled fields of the open countryside – how exciting it was to find a stream running along a paddock's edge! – they quickly overcame their fear of the strange flat-faced creatures who walked on their hind legs, and carried on into the neighbouring groves.

Ony and Belka, however, wanted to feel the water, so, with tumbles and tussles, they headed upstream, where they soon found themselves in the shaded underside of a rotten trunk. Growing from it was an odd round object, creamy white and smooth as a newborn; they perceived in the earthy scent of this strange orb that it was something edible. While Ony went to it, Belka stayed back, repelled by its alien nature.

Tentatively, Ony gave the curious thing a nudge – and the moment his muzzle made contact, a puff of dust exploded into the sky, sending a fine mist of barely visible particles raining down. Belka scampered away with a yelp of shock, but Ony, whose twig of a tail swished back and forth, wasted no time gulping mouthfuls of the orb. 'Mushroom,' he announced.

Act first, think later: that was Ony.

The pups returned to Creche in time to find Levka heading off to scavenge. Ordinarily, Ony stayed in the sheds at such a time, but enraptured now by his first taste of the outside world, he hungered for more adventure, and joined his mother on the journey north to town.

Everything that moved was a distraction to him, but Levka was patient with Ony, and they eventually came to a row of shops. In the middle of the alley that ran along the back, a door stood open, from which a strong, meaty odour wafted out. The scent drew Ony closer, but Levka held the curious pup back. 'Never go through a door unless you have to,' she warned. 'People aren't the same inside as they are out here in our world.'

But the odour had bewitched him. This was flesh of a kind he'd not yet encountered: raw and fresh. While Levka pawed through an open rubbish can, Ony stood at the very threshold of the door, desperate.

A voice boomed out into the alley. 'Aww! Does puppy want a treat?'

Ony sprang forwards, unleashing a sharp command from Levka to return to her side. Then a giant man, stained with blood, emerged in front of them. In his hand was a handful of chopped meat. 'Here you go, puppy,' he said with a smile, then placed the food on the dusty ground and vanished back indoors.

Again, Ony leapt ahead, and again, Levka caught him. 'Me first,' she huffed. She went to the food; her nostrils twitched with concentration. Then, while Ony whined, a clump of the stuff vanished into her mouth. But still she kept her son back.

The grinning face of the butcher appeared around the open door. 'That nice, pretty girl? Let baby have some now.'

Levka brought her head up from the pile of meat. Keeping her gaze on the man, she backed slowly away. 'Come,' she said, and, with Ony groaning disappointedly as he followed, she sped off into the street.

By the time Ony caught up, Levka was on her side on the pavement. Breath came fast from her panting jaws. Her eyes seemed to see nothing.

Ony began crying, but she offered him no comfort.

From Levka's mouth, froth bubbled. Her breathing began to rattle. 'Ony,' she said, 'you've got to do whatever it takes to protect your children.'

'Mama,' said Ony, shimmying back beneath a parked vehicle. 'What's happening?'

But she was already gone.

Ony's paws barely touched the pinefall as he raced from the chasing pack, yet still – somehow – they were on him. He should have shaken these boys way back. They weren't fast dogs, and the density of this section of forest ought to have kept him well hidden.

With the airstream intensifying the heat of his wound, a sudden connection occurred to him. It was his blood: the open cut was making a trail!

Ony skidded to a halt on the slope of a valley and cocked his ears, which twitched as he took in the sounds of the environment. Whorls of pine limbs were shivering delicately on the trees, and at the valley's foot a brook was gurgling, but there was no sign his assailants were approaching, yet.

Finding the stream's low banks sticky with mud, Ony dropped his front and began to push his ribs along the wet soil, and when he was sure the slash in his side was stuck well enough, he hopped back up onto the gentle slope. But just as his paws landed on the carpet of pine needles, Han and Feliks appeared at the top of the dell.

'Here he is!' yipped Han, as the other dogs came abreast to make five against one.

Ony turned and leapt over the brook.

'Look at him, skulking off with his tail between his legs,' yowled Feliks. 'You'll pay for what you did to Starla!'

'Your alpha will decide that,' said Ony.

'You'll pay!' barked Feliks, and the pack advanced. 'And Belka, too. I expect you'll be fancying a litter soon? Well, you'll see what kind of welcome they'll get in our town!'

Ony sprinted off, pursued by the others. But his swiftness was unmatched, and with his wound now held shut by the mud, they'd struggle to stay on him this time.

When the woods eventually thinned and he came out onto a glade, Ony saw, beyond the rail tracks, an area familiar to him. An old lady in the dwellings around the corner from here shared treats, but his priority was to remain invisible; it wouldn't do to be spotted by other free-ranging strays who roamed these parts. So, cantering over to an upturned barrow beside a mound of manure, Ony curled up beneath it to rest, thankful that the earth wasn't frozen, as it had been just half a moon ago.

As the day wore on, Ony grew more confident he'd given the boys the slip. A smile spread across his lips: he may have been smaller, and there wasn't a lot of meat on his bones, but he could outthink the best of his rivals. Still, caution was essential. Feliks and the others would be back at Hospital soon, whose fields their leader roamed, and once news of Starla's death was conveyed, scouts would be dispatched. Though Ony longed to be back by Belka's side, he could wait. It wasn't worth the risk of leading an outraged pack straight to her den.

By the time the sparrows began to convene in the treetops to chatter about their day, Ony was certain he was safe. Creeping out from under the barrow, he made his way to the centre of town, until the human dwellings began to block out the sky. It was a mystery to him why they preferred to live in such confined places. Like Belka always said, though, it was a waste of a dog's time to question the wisdom of peoplekind.

One after the other, the drab buildings stretched on until Ony eventually reached the sharer's door. To his relief, he found her at home; from inside, a song came drifting. Another of their mysteries, their songs. It seemed to be something they did when they were happy. Or sad.

From the day without a yesterday, went the voice,
To the day with no tomorrow.
The Party stands beside me
In my joy and in my sorrow.
Though our enemies may seek to end
Our gallant, glorious ways.
The Party will protect each friend
Who labours through the days.

The old lady, as always, was alone, and was busying herself folding garments over a line. The scent had been completely removed from the fabric. What compelled people to want to mask their true character this way? Odour mattered so much to a canine, but evidently very little to them. They even tried to mask the natural scent of their pets, too – though why those spoilt dogs allowed their masters to do it was beyond the limits of Ony's understanding.

Entering the dwelling was unthinkable, so he gave a polite bark to bring the old lady peering around the open door. 'My Golden Boy! Haven't see you in a while.' She stooped to stroke him, prompting an unthreatening growl. 'Yes, yes. I know you don't like a fuss. You like a treat though, don't you?'

Ony loudly smacked his chops. He knew very few words of the human tongue, but "treat" usually signalled something good; sure enough, the old lady then brought out pickled vegetables and set them down on the tiles.

He looked at the food, then at her.

'Still don't trust me?' she said, and made a show of popping a morsel into her mouth. At that, Ony devoured her offering.

From the threshold, he scanned inside her dwelling to see a bag on wheels and a stack of small cases, but little else. Usually, people liked soft things around them – natural surfaces didn't seem to satisfy them – but nothing to sit or sleep on was evident here. It didn't really appear lived-in at all, at least not in the way families usual lived, amid their chaos and their clutter.

The old lady resumed her song. Was this one born of gladness or woe? Ony couldn't possibly know. It was soothing, though. Laying by the empty plate, his eyes began to grow heavy, but just then a young woman appeared from out of the next house, with a child in her arms.

'Oh, it's you! I thought perhaps your son was moving back in. How's he getting on in the capital, anyway? Has he settled into his new role in the Party yet?'

'I wouldn't know, dear,' said the old lady, pulling shut the door. 'You know these Party types. More important things to think about than the likes of their mothers.'

The neighbour smiled shyly and nodded. 'Heading off to Chernobyl?'

'Yes, yes. Few shifts in the canteen keeps things ticking along.'

'You should be enjoying your retirement, Mrs Ogilvy.'

'On the measly pension they pay me?' she said, shuffling away towards the roadside shelter. 'I wish.' She turned and gave Ony a wave. 'See you soon, Golden Boy.'

Ony pushed out his behind and stretched his forepaws. He ought to have felt rested, but the dark threat Feliks had issued in the woods earlier still troubled his mind. This wretched pack meant to hurt Belka and him.

With Sun nearing the horizon, the shadow before him was long. Pyotr, Ony's quick-tempered father, was going to demand an account of today's brawl, but that would have to wait until morning. Right now, the only thing that mattered was alerting Belka.

He sprinted until the sparkling river came into view, his side burning with the sting of claw marks. As soon as Feliks had realised Starla was in trouble earlier, he'd struck out at Ony's rear: a decent blow, in fairness to him. But by then the damage was already done. If Feliks had really wanted to save his pack mate, he should have joined the scrap sooner.

Still, that wasn't Ony's problem. The elimination of a rival was to be celebrated. Hopefully a litter would soon be growing inside Belka's belly, and this way the world they came into would be that little bit safer. Pyotr was going to be angry, of course, but Ony felt it was worth it. A reputation for ferociousness could only help a free-ranger like him.

Waiting at the roadside for a vehicle to pass by, he became aware of a shuffling in the shrubs behind him. A faint canine scent caught his nostrils. This was odd: Belka's meadow, hidden behind the hedges on the other side of the road, wasn't well-known. Other dogs simply didn't come around these parts.

Ony's hackles rose. An attack was coming. He took a cautious step out into the road – and the moment he did, an explosion of rustling sounded from the bushes.

Feliks, hurtling towards Ony at top speed, sprang off the curb, his fangs unsheathed from his lips. As the bigger dog sailed through the sky, he held his muscular forelegs out in front of him, intending to take Ony down.

With a swift side-step, Ony was able to evade the pounce, and Feliks was sent skidding on his claws. Capitalising on the stumble – it was the last thing any rival should do against him – Ony darted in to clamp Feliks's throat between his jaws, and he shook him violently from side to side.

A metallic taste settled on Ony's tongue, followed by a hot liquid pouring into his mouth. But not once did he release the pressure upon the gristly, lumpy tube between his teeth.

Feliks's growling became a whimper, then his whimper became a wheeze. And after that, he made no noise at all.

With blood and flesh dripping from his jaws, Ony stepped back to survey the gory scene. His heart thudded against his breast. Another moment, and Feliks would have got to Belka before he could stop him.

Panting heavily, he was focusing on steadying his breaths when he became aware that he'd been cast into shadow. He peered around to see Pyotr standing above him, and dropped at once to the ground beneath his father's wide frame.

Pyotr's face seethed with fury. Teeth bared, his eyes betrayed a savage intent. 'Get up!'

Ony leapt to his paws. 'Father, he tried to—'

'What have you done, Ony? This was Sergei's only son!'

'I'm sorry, father.' The intense energy that had coursed through him was beginning to wear off, the horrors of the day now hinting at their true weight.

'You've made an enemy of the most vicious pack leader in this town,' said Pyotr, dragging the eviscerated carcass over to the grass. 'Now I have no choice. All the packs – and the free-rangers like you – will meet tonight on neutral turf.'

Ony whimpered to think of the outcome of that assembly, but Pyotr paid him no mind. 'This territory battle has gone too far. Do you have any idea what your actions will cost me?'

But Ony couldn't possibly know the answer to that.

From across the road, a faint whining alerted him to the presence of another canine. Belka had seen the exchange, and her expression cut into Ony's heart so deeply that he heard nothing of what Pyotr said next.

The look on Belka's face was of a kind he'd never before seen. From where Ony stood, his beloved mate appeared frightened of him.

2

THE ASSEMBLY

BEFORE HER DAY was so tragically spoilt, Belka had been in the city, keeping an eye on the pups of a dam who'd gone off scavenging.

The small litter was sheltering from the noon glare beneath a parked vehicle. Having come into the world after the frosts, these pups took for granted that Sun's rays brought warmth now as well as light, but to Belka the feeling of its radiance seeping into her auburn coat was a joy like no other, and she was unwilling to miss a moment of it.

Her very spirit seemed to be thawing. Memories of winter's silver dust, of days devoid of shadows, would soon grow dim, and twilight's golden skies would be alive again with dandelion down and poplar dander. Cheered by the thought that life was about to get that bit easier, she stretched out her forepaws, exposed her belly to the blue canopy and smiled. Soon, she would be filled with pups of her own.

On her back on the hard ground, Belka surveyed the faces of the passing city folk. They seemed to be out in greater numbers today; many of them were heading off on the long, juddering vehicles in the direction of Plant. She wondered if people, too, preferred summer to winter, and whether, in their busyness, they even noticed the change at all.

'Have you seen him yet?' said her friend Lyuba, awaking beside her with a yawn.

'Not yet,' said Belka, stiffening to see one of the pups emerging from out of the vehicle's shade and into the busy street.

'What do you think they wanted with him, anyway?'

'Just a talk.'

Lyuba gave her friend's muzzle a quick lick. 'Ony's not capable of just *talking*.'

Belka sighed. 'I know your mind's already made up. But you don't know him the way I do.'

'I know Len.'

'That's different.'

Standing swiftly, Belka went to the kerb. With a gentle hold, she took the roaming pup by the scruff of the neck and placed him back beside his sleeping siblings.

Lyuba wasn't done, though. 'Len changed the moment that man killed his brother.'

'But Len always had an aggressive streak. That's why you fell for him.'

'It did something to him, Belka, seeing his brother die like that. He couldn't control himself anymore. And that was just a brother. Levka was Ony's *mother*.'

'Ony is no devil dog!' scowled Belka. 'He's hurting, that's all. You know, these scars of his would heal a lot faster if he hadn't been shunned.'

Lyuba let out a grunt. 'Ony could have roamed with any one of the packs, but he chose not to. He shunned himself.'

Belka stood and stretched. Satisfied that the curious pup was in no danger, she made to step down from the steps in search of a snack when she noticed Laika approaching.

'Have you heard?' said Laika, excitedly licking Belka's face.

Belka stared blankly at her friend.

A wide grin spread across Laika's mouth; she always did like sharing bad news. 'Ony *killed* Starla!'

Lyuba shifted on her paws, and although she said nothing, Belka thought she heard her friend say: 'I told you so.'

Shattered by the news, Belka, keen now to be alone, sprinted off at once.

~

Halfway to the river, Belka stopped to rest in the playing fields, where some children were chasing a ball. Faint hunger stirred in her belly – she hadn't eaten since last night – but for now Sun's special kind of nourishment was enough. She curled up at the edge of the yard, and with the worries of the present weighing so heavily, she let her mind relive the summer past.

Her lips curled into a smile as she remembered playing with Lyuba and Laika, tugging a piece of rope and leaping for damselflies, coaxing the littler pups into the spring waters with playful nips. In spite of the awful poisoning of Levka, they'd all found fun in everything then; Belka especially loved to cavort in the long stream that snaked through the pines.

She remembered skipping deeper into the woods where the moss was softest. But something's wrong. The group's starting to separate much too hastily. The tiny ones are wandering away in different directions – Belka gives a yip for them to stay together but she can't herd them, and now Lyuba and Laika are out of her nose's range and some of the pups have got into the stream and it's suddenly dark and some wolf dogs have appeared.

With a loud smack, the children's ball fell out of the air, pulling Belka out from what had become a nightmare. Knowing she couldn't hide from the present – not even in her dreams – she began to softly whine. What could have gone so very wrong at Ony's meeting that Starla should have lost his life?

One of the pack dogs must have struck out first. Ony was impulsive, but he wasn't stupid, and he'd have known he was outnumbered. Whatever it was that had provoked a violent reaction, though, Ony wasn't the type of animal to back down once the first blow had landed.

Belka yawned and scratched her side. He'd be along soon enough with his own account of it. Hopefully, if the elders were fair, as she knew them to be, he'd get off with a warning.

Passing by the buildings of Hospital, Belka made her way east to the river and was glad to get back to the meadow and its large oak tree. Its protruding roots, gnarled like the fingers of the old people who fed her scraps and ruffled her neck and told her she was a good girl, would offer an ideal den for the pups she and Ony would soon make.

The fisherman was still absent from the water's edge. She'd missed the sound of his voice this morning. A person chatting away to themselves was comforting, and it seemed to Belka that the feeling was mutual; the hearts that beat inside people often quietened when a dog was around.

The man in the neighbouring meadow was there, though. His business was more mysterious. Wearing a shapeless suit and a strange net around his head, he hung around the little huts at the edge of the field, taking – or giving, she wasn't sure – something from the bees. But they didn't seem to mind him. In fact, they seemed to be friends. He spoke to the insects as a man would a dog and it may have been the case that the bees spoke back but Belka, who'd learnt the hard way about their barbed bottoms, wasn't prepared to get close enough to find out.

Just as she settled into the oak's roots, the fur along her spine bristled. A wailing coming from the road signalled a dog in agony. She sped through the hedgerow at the meadow's top, to be greeted with a scene that wrenched the air from her lungs.

Pyotr, one of the fiercest of all the city's pack leaders, was standing above Ony, whose muzzle was glistening with the lifesource of another creature. Beside them was the spent body of Feliks, his head contorted beneath a torn neck. Although Pyotr's eyes flamed with rage, he was allowing Ony to stand.

Unable to hear the exchange that took place – blood rushed through her ears as her heart raced – Belka watched as Pyotr dragged away the body and sped off, leaving Ony amid pools of Feliks's blood. As she locked eyes with her brooding mate, more questions than she could possibly process flicked through her mind.

She called out. 'Ony!'

But Ony simply stared, too shocked by it all to respond.

'Foolish dog!' said Belka. She gave him a nudge with her snout, and made her first strides across the road back to the riverside meadow. 'Come with me.'

Ony complied, and the pair stood side by side on the riverbank, watching the torrent as it headed south to some faraway place. Sun hung low on the horizon, mirrored in the west by ghostly Moon, which was beginning to solidify in the first gloaming of dusk.

Belka blew out a huff of air from her nostrils. 'Starla *and* Feliks! It doesn't matter if it was an accident, Ony. Two killings in a single day won't go unpunished.' She began to whine. 'At least there's no pups in me yet.'

Ony brought up a hind paw to scratch behind his ear. 'What do you mean?'

'Even if the pack leaders rule to spare your life, everything's going to change for us now.'

But Ony returned no reply. Vacantly, he coiled his body around to face the other direction, then ran.

Belka stood at the river until the skies bruised to darkness, then went back to the tree and drifted off into a dreamless sleep, where she was likely to have remained curled up in a tight coil until morning.

A distant howling deep in the night, however, roused her from her slumber. It wasn't uncommon to hear dogs calling out into the open air, but this particular holler was mysterious. The alphas howled when they wanted to form a pack – an event that had grown in frequency with these blasted turf disputes – and they sometimes used their howls to let other dogs know if allies were nearby. Yet the type she was hearing now, here at the dawn of her third summer, was new, and stoked within her an unusual kind of unease.

Belka ran across the meadow and onto the roads to see two dogs heading towards the calls. 'What's happening?' she yapped.

'Pyotr is assembling the packs on neutral turf. Some devil dog has been killing others.'

'They're saying it's Pyotr's own son,' his friend added.

The pair sprinted off, but Belka stayed right where she was. What point was there attending such an assembly? The fate the elders decided for Ony wouldn't be reversed because of her protests.

But the howling was irresistible.

It was sounding now in every direction, a mass canine chorus she knew herself to be a part of. Against her will, she found herself gravitating towards the source.

It seemed to be coming from Plant.

The expansive site was still quite a distance off when the call of the dogs abated, and as the howling ceased, so did the anxiety of instinct, allowing her to think clearly again.

No. She would *not* be a part of their assembly. It was likely that tonight was Ony's last on earth, and she would not bear witness to her mate's destruction.

~

Pack by pack, the dogs had begun to assemble in the softly lit grasslands beyond the perimeter of Plant. A high volume of people shuffled around the main site, which was unusual for this time of night, but the serious business that concerned them would be undisturbed by the outcome of the meeting – whatever that stood to be.

The animals lay around in a state of alertness. News of Feliks's death had travelled fast, and all present anxiously awaited Pyotr's response. Sergei still hadn't arrived, though, prompting much speculation: would the bereaved father even *consider* a truce should Pyotr request one?

Ony was scrapping with the arriving strays. Foolish mutts, all. His rivalry with Sergei's empty-headed brutes should be of no concern to the rest of them, but the extent of their ill-feeling toward him was becoming clear. Their eyes seared with violence.

With their number growing, Ony soon realised he could be easily overpowered, so skulked over to the edge of the grasslands and lay down alone, sniffing in each direction for traces of Belka. She'd kept away, and who could blame her? It wasn't reasonable to expect her to watch as he was savaged to death.

Of course, with the street lights faltering, there was always the chance she'd slipped in without his noticing. Blindingly bright one instant, dim the next, these electric lamps seemed to have a mind of their own tonight. Indeed, just as Sergei finally arrived, the bulbs failed completely. No dog needed light to know the huge hound had come, however. His furious energy was unmistakable.

As Sergei made his way to the centre of the grasslands, the atmosphere bristled. A slow ballet of sniffing commenced between the pack leaders. Ears remained fronted. Tails swished. Hackles were pointedly lowered. Sergei, with more reason than any to want a fight, signalled with his body that he hadn't come to cause mayhem, which caused the audience to settle: many that had wanted to greet each other, but were unsure if they should, imitated the elders' behaviour and after a few tense moments, all dogs lay.

Pyotr began his address. 'Fellow dogs. By now, you'll know the circumstances that have brought us together. I'll always regret that I let tragedy strike before calling this overdue assembly. But better late than not at all.' He turned to the other alphas beside him. 'Maks, Bimka, Danil, Dima – to you, I offer thanks. I know how much you care about the welfare of this city's dogs, which is why each of you will feel – as I do – that you've failed. But being here tonight communicates a message: we won't allow things to go on as they are. Together, we must work to set things right.'

The street lights flashed on again with fierce intensity, revealing to Pyotr the full scale of the gathering.

'Look around you. Have you ever seen so many dogs gathered together? Bimka here is the oldest among us, but I doubt if even he has witnessed an assembly like this. We should celebrate our numbers. Many of us can remember lean times, but these days things are so much better for us all. The human folk show more fondness now, ever since sweet Levka was so cruelly killed by one of them.'

Ony, set back from the other attendees, felt his heart tighten at the sound of his mother's name.

'Even though the work of the people is a mystery to us,' continued Pyotr, 'it's easy to see they're prospering here, and this is good for us. But like all things, there has to be balance.'

Many of the dogs studied the reactions of the elders while Pyotr spoke. Nothing could be read in their faces though, as yet.

Pytor dipped his head. His energy shifted; he was coming to the point. 'Such high numbers are forcing a territory war on us.'

Dima stood, his face twitching with barely-concealed hostility. 'It's only a war of territory when certain dogs fail to respect the preferred spaces of others. When rogue males – barely pups in our memories – think they can go wherever they please and start trouble with whomever they wish.'

'No dog here would disagree with you, Dima,' said Pytor. 'But look at it this way: in the past I could walk from Stadium to Dock without attracting trouble. If I do that now, I'll be savaged. Put simply, there are too many of us here. So, for that reason, I'm proposing that some of us move out from this small city.'

Grumbling rose into the night sky before Sergei, finally, spoke. 'And push out into the wolf wilds? Let me ask some of my boys if they'll be volunteering for that honour.' He turned towards two of the larger dogs. 'Han, Gleb – are you prepared to steal from out of the mouths of wolves?'

An explosion of barking from the brothers confirmed they would not. Many dogs joined in with their protest to create a chorus of howling.

Sergei's contribution sent a ripple of tension around the watching packs. With all eyes upon him, he rose from the grass. But the moment he did, the surrounding lights blinked off, and the gathering was once again plunged into a darkness which, save only for the pale glow of Moon, was total.

A din of anxious growls rose, then, when the lights came on again, hushed.

Sergei's voice was strained with emotion. 'There hasn't been a day since Sun first shone when a father didn't lose a child. Today was my turn, and it's an experience that has ripped out my heart.' He looked around the fields until his eyes settled on a far corner. 'Ony!' he called out.

While Ony made his way to the centre of the field through a corridor of snarling dogs, Sergei continued.

'What happened today was nothing to do with some turf dispute. The only war of territory that exists here is the one in this youngster's head. We strays have never found it difficult to share before. We're the same kind, after all.'

Ony surveyed the naked rage on the faces of the audience.

'The deaths of Starla and Feliks occurred because we have a devil dog in our midst, one who threatens the stability of our entire society. Ony will no doubt believe what he did today was right, but he will not be given the opportunity to explain himself. It's already late enough, so I will say only this. And I say it to you, Pyotr. We all appreciate what you've done in calling this assembly. But if your son is sighted in these parts after Sun rises, it will be the day when you, old friend, taste the grief of losing a child.'

Upon these words, Han and Gleb came forward with teeth unsheathed.

'Not now!' barked Sergei. 'I wish never to sniff this crazed loner again, but I will spare him his life. Ony, your participation in the rest of our meeting is not required. You're free to live out your days beyond the edge of our city – but go now, or I'll hold these dogs back no longer.'

Ony cried as Pyotr stepped forward to clean his muzzle of the blood of two slain dogs. Then his father's ears suddenly flicked upright, and he pulled away with a growl. 'Go,' he snarled.

Sergei turned to Han and Gleb. 'Ony is banished from this town. He's heard my command. Now, see that he obeys it.'

3

SUNRISE AT MIDNIGHT

ON A HIGH VERGE that ran along the rail tracks, Belka settled onto her underside and fixed her stare ahead.

Plant, towering on the horizon, was skylined by Moon's bright glow. She gave a nod of her head. Pyotr had chosen the grassland around that vast site because it was neutral. But the wise old alpha knew, too, that fewer people would be disturbed by the dogs in the event their assembly exploded into violence.

That hadn't happened though, yet. In fact, it had been quiet now a while. The act had been done already, perhaps. Her heart ached at the thought of a lifeless Ony.

The streetlights, which had been blinking all night, suddenly flickered off, and the silent dark persuaded Belka that now was the right time to head back to her tree. But just as she was about to get up, the skittish rapping of claws against hard ground caught her ears. Something was approaching, and it was moving fast.

From the other side of the tracks, Ony came speeding along the road, followed, at some distance, by a pair she strained to identify as Han and Gleb.

Belka gave a bark. The brothers from Sergei's pack flashed her a glance but continued with their chase, and were quickly gone from sight.

Her mind raced as she tried to interpret what she'd seen. Was it that the elders issued the command to kill Ony, and he'd fled for his life? It couldn't be. Ony was as fast a dog as any, but with the assembly taking place in grasslands he'd be surrounded on all sides. If the will of the alphas was that Ony should die, his heart would be troubled now by no thumping.

She rose to her feet with a vigorous wagging of her tail: the pack leaders had spared his life! They'd shown mercy, and merely banished him from the city boundaries, sending Han and Gleb after him to ensure he did as they instructed. The chase was in a northerly direction: they were driving him out into the wilds beyond Stadium.

A sense of relief overwhelmed Belka. The very moment that impulsive mate of hers had killed Feliks, a big change was assured. But at least this way – if she was able to find him beyond the city – they could be together to raise the family they so craved.

In front of Stadium's main entrance, the chase came to a halt.

Flashing in and out of darkness as the street lamps strobed, three dogs stood in a triangle. While the flanks of Han and Gleb heaved in and out, Ony appeared unwearied, fresh as though risen from a nap.

'What happened to you, Ony?' said Gleb, panting. 'Why did you go so bad?'

Ony, scanning the environs, offered no reply.

'I think,' said Han, 'that he's got something to prove. I guess he made things tough for himself, taking off so young. You had to go vicious to survive, didn't you?' A smile opened up Han's exhausted face. 'Remember last summer when he took that chicken, Gleb?'

All three dogs let out a snort of amusement. 'I didn't

even think your little legs would get you up onto that man's table.'

'That clucker was bigger than you. And it was iced,' added Gleb. 'He nearly broke his neck dragging it out, didn't he, Han?'

'But you didn't even hesitate, Ony. Even as a pup you were tough. Feliks and Starla underestimated you today.'

Ony looked from Han to Gleb, then around to Stadium. 'Boys, there's nothing but wilderness that way. I'll be wolf food.'

Han, bemused, tilted his head. 'That's the point, Ony. You heard what Sergei said.' He bared his teeth and began to growl, but before he could pounce the southern horizon suddenly lit up.

This flash, however, wasn't caused by streetlights: it was doubtful if all the world's electric lamps combined could have matched the brightness of whatever had caused this.

A moment later, an even bigger flash exploded the entire sky, and then, just a few nervous heartbeats after that, came the sound.

Glass exploded in every direction as a shockwave coursed across the land. The loudest noise any of them had ever heard, it pushed the dogs sideways as it thundered into them.

'What was that?' whimpered the brothers. In the south, a line of pretty blue light was shining so brightly even Moon was dimmed by it.

'Ony!' cried Gleb. 'What was that?'

But the young troublemaker had already bolted off into the wilds on the far side of Stadium.

Belka was overcome by a need to show gratitude to Pyotr and Sergei. They were good leaders – merciful and wise. If she left now, she'd catch them, perhaps.

Springing from off the verge, she was at the crest of a bounding leap when the sky suddenly lit up with a flash as bright as noon. The shock of it scuppered her landing and sent her hurtling to the ground beside the tracks.

Plant had turned orange.

Then came a second flash, even bigger than the first, and a column of blue light shot into the further reaches of the night sky, followed soon after by a wall of sound which came barrelling up the tracks, an explosive wave that would have knocked her clean off her paws if she wasn't already on her side. The force of it unleashed a yelp, but amid the alarms and shattering windows, it was lost.

A strange shimmer, like the edges of her eyes were suddenly underwater, sullied Belka's vision. Laying down on the grass, she took some time to deliberate what to do next. Heading back to her oak tree to put an end to this awful day appealed most, but it was the wrong thing to do. The pack alphas *must* be shown proper respect for their handling of Ony, even if it meant heading towards the unnerving glow on the horizon.

She took off south along the banks of the rail line, straying east when she came to the Park road. Then, as she approached the wooded boundary of Park, the screams of a siren startled her onto the grass, and she cowered as a row of vehicles came speeding by. There were cars and trucks and, following up behind them, a water engine with its lights flashing.

She turned her mind again to her meadow; nothing would give her greater pleasure in this moment than curling up into the oak's protruding roots.

When the traffic settled down, Belka crossed to the Park lawns, and from there a bridge across the tracks took her onto a paved avenue between two long rows of dwellings. Unusually for this time of night, many people had come out from their homes, and were gathered on the tiles between the buildings. Among them were dogs on leashes.

A few of the pets looked to Belka expectantly, as though she might know just what on earth was going on around here, but most simply seemed put-out to find themselves wrenched away from their treat bowls and their soft beds.

A short-legged female, her fluffy white coat as pristine as new snowfall, was sat in the lap of a tearful child. The pet called out as Belka came by. 'You there! What was that enormous bang all about?'

Belka halted and dropped onto the stony ground beside the wall. 'Plant,' she said. 'It lit up.'

'Plant? You mean, *Chernobyl*?'

Belka tipped her head to the side, confused. Pets who grew up in the homes of people came to know the human tongue, but for the dogs who lived naturally, the only words they picked up were the occasional ones brought to them by some runaway who'd fled a cruel master. For the most part, it was all just sounds to Belka.

The child began to sob loudly. An older lady crouched low. 'Come now, Sofiy. Look! Here's Jayla!' She guided the child's hand over the pet's head, and the child calmed some. 'Let's finish your story, shall we?'

Belka watched as the lady opened wide a papery object and began to speak in an odd way.

'So, the brave knight took out his sword. The dragon swooped down with his mighty claws, but the knight wasn't afraid and, lifting his sword high into the air, he plunged it into the heart of the dragon and the terrible beast tumbled to the ground in a great ball of flame.'

Now the child was smiling. Such mysterious creatures, people.

Belka gave a soft snort to the lapdog. 'What's this?'

'We're reading a story,' replied the pet, to Belka's bafflement. 'Sofiy loves stories. This one's about a dragon who woke in his den after a very long sleep. He imprisoned the princess and blew his horrid infectious breath all across the land, but the hero knight has slayed it and is about to rescue her.'

Belka felt her hackles tremble at the mention of such an awful creature. She would have liked to know more, but a sudden commotion sounded from the far side of the avenue.

It was the people. As was so often the case, their anxieties were making them quarrelsome. Two men were shoving each other. A couple of women were shouting.

'You *would* say that! We've all heard the news that Vasily has been promoted again.'

'This has got nothing to do with my husband's position in the Party! I just think it would be better not to act until information is shared.'

'We could all be dead by the time the Party thinks of the likes of us!' protested the first woman, to a cheer from the rest of the onlookers.

Belka left the people to their pointless bickering. What difference did talking make, if neither really listened to what the other had to say? She sprinted across to the east of the paved avenue, to a patch of earth where the human folk grew vegetables.

At the far side of these fields, Belka saw the outline of some strays. Glad to have some company, she approached.

As she moved closer, she recognised Han and Gleb. The wearied brothers were watching another dog sniffing around in the turned soil. Nervously, she went and stood near the pair, afraid they may hold her accountable for Ony's actions. But her worries turned out to be unfounded, since the brutish brothers were far too distracted by the behaviour of the animal in front of them to give her a moment of thought.

'Who's that?' asked Belka. 'And why isn't he at the assembly?'

Gleb whimpered. 'We think it's Sergei, but his face is

so mangled. Do you think he came after us to check we did as he commanded, Han?'

Belka watched breathlessly as the unsteady creature before them shuffled around in the soil. Oddly, the dog gave off no scent. In fact, nothing around here seemed to smell of anything at all.

Gleb inched closer. 'Sergei? Is that you?' He turned back to Han and Belka. 'It is him. I think he's hurt.'

The chest of the old pack leader was expanding and contracting. A heavy wheeze accompanied his laboured breath. He kept his snout at ground level.

'We did as you ordered,' said Gleb. 'Ony's gone.'

Belka, moving ahead, brought her head low. 'You spared his life,' she said.

Sergei weakly lifted up his face, but where his skin ought to be there was now only exposed flesh that wept with blood. His eyes were misty like heavy morning fog; he looked right past the horrified trio. Then, with alarming suddenness, his spine heaved in a wave that rolled from his hind quarters to his neck, and he vomited violently onto the soil.

Belka stood back. What was happening to this fierce old alpha? Was this grief for the loss of his poor son? The assembly had been too much for him, perhaps, and he'd had to leave prematurely.

She turned. 'I have to go now and thank Pyotr.'

Han and Gleb ran with her as she made her way to the grasslands of Plant. A thick column of smoke was billowing up ahead, the sky around it aglow. Belka remained silent, but the brothers, probably because they were as frightened as she was herself, muttered away mindlessly.

'Did the people make this happen?'

'They must have.'

'Why?'

'I reckon a scrap started up between the packs after

we left. If they made too much noise at this time of night, the people would have attacked the assembly.'

'But our friends were there. All our brothers and sisters!'

Crossing the rail tracks, the trio came to the empty vehicle yards surrounding the office buildings. A man in white coverings was doubled over a wall, retching. On the other side of the yard a woman was laying on the hard ground, the skin on her face blistered and moist, as Sergei's had been. Although Belka was curious, she kept away from the fallen people, whose fretful energy was increasing her own stress.

Machines with flashing lights on their roofs sat haphazardly on the roads. Their doors were wide open, but no passengers were inside. Uniformed men, their faces scored with worry, were gathered in a conference. One of them was laying on the ground, noiselessly rolling back and forth as though some great pain had taken his voice.

In the open yards around Plant, water engines stood front-to-rear like a giant wall. Just visible beyond, men in rubber suits were holding powerful hoses. Everywhere was aflame.

Han shrieked. 'They did all this just to destroy some dogs?'

Their paws barely touching the earth as they took off across the grassland, the trio ascended a shallow bank at the edge of the field where, finally, Belka got a direct view of Plant. Human inventions of all shape, size and material – things that just a short time ago were concealed behind walls – now jutted out into the outside world. Fires raged in and around the site: on the lawns outside, on the walls inside, on sections of the adjoining roofs.

The heart of Plant was mere rubble now.

Distressed, Belka and the brothers sat before the

ruined building, the mysterious blush of the horizon reflecting in their eyes.

Some time passed before they even noticed that their friends were standing nearby on the verge.

'You're alright!' yipped Han and Gleb as they ran across. 'We thought something serious had happened!'

Nik and Lucie, with an odd sluggishness, turned to regard the brothers. Looking at their eyes, Belka could see they'd had a terrible shock. She moved in to sniff at the pair, but their scent was that of something without life.

'How did you get away when the people started attacking the assembly?' asked Gleb, as he licked at his friends.

Lucie's head tilted. 'We didn't try to get away. Most of us went in for a closer look. And as for people—'

Han interrupted. 'That's Pyotr and Bimka down there!' he yelled, nodding to the smoking pillar cascading into the air and the smouldering debris at the foot of the ruined buildings.

Belka's vision, still shimmery, was beginning to bother her, and she struggled to even identify the pack leaders. Halfway to those dogs, chunks of blackened rock were scattered on the ground, and these seemed especially difficult to focus on. 'What happened here?' she asked, blinking her eyes.

Nik's head drooped. When he spoke, it was with a blankness that made him seem absent. 'The assembly. We were finishing up. Two great bangs. The windows, they just blew apart. Steam came shooting out from every floor.' He motioned towards a vast disk of metal that stood diagonally where the roof once was. 'That huge thing there burst out of the top and fire came raining out of the sky. Then the whole front peeled away and flopped onto the road.'

Plant's exposed innards warmed the five dogs as they stood by. Many men were gathering, some dressed in their working suits with their caps on their heads, and others dressed as at leisure. Some lay on the ground calling out in pain and confusion, and some seemed less like men than the piles of clothes discarded sometimes in the wheeled bins outside their dwellings.

More and more vehicles were arriving all the time. Where were they all coming from?

The choking air was getting too much for Belka to bear. Reaching Pyotr as quickly as possible was her sole concern now; she longed to be far away from this chaotic place.

As she negotiated the rubble, she ignored the screaming man whose clothes were being cut from his oozing red body. Then, at the corner of the main building, she finally saw Pyotr, standing beside Bimka, Maks and Dima as they gazed inside the awful carcass of the smoking building.

She stepped forward to greet the elders, noticing again how their bodies smelt blank. The muzzles of the old dogs seemed curiously wizened, like forest fungus going to rot in late autumn. Their noses were dry, and a glassy film misted each of their eyes.

His head held high, Han spoke. 'Pyotr, Ony is gone now.'

But none of the pack alphas seemed to be interested. Staring into the wreckage, it was as though they were in a trance.

Belka readied to offer her thanks, but before she could speak, an entire wall inside the structure collapsed to the ground in a cloud of debris, revealing, at the base of an unfathomable column of smoke, a kind of fire Belka had never before glimpsed. This inferno was different from the kind that leapt and skittered like a pup at play; glowing with a heat of astonishing intensity, this furnace was like the Sun itself rising from out of the exposed guts of Plant.

While the others continued to gaze into it, Belka turned away. Nothing in her life had ever repelled her like this choking heat, but it wasn't the heat alone that so reviled her as much as the thought that something somehow *alive* was causing it.

Expressing her gratitude to the elders would have to wait.

Right now, she wanted nothing more to do with any of this.

4

THE SHIMMER

WAKING at dawn beneath the oak's boughs, with a throat as course as gravel, Belka went straight to the foot of her meadow to lap water from the river. Since her vision was still blurry from last night's tumble, she stood in the fisherman's shadow to prevent Sun's morning brightness from dazzling her eyes.

Back again after yesterday morning's absence, the man had set up his line and was digging in the earth, repeating the same phrase. 'I don't understand. There's usually loads of them.'

The friend who'd come along calmly shrugged. 'We could always go to the shop.'

'And waste an hour? No – they're here.'

The fisherman went to a case to fetch a sharp metal implement, and soon a mound began to grow. When the dug up soil reached Belka's height, he plunged his hand into the ground and held aloft a knot of writhing worms. 'Told you!' he laughed. 'Just gone deep, that's all.'

'Deep? What could possibly make earthworms retreat half a meter into the ground?'

'Fear of all the trout in that river,' replied the fisherman, and both men chuckled.

Although her throat still burned, Belka ceased

drinking and made her way along the riverbank to the neighbouring field, where the man was tending to his little wooden boxes. His netted headdress lay on the ground beside his feet. With his hands on his hips, he spoke curtly to the kennel-like structures. 'What's the matter with you?'

Noticing Belka as she trotted along the track towards the road, the man turned. 'Sweet girl,' he said, sheltering his eyes from the low dawn sun with his hand, 'do *you* know why my bees won't come out?'

They were funny things, people. Just what *were* they? Ony once speculated that humans were a kind of dog. That didn't sit right with Belka, though. Their emotions, for a start, were so different. The bee man, just like the fisherman, was troubled, yet gave the impression all was well. But a dog would never wag her tail because she wanted somebody to *think* she was happy. A dog's tail was honest.

In a lot of ways, people – whatever they were – were incomprehensible creatures. What would compel them to hide things about themselves that were true, yet exaggerate things that were not, like the butcher who made Levka believe he was kind when he was anything but? A dog just had to accept that, for the most part, people were unknowable beings and as such should be left to their own business.

At the head of the meadow, Belka emerged from the hedges and crossed the road. She looked nervously east to where Plant was situated; instinctively, she knew her painfully arid mouth had something to do with the explosions that had rattled the world last night.

Curiosity overcame her. Just hours before, Plant had been a mighty inferno. Was it still?

She *had* to know.

She sprinted without pause until she reached Park. Though Plant was still a long way off, the air had turned dry with a metallic bitterness.

At the bottom of Wheel, in the walled-off square, Belka noticed a group of people swarming around a concealed individual. Happy to leave them to get on with their business, she trotted past them, but right as she did, the crowd broke apart to reveal a woman at its centre.

Belka halted dead in her tracks. Had she really seen what she thought she had? With extreme caution, she inched closer.

Like wavering air above a flame, the woman was surrounded by a kind of fuzzy aura. But since she alone appeared this way – everybody else had a clearly visible edge – Belka grew instantly fearful. The odd phenomenon she'd observed last night, of things enveloped in shimmering air, had nothing to do with her own eyesight. A new, and very strange, kind of substance had arrived in the town.

One of the people noticed as Belka crept nearer, and began to shout. 'What are you looking at, mutt?'

'Go on!' said another. 'Shoo!'

But Belka was transfixed by it. It was as though the woman was a source of heat – only, it wasn't heat. Heat was a changeable state: she'd learnt that while still a pup, huddling in with the litter after a fall through thin ice. Whatever this was, it was fixed to the woman like a permanent kind of watery cloak. And it was clearly distressing to her: she was crying. When the woman suddenly vomited, a bystander started crying too, and with that the energy of the crowd grew too intense for Belka, who bolted to the other side of the yard to pick up the rail tracks.

She proceeded south until her curiosity about the state of Plant was eventually satisfied. In an unbroken column, stretching up as high into the sky as it was possible to see, raspberry-coloured smoke was billowing.

Plant was not back to normal.

And perhaps, she supposed, as she observed

countless and unusually large vehicles that flashed and screamed, it would never again be like its old self.

The spring air on the outskirts of the Plant site hung heavy with a repulsive force. As Belka neared the ruin, she saw again those scattered chunks of scorched rock, ejected from the building by the explosion.

The same shimmery fuzz that cloaked the crying woman was now visible everywhere, though nowhere more than at the gaping fissure that cleaved the central building in two, out of which smoke was ceaselessly pouring. This strange aura had a quality Belka found hard to turn away from. Was it hot, or was it cold? It seemed somehow to hold both properties at once, and for that reason, simply couldn't be trusted. Living things of all kinds would be better off away from it: the earthworms knew it, and so did the bees.

The warmth of Plant's interior could be felt even from this distance. Many men were gathered, wrapped in coverings that hid every inch of their skin. At regular intervals, water engines stood by, as well as smaller vehicles with their lights flashing; both types of machine were growing in number with each passing moment, and the eyes of the men who controlled them burned red with exhaustion.

Several dogs, including Han and his brother, Gleb, were gathered across the road. Approaching with caution, Belka decided to forego the customary waltz of sniffing. There was no point amid air this choking and scorched.

Lucie was there, although her mate, Nik, was nowhere to be seen. Belka went over and nudged at her head, which was slunk low. 'Are you alright?'

Listless Lucie offered no response; she simply kept her gaze fixed on the long-haired dog in the centre of a grassy clearing.

'Who's that?' said Belka.

Lucie turned, blankly. 'Choom.'

'What's he looking at?'

'Some kind of stone,' replied Han.

Belka strained to see the object. A wedge of rock, black as moonless midnight, snapped into focus. Nothing beyond the site of the ruined building itself seemed quite so alive with the frightening energy as this lump of blackened stone. She let out a sharp yelp.

Han and Gleb looked at one another. 'What's wrong with her?'

When Belka yelped again, Choom turned to face her. 'Get away from it, Choom!'

'Why?' asked Han. 'What is it?'

'It's covered with the shimmer,' Belka growled. 'I don't think it's safe.'

Puzzled, the dogs looked from the rock, to each other, to Belka. 'The shimmer?'

Belka flicked her head towards the vast scar of Plant. 'Like that stuff,' she said. 'That watery air all around the smoke.'

The dogs cocked their heads to the side.

'You don't see it? Choom!' she suddenly called. 'Come away from that rock!' But Choom went closer instead, taking his muzzle in for a good sniff.

Lucie, whose face was a grimace of nausea and worry, began to whine. She'd run out of patience. Han twisted his body away. 'Alright, alright,' he said. 'We'll go find Nik now.'

The dogs made their way to the dwellings nearest Plant where, during the night, people had crowded into the streets to watch the chaos unfolding. But now only a handful of them were outdoors. Were they, too, distressed to see so very many vehicles dashing through – and above – the city?

'So this was where you last saw Nik?' said Gleb, turning to Lucie, who seemed too distressed to respond.

Han gnawed into an itch. 'Well, even if we've lost our noses, we've still got our ears and eyes.'

Belka gave a nod: there was nothing in these parts that wasn't touched by the same lifeless, metallic odour.

Han, beginning to cough, approached the buildings. 'Let's try around the back first.'

Belka followed them around the corner, and her eyes immediately went to a body. It was Sergei. His burnt face was drooping over the lawn onto rocky soil, and pools of vomit lay beside him. On his hind quarters were deep red burns.

Another body lay just beyond Sergei. It was Pyotr. His face was slick with blood where his musculature was exposed; it looked as though he'd eaten flame. Near enough to his fellow elder, Belka hoped they'd been able to find comfort in each other when the end came for them.

She stood, dumbfounded. All day, she'd been hoping to find them, to express her thanks as she should have done when she saw them last night. What was she supposed to say now they lay discarded before her like piles of burned trash?

Stepping forward, Belka started to offer her gratitude to the dead animals, but she swallowed back the first of her words when Lucie began to mournfully squall nearby.

Running with the others, Belka went to investigate the source of the cries. All they could do was watch while Lucie fell to the ground beside the body of the deceased Nik. It was doubtful whether the poor girl would ever stand again.

But why did a vaporous halo surround each of these dead dogs? How could this shimmering quality live on even after the creatures it veiled had passed?

Gleb came to where Han and Belka were stood. 'Who did this?'

While Han answered his brother, he kept his eyes locked on Belka. A hostility burned inside him. 'This all happened right after Ony ran.'

Belka had nothing to offer, but held Han's gaze.

'He's a smart boy, that one,' said Han. 'Not the type to just roll over and accept his punishment.'

Belka began to pace. 'You can't be saying what I think you are.'

'You weren't there either when Plant went up were you, Belka? He warned you to keep away, didn't he?'

Belka centred her weight as her hackles came up. She responded blankly, in case her voice carried any tone which might be taken for aggression. 'Han, you've seen Plant with your own eyes. Nearly every dog present at the assembly last night is either dead or dying. With what unnatural powers could Ony have plotted that kind of devastation?'

'Why don't you tell us? You're the one that keeps going on about this "shimmer". What funny business are the pair of you involved with?'

Gleb started to growl.

'Don't even think about birthing Ony's evil babies in this city,' said Han, whose teeth suddenly looked very sharp.

Belka turned and sprinted, and the brothers gave chase. But before any ground was covered, they stopped again, startled by the sight that met them around the corner.

Choom was laying on the ground, shaking. A bloody secretion was foaming from his scorched muzzle. Soon, he was going to be indistinguishable from poor Sergei and Pyotr.

Belka recoiled, then her eye was directed away. In the grassy clearing behind the injured dog, a child was running toward a piece of blackened rock which shimmered almost as intensely as Plant did. A man – perhaps the boy's father – stood idly by. Belka let out a purposeful bark, but neither the child nor the man paid any attention.

With no time for a second warning, she sprinted at the

boy and leapt into the air. Just as he was stooping to pick up the dreadful object, all four of her paws connected with the child's body, and he rolled over onto the grass with a piercing scream. The boy wasn't out of danger yet, though, so she took his sleeve in her teeth and dragged him away from the dark debris whose vicious heat blazed against them as they slowly passed it.

A flash of pain suddenly rocked her side: the child's father had flung a sharp stone.

She could take no more.

As fast as she could, Belka retreated from the scorched grasslands of Plant, and ran and ran until she reached the river. Exhausted in mind and body, she collapsed into the nook of her oak tree.

She turned to her side to seek comfort from Ony, then gave a whimper as she remembered she didn't have the first clue where in the world that feisty boy was.

Last winter, when the meadows iced and a dog couldn't tell the still grey air from the surface of the roads, Belka stumbled across a face she hadn't seen since they grew up together as pups.

It was in a part of the city she tended to avoid, close to the dwellings, where she saw him. Down at the bottom of a bin, feasting on some boiled-down bones, was the boy whose mother was killed by a man. It was little Ony.

Scavenging alone had been going badly for Belka. Most strays went straight from the Creche lands to join packs, but she'd preferred the freedom to range at her leisure. It was an arrangement which might have suited her for the rest of her days – were it not for the battles each and every mealtime demanded. With their greater numbers, her rivals muscled her out of the way before she could get so much as a sniff of a choice morsel, which was why the meaty aroma drifting up from the wheeled bin seemed too good to be true.

Indeed, it was, since already snacking away inside it was a dog. Peering over the rim, she recognised this sole competitor at once from his golden fur. How long it had been since she last saw him she couldn't say, but it was long enough that she'd actually grown taller than him. 'Ony?' she called down. 'What are you doing here? I thought you left the city after Levka died.'

The wretched animal, his ribs rippling through his flanks to make his hunger visible, looked up with terror-filled eyes. But instead of brawling with her, he shuffled over, and she jumped down to feed next to him.

Side by side, the pair gulped down the meal. Then they took off together to wander – and continued to do so over all the moons that followed.

Ranging with Ony came with increased risk to her wellbeing; the scrappy little fellow nipped at trouble's tail wherever they went. But reminiscing about their puppyhood warmed her frosted spirit on those dark days. Provided she never mentioned the topic of Levka, whose sad death seemed to have fractured the boy's heart into pieces, the pair got on just as well as they had in Creche's open fields.

One day, Ony turned up at her riverside oak looking agitated. They were friends with a shared history, so it was odd that he should suddenly be looking at her with such animosity. Half a rat lay among the protruding oak roots: this, it appeared, he was coveting. She'd given a snort, not of jealousy, but of disappointment. Why all of a sudden did he regard her as a threat to his resources?

She stood and turned to face the city. 'You're welcome to it,' she said with a sniff. 'I'm more than capable of finding a meal on my own, you know. I'll leave you in peace.'

Ony was stunned. 'Why are you saying that?'

'Your face,' she replied. 'I can see you'd rather I wasn't with you right now.'

He went up to her and licked her ears. 'The opposite is true, sweet girl. I want you with me always.'

How bittersweet, the memory of it was. Presently rising alone in the oak tree's gnarled roots, Belka bristled with apprehension. Her bond with Ony had grown deep in the year since that day; understanding him as she did, she had no doubt he would make an attempt to come back to the city, and when he did, it was likely he'd head straight for Plant. Since he'd left before catastrophe struck, he would know nothing of the murderous poison that ruined place spewed.

Sooner or later, she had to warn him.

Crossing over the field beside her own, Belka saw the men at the river's edge packing up to leave. They'd done well, judging by how their bags bulged with fish. They seemed so happy.

She licked at her sore side, which hurt twice as bad for how she'd come to earn it. She'd helped that little boy, but his father lashed out. Incomprehensible creatures, people were.

As she cantered along, she kept her eyes on the horizon. In the distance, flying machines were silhouetted against the fading daylight. These whirring vehicles were pouring out various substances over the smoking buildings while giant jets of water arced from the ground into the terrible fissure. But nothing the people had done so far had caused the shimmer to retreat. In fact, pockets of it could be seen across a much wider expanse than before: a ghostly vapour here in the pines, a rippling spectre there above School.

It was even, she noticed as she glanced down at herself, all over her belly.

5

THE SICKNESS CREEPS

ONY WAS FAMISHED.

The night before last, Han and Gleb ran him into the wilds, and since then he'd found no snacks beyond the droppings left scattered in the briar patch. Today, these would not do. Today, he desired the flesh of the creatures whose fluffy tails those little brown balls spilled from.

They suspected nothing. Ony, still as the statues on the avenues of Park, skulked behind a birch's papery trunk, his keen eyes fixed on the many rabbits grazing peacefully amid the thicket.

Beneath the briars, in the centre of the thicket, was a warren, into which, at the sound of a single swish of brambles, the rabbits were ready to bolt. Any hunter working this patch was sure to be disappointed; as far as grazing grounds went, this was as near to perfection as any prey species could hope to find.

But it had one flaw:

People.

Positioned near the warren were rail tracks where vehicles as long as the horizon itself pulled carts to and from the city. The men who drove these inconceivable engines were no threat to the nibbling creatures, but the commotion of their journey shattered their peace – and deafened them to clever young dogs.

The whole area had exploded with human activity, which had gifted Ony an advantage he meant not to squander. Since Sun rose yesterday, flying machines came, too, and wheeled vehicles shrieked and flashed as they sped south along the roads. The herbivores were distracted; their defences were weakened.

The sight of their white backsides had cheered him when he awoke yesterday. In strange environs, it was comforting to learn that the world beyond the city was – at its surface, at least – still recognisable. Since then, he'd kept his distance from the rabbits, though never once let them out of his sight. As far as rabbits were concerned, if they knew you were there, you'd already lost; the ambush, when it was time to launch it, had to count.

Late last evening, as Sun was setting on a day of ceaseless commotion, Ony smelled a fox approaching. This was lucky: in their panic, the rabbits rushed westward through the thicket before suddenly vanishing into the ground, disclosing their secret bolt hole to Ony's spying eyes. Armed now with this knowledge, all he had to do was find a way to block it.

Remaining in position all day behind the fallen birch, Ony had noticed a small ribbon of road past the hedges on the other side of the tracks. Every vehicle which headed south did so on that road, and Ony worked out that the ones with the flashing lights – of which there were *a lot* – could be seen before they were heard. This made his task easier.

He'd already found the perfect piece of bark. It was wide enough to cover the bolt hole, but shallow enough that he was able to drag it. Waiting for the road to become illuminated, he'd scurried over to the chunk of rotten bark, then, as the vehicle passed nearby with its awful wail blaring into the sky, he'd pulled it closer and closer until it sat now with him.

The time to reveal himself was almost here. But first, with his usual method, he needed to position the rotten chunk of bark over the warren's entrance. There could be no avoiding being slashed or gouged by the dense tangle of brambles on the way to it, but that was just pain – and since when did hurting matter? So long as he kept low, he could avoid the worst of their barbed vines. But if he did become ensnared, the rabbits were sure to hear his struggle. For this reason, what he was about to attempt was the riskiest part of the whole venture.

Daylight was failing. Another night with an empty belly was unacceptable. It had to be now.

He stayed as still as he could, willing one of the vehicles to light up the ribbon of road. Whatever it was that was so important down in the city today, its people were bound to need another.

Sure enough, the stone wall that fringed the road soon flashed blue and red. He gripped the piece of bark in his jaws.

Already its screams became audible. In seconds it would pass, deafening the rabbits to his secret plan. He yanked at the rotting piece of tree bark, moving backwards towards the innermost sanctum of the thicket, closer and closer to the bolt hole as the scream of the vehicle grew in volume. Thorns ripped at him, but he paid them no heed as he approached his target.

When the vehicle was almost at its closest point to the briars he let the bark drop, then began nudging it forwards, and as the wailing engine moved away, he pawed at it until the warren's mouth was fully covered. Then, as carefully as he'd approached, he crept back to his vantage point.

The rabbits were clueless. Ten or so of them were scattered around the thicket. Ony fixed his glare on the one furthest from the burrow.

He crept from behind the broken birch and made his way covertly around the edge. Then he sprang.

No sooner did Ony's body leave the ground than the rabbits darted for their subterranean sanctuary, but one by one the animals were met by a brand new door. Changing course, the shocked rabbits leapt past the bolt hole and on into thicker briars where minor entrances were no doubt hidden. But the rabbit farthest back, whose view was obscured by the panicking colony, collided with the rotten chunk, and before it could even consider an alternative, it was pinned beneath Ony's sharp fangs.

By the light of dusk, Ony was trotting along an unsealed track when the faint outline of a person appeared ahead. The shape was moving slowly, and appeared to be pulling something behind itself. But the hot dinner bouncing in his jaws was making him salivate and dulled any sense of caution, so he simply carried on past the shape, which now materialised into an elderly woman.

When he'd moved on a few steps beyond her, a familiar voice called out. 'Yes, yes! What has my Golden Boy got there!' It was the old lady who sang her happy/sad song and fed him vegetables. 'Look at that!' she said, pointing at the rabbit. 'You're eating better than me tonight!'

Ony tightened his bite with a growl.

'You needn't worry about me,' she said, nodding towards the trolley she was hauling. 'I've got everything I need right here. Well, enjoy your meal.'

Ony waited a moment while the old lady struggled ahead. Then, at a distance, he followed behind.

At the end of the track were a clutch of crumbling homes. After fumbling at a gate awhile, the old lady went into a garden. A bell-like sound was ringing at intervals inside the house, but it prompted no urgency in the woman, who searched calmly through a bag for the metal object which she used to push open the door. The ringing stopped just before the woman disappeared inside.

Ony dropped the rabbit into the tall grass of her garden and approached the dwelling. From the threshold of the door, he surveyed the interior. The lady was sunk into a soft seat, humming in just such a way that a deep sense of serenity washed through him. He dragged his rabbit over, and in total peace he ate everything but the fluffy white tail.

Every now and then, the slow shuffling of feet sounded from inside, along with bursts of shuddering coughs, but eventually the old lady grew silent.

Curling up, Ony let his eyes close. Life had become so complicated so suddenly. On the edge of sleep, just as he was considering what he might do with himself tomorrow, the ringing bells began again, startling him up onto his paws.

More shuffling, then the ringing stopped.

'Da?'

As people often did when they were alone, the old lady talked to herself. Now though, she left odd pauses after each new thing she said.

'It happened during my shift. In the kitchens. Yes, yes.'

...

'But how long might that be? People are already starting to get sick.'

...

'"*Incident*"? Is that what the Party would have us call it? Son, the entire reactor was—'

...

'But why are they delaying? An official announcement should be made.'

...

'The greater good? If you say so.'

...

'Me? No, I'll stay where I am. Yes, yes. I have enough to last.'

...

'Yes, yes, the bottom drawer. I'll get your money, son. But I won't let them take me.'

...

'I tell you, your father never just stood by like this after the explosion in Kyshtym back in 57. The Party should be ashamed.'

After she said that, the lady stopped talking to herself and, as Sun vanished over the horizon for another day, Ony finally drifted off into a sleep filled with fitful dreams.

He was awoken in the dead of night by the rustling of an approaching animal.

With ears pricked high, Ony stood. He crouched as low as he could; moon wasn't as bright as it had been during Pyotr's assembly, when it was ripe to bursting, yet the ghostly pallor it now lent the dark countryside would be sufficient to skylight an approaching rival. In the trees beyond the garden fence, twigs popped and foliage crumpled.

Ony inched out of the garden and into the dirt road.

Belka was right in front of him.

He was too shocked, initially, to greet her – why hadn't he smelt her? – but within seconds they fell into the customary waltz of sniffing and nudging, jaws open wide as they butted at each other's faces. Belka's movement appeared strained; a nasty cut ran along her side.

They lay together in the garden. There was a lot to say, but given the hour it would wait. Before closing his eyes, Ony asked a single question:

'Why can't I smell you?'

Belka wriggled into the earth to make it yield to her shape. 'Something's happened down there. Nothing seems to smell of anything much anymore.'

Curled around each other in the long grass, the pair – finally able to settle – fell instantly to sleep, awaking just before Sun came over the horizon to the sound of plates being placed on the hard ground.

Ony, having spent almost two full days alone in the countryside, was more excited by the sight of Belka laying beside him, but Belka wasted no time springing over to the porch, gulping down the pickled vegetables the kind old lady had diced up for them.

'So Golden Boy has his Golden Girl, yes! Let me see, you must be about two years old, the pair of you? Well then, there'll be a litter growing inside you in no time!' Belka approached to show thanks, but when the old lady began violently coughing, she halted.

'No!'

Ony turned to her. 'What?'

'The air around her,' said Belka. 'It's shimmering.'

Ony tilted his head to the side in confusion.

'What a pretty pair you make,' the old lady said, when she'd regained control of her breathing. She went to pat Belka along the flank, but Belka, who looked suddenly distressed, retreated.

It wasn't like her to spurn human affection. The only time Ony had seen such a disturbed expression on Belka's slender face was in the moments after he'd killed Feliks.

The old lady laughed. 'So you're a shy one too? Made for each other, aren't you?'

~

By midmorning, as they roamed through a glade deep within the trees, Ony noticed that Belka's scent had returned.

The woodland surrounding the crumbling village was old growth. Things made by people tended to fall to ruin over time, like the old lady's house, yet the natural world seemed to thrive when it was left alone. Oaks as ancient as these forced peace upon a creature; a dog's entire life was the trickle of a raindrop down the edge of its trunk.

But all dogs knew that nothing stands tall forever. Even mighty trees topple in the end, and three had fallen in such a way as to form a perfect triangle on the mossy forest bed.

Ony deviated from their path to investigate. As he passed through a line of shrubs, a startled woodlark took off from the ground to perch on a nearby branch. The bird could only protest as Ony discovered, in the dead centre of the triangular clearing between the logs, four eggs in her nest.

Two each.

He called for Belka, and crunched through the first of his share. Something tasted a little off, but who was he to complain about a fresh meal? He went for the second as Belka arrived.

'Ony, no! Spit it out!'

Ony stopped chewing.

'Spit it out!'

Despite his excitement, the graveness of her expression made him obey. From his mouth, lumps of blood fell onto the turf.

'They're spoilt,' Belka said. 'All of them.'

Ony ran a claw through the centre of the remaining eggs. Each one opened with a slithering blob of blood. 'How did you know?'

Belka turned shyly away.

'What's wrong?'

'Plant's spoiled air. It's travelling.'

After Belka whined these mysterious words, neither spoke for some time, though each knew the other wanted to say something. They walked in silence until they reached the ruin of a long-abandoned dwelling, whose single stone wall offered shade. But neither napped.

'I didn't mean for either of them to die.'

Belka kept her eyes on his own. She was good at this; somehow, his lovely girl always knew when there was something he needed to get out.

'I could take it when it was aimed at me,' Ony said, sadly. 'But why did he insult mama? Before I even knew what was going on, Starla was dead.'

'He shouldn't have said anything about Levka. She didn't deserve what happened to her.'

'That's what bothers me so much,' said Ony, resting his chin on the soil. 'It was meant for me. She saved my life when she tasted that meat first.'

Belka sidled closer to Ony until her head was resting on his neck. Then, as though she'd suddenly remembered something, she quickly drew back.

'As for Feliks, well, he would still be alive if he hadn't threatened our babies. That was the main lesson I learnt from my mother: the safety of your children is the most important thing. You can't let anything cause them harm.'

Belka turned away. Once again, Ony perceived embarrassment on her face.

Birds chirruped in the trees as time ticked wordlessly on. As yesterday, distant vehicles wailed. The countryside air that had been so fresh when they woke now seemed stale somehow. A metallic taste settled in their mouths, their throats feeling suddenly dry.

Eventually, Belka spoke. 'There's something you need to hear, Ony. I wish it hadn't fallen to me to say it. Your father. He's dead.'

Ony bristled.

'Not just Pyotr. Sergei, too.'

His head cocked to the side.

Belka steadied herself. 'Something happened to Plant.'

'*Happened?* Like what?'

'A huge part of it is gone. It burst.'

A memory took shape in Ony's mind. Stadium. Han and Gleb. The sky lighting up in the south. He let out a snort. 'There was an incredible noise.'

'That was an explosion. The dogs from the assembly who hung around to investigate are dead, and many others have become sick.'

Ony took some time to process the information; when he spoke again, Belka appeared surprised by what he said. 'The most important thing is the safety of the children we're going to have. They'll have a better life with these dogs gone. Soon, we can return to our home.'

A look of puzzlement descended upon Belka's face, as though something had taken purchase in her mind and wouldn't let loose. 'The explosion. Ony, it... it didn't have anything to do with you did it?'

'I wasn't there, Belka.'

'I know. But Han has accused you of something very odd and what you just said has made me nervous. Han thinks *you* caused it all to happen.'

'I didn't.'

'I know. But they're going to kill you if they see you, Ony.'

Ony grunted softly. 'Plant will kill them first by the sounds of it. And if it doesn't, I'll do it myself.'

Suddenly, some unseen force, as though the air were full of horseflies, appeared to be agitating Belka.

'What are you looking at?'

Belka turned away without replying.

'Come on,' said Ony. 'Let's see if the old woman has got any more snacks.'

'*Da, da,*' said Belka.

Ony smiled. '*Da! Da!* Why does she always say that?' Standing, he gave Belka a playful shunt. 'We'll wait up here a while before we go back to the city.' He span in a single circle in front of her. 'I think this business with Plant could be the making of us, you know,' he said.

But although she voiced no words, Belka's face said that she didn't share that belief.

6

THE DOG FACE MEN

FOUR DAWNS since Belka found Ony in the old lady's garden, the bell machine, as it had done every morning, roused them from their slumber with its ringing.

Usually so calm as she spoke into the device, now the woman seemed upset with it. 'Yes,' she said into it. 'Yes, yes.'

Ony, discomforted by her angst, stood and began pacing, observing how she scrunched her eyes tight and jabbed her finger into thin air.

'I have no choice – I've run out, son! I'll call when I get there. Yes, yes, I know. The bottom drawer.'

Some quiet moments followed, then the front door slammed shut and Dada, as they'd come to call her, came up the path. Knowing full well that no snacks had been set down, Ony went to the porch anyway.

From the garden gate, Dada gave a shrug. 'I'm sorry, Golden Boy. Barely anything left for myself.'

The pair were following her out of the garden when a vehicle came around the corner. This was unusual – there weren't any roads in these parts, just imprints in the ground where the grass didn't grow – but even more odd was Dada's reaction. The old lady, straining her eyes to see the words painted on the side of the juddering thing as it approached, grew suddenly grave; both dogs felt an anxious jolt as the old lady swallowed hard and began biting her lower lip.

The vehicle pulled up beside them and purred like a very strange cat, while fumes from the back belched out into the clean rural air. Then a pane of glass dropped down, revealing men inside. Only, they weren't men at all. Were they? They certainly didn't look like people. People had faces: browed eyes, tall noses, mouths with square teeth. Whatever these beings were, their faces were conical, almost as though they had snouts, and their eyes were round screens of glass. They looked almost dog-like.

A muffled voice came from one of the creatures. 'Are these your animals?'

The head of the elderly lady bounced up and down. 'Da. Da.'

Facing one another, the beings in the vehicle nodded sharply, and their machine crawled off.

When the old lady crouched to pet her, Belka, who'd only grown more aloof around her as the days had passed, spurned the offer of affection. Dada smiled sadly and pushed the gate tight. 'You two will need to be very careful,' she said, peering down at them, then shuffled off up the track.

Ony nudged Belka to stir her into action, but as was usual now, she recoiled from him, too. Not even his climbing game interested her very much anymore. They always played that one when their talk turned to the litters they hoped to raise together, though those thoughts seemed far now from Belka's troubled mind. His heart ached to observe her disinterest in the family he so wished to gift her. His reputation, finally, must have coloured her impression of him.

At the end of the track, Dada stopped and turned back to the advancing dogs. 'Follow me in the village all you like. But when I go back to the apartment, you're not to follow me. Do you hear me, Golden Boy?'

But Ony couldn't possibly decipher what she was trying to tell him.

Driven by the heat of Sun, Ony and Belka went into the shade to nap, but soon hunger hauled them back up onto their paws. They tracked Dada north, to where more crumbling houses stood, eventually picking up the chatter of women as it drifted into the blue afternoon sky.

Outside a dwelling that was indistinguishable from Dada's own, she and another old lady were sat on stools, hammering walnuts on a metal plate. When they saw the dogs appear, Dada waved across at them. 'I didn't think you two would be far behind,' she said, popping a knotty piece of flesh into her mouth. She held out some of the excavated walnut meat, drawing Belka closer from the gate. 'Come on. You won't like it, though.'

While Belka sniffed at it, the neighbour began a slow nodding of her head. 'I had a feeling all through Friday that something bad was going to happen,' she said. 'The way the power kept surging. And the lights: on, off. On, off.'

Ony looked at the snack on the ground. Since the old humans were gulping the same stuff, he deemed it safe, and proceeded to crunch his portion, and in this way, with the women first cracking the shells then sharing out the contents between the four of them, he and Belka lay near while the people continued their conversation.

Raising her fingertips to her temples, the neighbour shook her head from side to side and looked down at her lap sorrowfully. 'I can still remember 1957. I hoped I wouldn't live long enough to see another incident like this. The Party will again act like nothing's happened, of course.'

The muscles in Dada's face tensed. Dogs could be expressive, but they couldn't do half as much with their faces as people could. Ony found it fascinating to observe, the way they wielded their features to express all manner of thoughts and feelings. They scrunched their eyes tight, opened them wide; they stuck out their lips and wrinkled their noses and made their brows dance.

'Did you see that news report on Monday?' said Dada. 'They certainly wanted people to think it was nothing. Well, if that newsreader had been in the canteen during the explosion she wouldn't have called it an "incident". I thought we'd been hit by American rockets!'

'It's a wonder you weren't deafened, dear.'

'The second explosion was even worse,' said Dada, clamping her teeth shut and making her eyes roll. 'The men were running about like my chickens used to on slaughter day. "The test has failed! The cooling system's been shut off!" It was pandemonium.'

As though some horrid memory had returned to Dada's mind, she folded into herself with her head in her hands, startling Ony and Belka. The energy in the garden had grown so tense that Ony stood in a state of alertness.

'We thought the bosses might show up, or some Party official from the Energy Ministry, but nobody did. So in the end we evacuated ourselves.' Although she was upset, her lips then formed a thin smile. She reached across to pat the woman's knee as she munched her mouthful. 'Good thing you stored last year's harvest away, dear.'

The elderly neighbour tossed some flesh to Belka. 'Spring couldn't come soon enough! Supplies are getting low now, though.' As she turned to face Dada, it seemed to the dogs that she was somehow holding something back, as though she wished to do or say something but wasn't confident enough to make it happen.

Dada sensed it too, perhaps, because she began to speak again.

'You're curious about the damage, aren't you, dear?'

The neighbour looked suddenly ashamed.

'You've every right to be. It's bad. Very, very bad. And

some of those poor workers. They were just—' Dada suddenly went silent, and Ony once again felt an anxious bolt shoot through his body.

'Just what?'

Dada directed a serious glance towards the other woman. 'A lot of men suffered terribly that night, dear.'

By now, Belka too had become agitated by the energy between the human folk and both dogs were up on their paws ready to roam elsewhere.

The neighbour's face was overcome with emotion, though whether it was sorrow or worry the dogs couldn't tell. 'They'll have to evacuate the town,' she said.

Dada nodded grimly. 'I don't understand why the Party is delaying. Still, it gave me time to come here, at least. I'll not let them take me to Kiev or Kharkiv.'

'But what will we do for supplies? How will we eat?'

'We have to hope the shops haven't yet closed, dear. There's still some power left in these old legs. I'm heading back to my son's apartment now. There's money there. He won't be happy, but I'll use it to get whatever I can, and then I'll bring it all back here and share it out among us. It will just have to last until the crops are ready.'

~

Ony was thinking about pups again, and felt like playing the climbing game. But when he tried to hop up behind Belka, she bolted away.

For days, he'd waited for her frosts to thaw, but very little warmth glowed inside her anymore. He'd never before seen her so despondent.

How to even make sense of it? If the business with Feliks and Starla was so upsetting to her, why had she sought him here? When Sergei sent him from the city, he'd given her a chance of a new beginning, yet here she still was after Moon had shrunk by several slivers.

On the cool tiles of an abandoned yard, she lay at a distance from him, angst scored into her pretty face. She looked around in the sky, fretfully, as though at any time a swarm of wasps might come raining down upon her and drive their barbs into her flesh.

'Sweet girl,' he said, when he could bear it no longer. 'What's troubling you?'

With her muzzle on the hard ground, Belka let out a sigh. 'Something's very wrong, Ony.'

'This isn't our home,' said Ony. 'We've got to go back to the city. When you see your oak tree you'll understand. Everything will be normal there again. If we leave now, we'll catch up with Dada. She has pickled vegetables there.'

'No, Ony. Things won't be normal. Plant is more than just one of their buildings. There's something different about that place. Something… alive. It's infected, and that infection is spreading.'

'Belka, please listen to me. If this is about Sergei's boys, you mustn't worry. I'll find a way to get Han and Gleb apart, then I'll take them. I know I can do it. Any dog who wants to stand in my way, I'll rip out his throat and leave him to bleed. We'll be free to live again in our own home, Belka.'

'Our home is gone, Ony. And soon, this place will be, too. The sickness, it's going to poison everything. It's already in Dada, and it's—' She fell silent.

Ony's head tipped sideways.

'It's in me too. And if you come too close, you'll be shimmering as well.'

The tension that had gripped Ony's innards suddenly loosened. So, her behaviour wasn't due to ill feeling towards him! He stepped across and licked at Belka's ears and neck. 'You've had a terrible shock. But it's just your thoughts that are making you suffer. It's stopping you from seeing what I can: this business at Plant is a gift to us.'

Belka began to whine.

'Try to focus on our future, when all this is over,' continued Ony. 'Han and Gleb and any other dog who wants to harm us will be gone, and we'll be free to make our family. Our pups are going to thrive.'

'But Ony, I think the shimmer has harmed my body. And it'll harm yours, too, if you catch it. Forget about fighting now. We need to get out of this place. Even if it means braving the wolf-wilds.'

'If I'm wrong, Belka, that's what we'll do. But I know that when I remove the threat of our rivals, things are going to be so much better for us. Not just for you and me, but for our pups, too. All those little mouths that are going to depend on us.'

Belka's eyes softened; his words, as he'd hoped, were bringing her comfort. 'If Dada didn't think it was safe, she wouldn't head back there, Belka. So we'll go too, together. Whatever it is we have to do to get the life we want, we'll do it. We *will* get the life we want, sweet girl.'

As Stadium shrank into the dusky horizon behind them and Wheel appeared over the treetops, Belka showed no enthusiasm for their return to the city. It was clear now to Ony that, much like the trolley Dada had pulled all this way, Belka's anguish had come along with them.

She hadn't been exaggerating, then. Things really were different. There were fewer people and fewer dogs, and although many strange machines whirred through the air, the traffic on the roads was scant, too.

Perhaps the biggest difference, though, was the sound of loud cracks regularly piercing the sky. He'd been away a while, but Ony was sure these weren't part of life before Sergei had banished him from town. With each sharp pop, the dogs – and even old Dada – jumped with shock. There was no rhythm to these ominous explosions – at least, no pattern that made sense to them. Mostly the cracks occurred individually, but occasionally five or six came in a burst, their violence ringing in the sky for some time afterwards.

When they finally reached Wheel, Dada, whose shooing away they'd ignored all afternoon, shuffled along to the west side of the yard. But since Ony and Belka were heading east to the riverside meadow, they halted and dropped down to rest. As their human companion vanished into the distance, Belka followed her with her eyes; as was always the case whenever Belka looked at the old woman, worry emanated from her core.

They proceeded on to the river, but the route Belka chose to get back there was so convoluted Ony gave frequent yips of frustration. With each twist and turn, he laboured to lock their course into his internal map, and each time he thought he'd got it figured out, she insisted they change direction once again. It was as though Belka were trying to evade some assailant waiting up ahead, when nothing – to his eyes, at least – was there.

When they finally reached the river, the crown of Sun was just dipping over the horizon. The soil beneath the oak was holding on to the day's warmth; Belka wasted no time curling up within the roots of the nook.

But Ony wasn't ready for sleep. 'I'm going now,' he said.

Belka yawned, then lay her chin flat upon her paws. She made no reply.

'Aren't you going to ask me where?'

'You're going to look for Han and Gleb, Ony.'

He went in and licked her behind the ears.

'Where do you expect to find them?' Belka asked.

'Plant.'

Belka began whining, but Ony simply gave an affectionate huff, then paced away.

'Do what you have to do, Ony. But those black rocks

are more vicious than the fangs in any dog's mouth. Keep well clear of them.'

Belka closed her eyes the moment Ony left. Her feverish brain conjured a world where every edge was softened with a watery cloak. Animals, buildings, people, trees: nothing existed in her dreams that had a clear boundary. The butterflies dancing in the forest were as much air as the air was itself, and even the very water of the rivers lacked its nourishing essence. From the sod of the earth to the farthest wisps of clouds, everything shimmered where its form should be fixed. And the pups she saw that suckled at her underside – these lacked anything of solid substance. Mere vapours, they were shadows more than they were living entities.

Though her sleep had failed to restore her, Belka knew further rest was out of the question: Ony might be confronting Han and Gleb right now. There were two of them, each bigger than him. How would he possibly defeat them both?

She stood and walked to where the field met the road, and began to pace. In the distance, those horrible loud cracks continued to pierce the night sky. Back and forth she went, to and fro, hoping for Ony to return.

Then something across the road caught her eye. Laying in the gutter was a dog.

She approached. Horror iced her heart in recognition of the animal splayed out before her.

This was Lyuba.

In the middle of her friend's head was a hole. Streaking out onto the road from this mortal wound were ribbons of wet lumps, blackened by swarms of flies. But the air around Lyuba's dead body was normal.

There was no shimmer.

She looked down the pavement towards the city. In the distance, a vehicle was coming onto the road from a side street, its lights shining into her eyes.

Halfway to the vehicle, in another gutter, was a

second heap. Cautiously, Belka went to it. It was Len, Lyuba's mate. Again, a hole marked the centre of his head, and again not a trace of vaporous air cloaked his lifeless torso.

Why didn't the air shimmer around these animals, as it continued to do around the remains of those who'd ventured too close to Plant?

She stepped onto the pavement. The vehicle was about to pass now, but it was slowing to a crawl as it came alongside her. Then the window came down, and a dog-faced man peered out through perfectly round, glass eyes.

Instinctively, Belka backed away.

A metal stick suddenly emerged from out of the window, and before Belka could even focus on it, the thing lit up at the end and an almighty bang exploded. A whistling sounded, then the hard ground beside her paws churned up with a puff of dust and debris.

As fast as her legs could carry her, she ran into the bushes.

So, these mysterious glass-eyed creatures were killing dogs!

There was no time for the sleep she craved.

She had to find Ony before they did.

7

GHOST TOWN

THE LANDSCAPE WAS CHANGED ALMOST beyond Ony's recognition.

Not six full days ago, these grasslands, where dogs had assembled on account of him, were peaceful. The entire Plant site now, however, was a chaos of activity.

Laying atop a hump of recently dug soil, Ony scanned an environment illuminated by the first rays of dawn. At every point on the vista, hordes of people worked towards achieving some common goal, much as they'd always done here before. Now, though, there was a frantic urgency to their task.

Questions he had no hope of being able to answer swirled in his mind. How to make sense of the flying machines that were dropping sand onto the steaming wreckage of the main building? Of the dog-faced men tossing topsoil onto a truck, which drove to the other side of the field and tipped it into a steaming crater? Of the folk in metal suits dumping barrows full of dark rocks into that same pit, as though something dwelt within that required feeding? He'd seen people conduct all manner of incomprehensible tasks, but none had ever struck him as more pointless than this one: they were burying the ground *in* the ground! What could possibly be compelling them to behave like this?

There were just some things, he supposed, that a stray wasn't supposed to know, and as such, he turned his mind back to his own affairs.

Upon the mound of soil, tolerating the discomfort of the choking air, he recounted his journey here. Finding Han and Gleb had been a bigger challenge than he'd thought; had he missed something? After leaving Belka at her tree, he'd passed the night skulking the empty streets, napping briefly in shrubland when the sky grew darkest. Though he checked every surface for traces of Han and Gleb, their odours were so faint where he found them upon the lampposts and shop corners and rosebushes that tracking them proved impossible. Their scent just seemed to vanish into thin air. It was as though showers had come down to wash their trails away – which was odd, since the weather had been dry.

He noticed too a strange correlation: wherever odours grew faint, his throat and eyes burned worse, and as he'd come ever closer to the Plant site, every scent became infused with the same vague aroma of scorched metal. He may as well have had no nose, for all its use in these parts.

With the large dumping vehicles presently nowhere to be seen, Ony decided now was as good a time as any to investigate the crater itself, and trotted down the soil and over to the slope. The sides of the pit he found were as long as a pine was tall, and had been reinforced with metal walkways. Its western edge, where the road was, was higher than the other three sides due to the incline of the field; when he got to the lower rim, Ony inched forward to get a good look at what was down there.

Inside the pit were rocks of the purest black. The instant he saw them, he remembered Belka's warning and quickly recoiled. The intensity of the heat was shocking – was this where Sun went to sleep at night? –

and as he backed away, he wondered how anything could be so agonisingly, ferociously hot.

Behind him, a noise sounded: paws were moving across the metal walkway, but before he could turn to look, a voice yowled down from the pit's higher rim.

'Cur dog!'

Ony looked up to see Han.

'What did you do to our city?'

With his paws frozen to the spot, Ony, fearing the worst, craned his neck around.

There behind him, in a baying stance, stood Gleb. His bared teeth were long and sharp, and the musculature of his body rippled with tension as he stood firm.

Ony issued a growl, but it was aimed at himself. He'd failed to get the brothers apart. And, worse, they'd manoeuvred to trap him right between them.

~

A curious thing was happening near the rows of dwellings.

Belka, trying her best to go unseen beneath the hedges of the avenue, was waiting for the right moment to run, but the dense line of people waiting to board the vehicles on the road was blocking her way. Struggling with bags full of luggage, their tempers were ill. The men yelled and the women fidgeted, while many of the children sobbed.

Patrolling the line were more dog-men. Some held hoses, out of which a thick foam came pouring to create a bubbly white carpet. As the people stepped forward, they left behind peculiar footprints in the foam of the brightest shade of purple.

One man was angrier than the rest, and confronted a pair of the suited dog-faced people. He puffed out his chest as he screamed into their faces. 'Why are you doing this on Workers' Day? Look at my daughter's face! She's heartbroken – we've been counting down for weeks for the grand opening of the fairground!'

'You said we could ride on the big wheel today, daddy!' whined a girl clutching a fluffy white dog.

Another man in the line became enraged. 'The fairground? Are you crazy, Lobanovski? The Party should have got us out of here days ago!'

'Shut up!' yelled the man with the inflated chest. The suited dog-people stepped up to him and the man struck one of them in the head.

Belka recoiled with shock when the man's dog face fell onto the floor. It was just another of their tools! These beings were ordinary people, nothing more, with snout-shaped masks covering their flat human features.

When the anguished folk got to the long vehicles waiting for them on the road, they disappeared inside. While Belka watched, she became aware that what had started off as a single bark was now a chorus of distressed yips which had risen above the din of the engines. These were pets and, as was typical with domestic canines, they were distressed to be separated from their owners.

The children now were hysterical with emotion. 'Why can't we take Bobo?'

'Jayla!' wailed another.

But the dog-men were simply herding the people onto the wheeled machines, and shunting away the animals with their booted feet.

Another vehicle, this one short and squat like a box, pulled up beside the long ones, causing Belka to retract deeper into the bushes: it was the dog killers who'd fired their terrible metal tubes at her last night. Two men stepped out from its doors. As yesterday, they wore the snout-like apparatus on their faces, and sitting upon their shoulders were the same exploding sticks.

Belka darted out from the rose bushes. She could wait

no longer for the people to conclude this business. If she didn't find Ony soon, the dog-faced killers would.

~

The fight was on.

Ony kept his eyes fixed on Gleb as his brother advanced down the crater's perimeter toward the lower rim.

'We warned you not to come back here,' growled Han.

Gleb, his face contorted with hatred, moved forwards, pushing Ony closer to the edge of the searing pit. Then, like a coiled spring let loose, he pounced.

Ony acted on instinct. While Gleb sailed through the air, he dropped onto his back in time to catch him. When Gleb's belly came down heavily onto all four of Ony's paws, he let his legs absorb the weight. Then, with every ounce of strength he possessed, Ony pushed his limbs out again, sending Gleb bouncing over his head, straight over the edge of the walkway and into the pit.

An agonised wail sounded as Gleb was consumed by the inferno. But Ony barely processed what was happening, because suddenly Han was on top of him, biting into his breast.

Ony knew there was only one way to survive this attack: he was going to have to run. But Han wasn't letting go. No matter how much Ony wriggled and lashed out with his jaws, Han kept him pinned to the platform while he looked for an opportunity to deliver a fatal bite to his throat.

Just then, at the high ledge, the juddering of an engine sounded: a box-shaped vehicle had rolled up. Han looked momentarily across at it, gifting Ony the slightest chance to pull himself free, but just as he'd managed to get halfway up onto his paws, Han seized hold of his back leg in his jaws.

With ferocious strength, Han whipped Ony to the side, sending him tumbling over the edge.

This was it. He was going to be seared into vapours.

As Ony slid down the crater side, he threw out his front paws wildly, managing to hook his claws into the metal grid. But raging heat was blazing up his underside, and Han was coming back to finish the job.

Above, the vehicle's door slammed shut.

Ony yelped with pain as Han sunk his teeth into his paws. It was time to enter the pit.

But just then a sharp crack split the sky and Ony, his gaze still linked with his rival's, saw the air become misted with blood. Han gave a cry of pain and bolted off, a perfectly straight cut marking his flank where something had glanced alongside him.

Scrambling back onto the platform, Ony looked across to the higher rim. There, in an odd patchwork suit made from sheets of metal, was a dog-man. He was holding out a kind of stick, from which a line of smoke was drifting.

Another terrible crack sounded as sparks exploded on the metal beneath Ony's paws. Paralysed with fear, he watched as the dog-man fumbled with his metal device, pulling it at either end to open it near the middle.

His belly and groin felt hot, and his paws were bleeding from Han's bites, but this wasn't the right time for pain, so Ony dashed down from the metal walkways and into the grassless field. As fast as his legs could carry him, he made his way to the trees, barely making it into their shade before the next bang sounded and something hot and fast whistled by his ear. Sparing no consideration for where the woods led – nor whether Han had similarly sought refuge within them – Ony sprinted eastwards.

As he ran further and further from the dreadful crater and the dog-men with their exploding sticks, he kept his mind on Belka's meadow. Soon the cool waters of its river would be soothing his body, flowing into his mouth in a constant stream until the fire in his throat was extinguished and he could once again taste the air of early summer and smell its fertile earth.

But with the warmth in his underside growing ever hotter, the meadow suddenly seemed very far.

~

Belka was puzzled: the strange shimmering air was behaving differently today. Every attempt she'd made to reach one of Ony's usual haunts was frustrated by the constant shifting of the sickness in the sky, so now, unsure quite how to proceed, she lingered aimlessly in the yard where Wheel stood.

No sooner did she drop onto her belly to establish a new plan, than a flash of orange caught her eye. Across the lawns at the top of the steps, Ony was passing by.

She leapt back onto her paws and ran across the yard. Keeping tight to the shrubs fringing the field, she got Ony's attention with a single piercing bark. He turned, and the tightness that had resided in her chest since he left the meadow last night instantly relaxed. He was alright!

But...no!

He approached and began licking her muzzle. 'What's wrong?' he said. 'I told you, this town is ours. Gleb is dead. And Han is injured. He—'

Her whining silenced him.

'What is it?'

Keeping low to conceal herself from the glass eyes of the dog-mask men who were ushering residents out into the road nearby, Belka knew this was no time to lose her focus. 'Nothing. It's nothing. Ony, those creatures with the dog faces are just people. And some of them are trying to—'

'Kill us. I know. We need to get away while they finish this business with the townfolk. Let's go back to the meadow for a while. I want to swim. I feel so hot. Belka?'

She jolted, startled that he'd noticed her looking at him with such horror. Turning to move off, she then became aware of a familiar voice drifting over from the road.

They crept through the shrubs to see Dada arguing with the suited men. 'But I have no business in the city!'

The men shoved her closer to the vehicle, prompting both dogs to immediately break cover and run barking at them.

'Golden Boy! Golden Girl! No! It's not safe for you here!'

One man took hold of the old woman's arms. 'Let go of me! Soldiers, please. My home is in the countryside. My son is Comrade Ogilvy. A Party member. He'll tell you. This was his place, not mine. I'm only here for supplies. Why are you putting my trolley on the bus? Let me go back to my own village!'

Ony gripped at the trouser of the man's ankles and pulled. Another individual clicked his finger against his thumb and signalled to a third man further up the line of people. 'Alert the exterminators!'

A swift kick drove Ony off.

Dada began to cry. 'Don't hurt them! They're not strays, they're mine. If I have to go to the city, they can come with me.'

'No pets,' came a voice from behind the mask.

'Closing the cargo doors,' yelled another one.

The old woman was frantic. 'What about the dogs?'

'No pets!'

A box-like vehicle pulled up at the end of the paved avenue. Two men got out, metal sticks slung over their shoulders.

Ony and Belka stood back.

'Go!' said Dada, kicking out at the dogs with a frail leg. 'Now!'

The pair ran a few paces into the bushes, while Dada was ushered to the steps of the juddering vehicle.

'Up,' the men said to her, and as she stepped aboard she turned back towards the dogs.

Contained in Dada's eyes was the most odd message. Neither Belka or Ony had ever seen anything like it in a human, but it was clear that Dada was telling them both she truly was their friend.

The old lady then began sobbing. 'Look what they did to our city! It's a living hell!' And with that, she vanished inside and the vehicle rolled away.

Ony and Belka sprinted back through the boulevards on light paws. But they barely made it any distance before Belka stopped again.

As she scanned the sky, Ony's head flopped over to the side in confusion. 'What is it? Do you see something?'

Belka began to whine. 'We can't go to the meadow, Ony. Or back to Dada's.'

'Why not?' asked Ony, with a faint growl of annoyance.

'Because the shimmer has spread even further. It's everywhere now. We'll have to go west. There'll be water for you there, Ony, I promise. We just need to keep going a while longer.'

They readied to run off, when the sound of an approaching pack caught their ears. As individual barks grew in volume, Ony assumed a fighting stance.

Belka bristled. Ony's old enemies had, somehow, survived the chaos of the past few days and were now here to put a stop to his mischief once and for all.

Emerging around the corner was a crowd of dogs, of all shapes and sizes. This was it. There were simply too many to fight away. Blood was about to be shed, and this time it was Ony's lifesource that would stain the gravelly surface of the road.

Ony let out a growl as the muscles of his rear legs twitched in anticipation, and within seconds the pair were surrounded by the large group of assailants.

'Wait,' Belka said to Ony, noticing that these animals were curiously well-groomed.

'Where are our masters?' they were yipping. 'Where are our masters? What's happening?'

Ony lunged at the nearest dog and struck out fiercely with his claws. 'This town belongs to us now! Get away from here!'

'No!' barked Belka. 'Step back, Ony! They're just pets.'

Ony retreated from the distressed animal, whose side was now scored with three bright track marks.

'We'll be killed if we stay here,' said Belka to the terrified creatures surrounding them. 'If you want to, you can follow us to safety. But keep up, or be left behind.'

With Sun about to vanish over the western horizon, they at last stopped running. His chest heaving, Ony collapsed onto a bed of soft needles. It was the furthest he'd ever run in a single sprint.

On weakened legs, he'd followed his mate as she hurtled out of the town. Before she'd chosen any new direction, he watched as Belka intensely studied the sky, and in this stop-start manner, with the pets in tow, they'd raced away into a changing landscape. First, the buildings became sheds. Then, fields. Logging yards followed next, then scrubland, and now, with only forest surrounding them, the journey was at its end.

Nearby was a pond, into which Ony promptly jumped. Unnaturally circular, it lay in front of an odd human construction. A tower stood beside a high archway, inside of which was a large, glistening bell. Across the arch were words which, even if the dogs had been able to read human markings, were indecipherable for the moss that blanketed them.

Those that were left of the pets that had followed joined Ony in the water as they gasped and panted with exhaustion. Belka, though, stayed on the ground, looking around in every direction. 'The sky's clean here,' she announced. 'For now.'

When Ony emerged from the pool, he caught Belka's sorrowful gaze. Something in the intensity of it made him fearful. 'You've been putting something off,' he said.

Belka turned away, whimpering. 'It's all over you.'

What did she mean? He was about to probe, but just then an engine came rumbling from beyond the buildings on the other side of the archway.

His ears pricked with alertness. 'Did the dog killers follow us?' He turned back to the breathless pets. 'Stay low, all of you!' he commanded, then led Belka away to get a clearer look.

As they moved through the clearing in the forest, voices began to drift across. Moving closer to assess the level of threat, Ony noticed all manner of curious stone creatures dotted around: a large fish leaping; three snake-like things covered in spiky scales. Then, at the edge of the grass, he saw a girl sitting at a folding desk. Masses of frizzy ringlets stuck out from beneath a cap that was emblazoned with a big red cross.

Keeping far enough back to go unnoticed, but close enough to see the girl making marks on the many papers spread out in front of her, Ony became aware that people were stepping down from the arriving vehicles. These people were not of the dog-mask variety and, thankfully, they didn't carry the terrifying metal sticks.

A small group went over to meet the newcomers, who threw their bags onto the pine carpet of the forest floor and made their way to the girl's table.

Ony and Belka inched closer. The discovery of people might just be a stroke of good luck. Perhaps they were sharers?

'Name?' asked the girl with the frizzy hair to the youngest-looking of the arrivals.

'Alek.'

'Date of birth?'

'April 26th, 1971.'

'You're fifteen, too! That's at least two of us, then.'

Ony observed in the pair that curious sense of pride people sometimes carried. But it wasn't as though either of them had a nice big bone in their mouth, which was the only reason he could think of for a creature to feel quite so pleased with itself.

'Happy Workers' Day, Cadet Alek. I'm Cadet Narmin. Welcome to *Fairytale*, the least desirable Young Pioneer Camp on the face of the Earth right now.'

8

FAIRYTALE

THE PETS WERE NAPPING when Ony and Belka returned to Archway.

While Belka went to drink from Round Pond, Ony slumped onto the moss. The leaping of his heart refused to calm; as he struggled to catch his breath, waves of nausea rippled through his insides.

Why did he feel like this? It couldn't just be the distance he ran today. He'd covered far more ground the night Han and Gleb chased him to Stadium, and he'd barely broken into a pant. It *was* hotter now though. That was probably all this was.

As the pets slept beneath the forest canopy, Ony watched them with savagery burning in his eyes. Every instinct was telling him to kill the lot of them. Belka wouldn't have that, though, and he had no desire to see her look upon him again the way she had the day Feliks and Starla died.

One thing was certain, though: these pampered creatures were in for a shock. The humans that had raised them were no longer around, but the animals' devotion to their masters was sure to persist. He'd seen it before, in a canine that found himself abandoned on the edge of the city. Ony ranged with him a while, but the creature was made wretched, the sickness in his heart forged by a bond that was broken.

These others would be just the same. And their heart-sickness was going to endanger he and Belka.

Although he wished to rest, Ony knew that action was urgent, so went and joined Belka at Round Pond. Ignoring her unwillingness to look at him directly – was he really so ugly to her now? – Ony raised the matter. 'They have no fear of humans.'

Belka's head dropped to rest upon her outstretched paws. 'It's a problem.'

'They'll head into the camp as soon as they wake. Pets aren't like us strays. All they want is to serve a master.'

'Perhaps we ought to lead them away from here,' said Belka through a yawn. 'Where there are no people.'

Ony yawned too, then flopped onto his side. 'Better just to assert ourselves over them. How hard would it be to make them see they're not welcome with us?'

Belka turned and held an intense gaze upon Ony's eyes. Her brow furrowed. 'You went near the black rocks, didn't you? Even though I told you not to.'

Ony readied to protest. He hadn't known what lay beyond the rim of the searing pit; he'd merely gone to investigate when Han and Gleb launched their ambush. Still, Belka wasn't wrong. He *had* been near those mysterious, terrifying lumps of stone. 'What are they?'

'They are death, Ony. Whatever business occupied the people at Plant, it wasn't anything we could ever understand. But I know this much – they've turned the sky into disease.'

Suddenly alert to the crunching of leaf litter, both dogs rose. Near Archway, a person was approaching. It was the young man who'd conversed with the frizzy-haired girl earlier.

The hue of their coats ensured Ony and Belka remained invisible among the foliage. Nevertheless, they kept perfectly still until the boy had passed.

Belka's face grew heavy with concern. 'How can we know which ones are dog killers?'

'We have to assume they all are. That's what we'll tell the pets.'

Letting out a grunt, Belka dropped her head. 'Assemble them, then. But control yourself, Ony. They've done no wrong by you.'

Ony's mind suddenly filled with images of Belka's future litters, and he moved closer to her rear side, but she pulled away. 'I need to go,' she said.

Confused, his head tilted to the side.

'There must be others who see the shimmer, Ony. If there are others who know what it is, maybe they can show us how to rid ourselves of it.'

'Where will you go?'

'Creche. It's far enough to the south that the dog-mask men may have kept away. I've got to go back and find my mother. Maybe she can help me understand.'

A thin whine escaped Ony's jaws, but Belka rose and gave a swish of her tail. 'The direction of the wind is in my favour. I'll be back before you know it,' she said, as concern flashed across her hazel eyes. 'Just get plenty of rest, will you, Ony? You've had a hard time.'

Belka took off into the woods, and at the sound of her paws scuttling against foliage, the boy passing nearby turned. He began to approach.

Startled, Ony paced away. But in the boy's outstretched hand was something that looked – and smelt – like a snack.

'Here, foxy,' the boy was saying. His face was friendly, but as any stray was wise enough to know, humans could use their smiles to deceive, so Ony held back. The boy then ripped the item into two halves, tossing one portion in Ony's direction; a while since he last ate, Ony gave a few investigative sniffs, but stopped short of taking it in his jaws.

'It's a dumpling. It's good. Look.' The boy took a large

bite. That was all Ony needed: he gobbled up the morsel from the forest floor. Salty, greasy meat in a thin skin of bread, it was the tastiest thing he'd eaten in a long while.

'Good boy. Want more? Come on then.' The sharer patted himself on his knees to entice Ony. But now wasn't the time.

'Thanks,' said Ony with a soft bark. Then he turned and went to the sleeping pets.

He found them in the scrubby bushes among the odd stone statues. It took him just a few moments to recount all he knew of the explosion at Plant and the chaos that followed it. They were invited to share what they themselves knew, but the ignorant animals knew nothing. Even the few that had heard the explosion admitted they'd simply snuggled deeper into their masters' beds, inconvenienced by the disturbance.

Turning to the issue of their current situation, Ony let his ears stand high. 'People are not what you think they are,' he said.

'People are so kind,' yapped one retriever.

'And helpful,' said a herder with a wide smile. 'Mine carries me everywhere. "How can he be expected to walk up the stairs on such little legs?" she always says. I love her!'

'You sheltered fools don't know anything about people!' growled Ony. 'They're more dangerous than a wolf-dog or a bear or anything else you could ever come across.'

'Not ogres,' said a terrier.

Ony's head tilted.

'Ogres are way more dangerous than people. They're bigger, for a start. And they have enormous clubs they use when they try to capture princesses.'

'And dragons,' added a fluffy female with a pure white coat, prompting a chorus of confused grunts. 'Dragons! You know, those beasts that live in underground lairs. They fly over the land, and breathe fire and poison. My master always reads to Sofiy about dragons.'

'Shut up, stupid dogs!' barked Ony. 'Dragons don't drive around in their vehicles and point metal sticks at you which blow holes through your heads. And as for Ogres – do they offer your mothers spoilt meat which makes blood froth from her mouth and the life leave her eyes? No. That's men. It was men that poisoned our sky and scorched our earth, and it's men that will put an end to our lives the instant they get the chance.'

Puffing out his chest, Ony walked along the assembled line. If any challenger was going to fight him for dominance, it was better they did so now. But, exactly as he predicted, each animal lowered its head in subservience. Ony might have been younger than most of them, but his life as a stray – with the scars of many a battle scoring his torso – elevated his status.

'If it had been up to me,' he snarled, 'I'd have eaten each of your pampered hearts. But Belka insisted you follow us here, and you did. We saved your lives, and now you owe us. All we ask of you is that you do *not* seek the affection of the people in this place. Do that, and you can consider your debt repaid. Do you understand?'

The assembled animals dipped their necks.

'If people know we're here, they'll come with their metal sticks,' said Ony, allowing just enough of his fangs to be seen to ensure what he said next wasn't taken as an idle threat. 'So roam this forest as you like. There's plenty of fruit and seed here. But if I see you beyond the line of Archway – even once – I'll kill you.'

Belka walked until Sun's beams crowned the treetops with a golden glow. Not quite hungry enough during the afternoon to risk the villages, the strain of a full day's journeying now it was at its end had become overwhelming. Without nourishment, she couldn't go on.

She stopped when a cluster of crumbling houses appeared through the trunks. Waiting in the saplings until she was sure there were no vehicles around, she trotted across the stony track and focused her attention to the tip of her nose.

Around the back of a dwelling that looked every inch the same as Dada's, she located vegetable scrapings. She really must have burned through her energy today; even after swallowing down the lot, she wanted more. The dams with their new litters used to say how their entire pregnancies passed with a desire to eat at all times of the day and night – did that explain her lingering hunger?

Flopping onto the grass that fringed an outbuilding, Belka braved a brief look at her underside. But she saw no swelling, only a mysterious, pulsating air, which clung to her exactly as she'd known in her heart it would. The thought of a litter growing within such a place was frightful: Plant's spreading air, so rotten and choking, wished only to starve all things of their life.

Not a sound came from the house. Straining her ears, she soon perceived that the entire area was bathed in silence. Urgent business must have called the villagers away, which suited her well given the time of day and her need for sleep.

When she next opened her eyes, dawn's light already washed over the lower portion of the morning sky; rare was a night without a single disturbance.

Now well-rested – not even her dreams had given her cause to stir – she lapped water from a trough and vacated the garden. She ran into the rays of Sun as it climbed out from the horizon, and used the canopy wherever she could to shield her eyes.

As much of her energy went to her senses as it did the muscles that propelled her further eastward. As long as scent was in her nostrils, the bad air of Plant was distant.

Her tail wagged to find so many natural odours on her route back to Creche: the musk of a weasel on the roots of a larch here, a buck deer's territorial spray along a gnarled cedar fence there. This was more like it.

But explosions in the sky near the southern boundary of the city soon brought an end to her carefree mood. They were wielding their terrible sticks again. It was clear from the echoes that the explosions were afar, but she'd seen enough of those devices to know that distance wouldn't save a dog from their violence.

Slowing now to barely a crawl, she proceeded with caution towards the first of Creche's sheds. As a pup, the commotion of the people's machines here had been constant. To find the area hushed was unusual, though nothing worth fretting over in times as tense as these.

When she came at last to the fields beyond the last of the wide buildings, she saw a circle of dogs resting there, and began to rush in excited circles. The mewling of litters in the sheds was as pleasant a sound as any she'd heard in her life. Soon, she was sniffing and waltzing with old faces as though the chaos of the previous days had never occurred; though, as far as her old friends were concerned, nothing out of the ordinary *had* happened beyond the din of heavy machinery coming to a sudden halt.

Unable to believe this, Belka probed. 'So, none of you answered the call of the alphas?'

'Their howls don't reach this far,' said Nazrin. 'And even if they did, their turf squabbles don't matter to us. There's nothing where the menfolk dwell that we desire.'

'But you didn't hear the bang that happened that night?'

'It's hard to hear anything down here with the machines always running.'

'What about the vehicles? The flying ones with their whirring? The ones on the roads with their flashes and screams?'

'Sure,' said Inna, 'we hear them. But that's their business. It's no concern of ours.'

Belka suddenly felt a sense of alarm. Her friends had been safe from Plant's horrid clouds, and from the terrible intent of the dog-mask men, and that was a relief to know. But the danger of the times had passed these dams by. Even if the killers in their box-like vehicles decided not to venture into the southern reaches of the city, the wind *would* change, and when it did the females of the Creche sheds would find themselves ill prepared for the horror.

A sudden rustling sounded on Belka's right side, and she looked up to see her friend, Lala, emerging from out of the shade of the bushes. She was downcast and exhausted in appearance, but that wasn't why Belka recoiled.

Lala yipped with agitation. 'Why are you looking at me like that?'

'Your belly!'

The tails of the other dogs began to wag in playful delight. 'Bellies tend to swell up when we're in pup, daft girl!' one of them laughed. 'You have two summers already – you should know that yourself by now.'

Belka fixed her eyes on her friend's swollen stomach, shrouded beneath a fuzzy aura. 'Lala, what about you? Did you attend the assembly?'

Lala turned away, shamed, but Mila pursued it. 'Why is Belka asking you such a question? Have you been mixing with the city dogs?'

'I wasn't there the night it happened,' Lala said. 'Fedir told me about it a few mornings ago. I only went to show him his babies in my stomach. But ever since we lingered near those horrid hot stones something's been wrong. Yesterday, I felt a pain. The pups inside me have always been so hungry for life, but now their fidgeting has stopped. I think… I think they're gone.'

A chorus of whining spread around the dams. 'Are you still in pain?'

Lala's head drooped. 'I don't know. It's hard to say when my heart aches so.'

Belka burned to hear of Lala's loss; as she slumped sadly onto the grass, it chilled her to consider that it may already be too late to warn these dogs of the danger. 'Listen to me, all of you,' she said. 'You need to stay away from Plant, and from any stones that gleam with the blackness of deepest night. There are men in vehicles who appear like dogs now. They wear strange, snouted masks on their faces with round eyes of glass. And they carry sticks which make dogs fall to the ground with holes in them.'

The females, clearly shocked, listened without interruption, but just as they were readying to question her, a voice came from behind, one that Belka hadn't heard since before the frosts descended. It was Galina, her mother, and just to hear her soothed Belka's agitation.

'My girl! Look how much you've grown! But there's nothing in your belly? Hasn't Ony given you his gift yet?'

'Mama,' said Belka, turning. 'Tell me you can see the watery air around Lala's underside!'

Galina turned to face the young female, then looked blankly back at Belka, who began to bark fretfully. 'Why am I the only one who can see it?'

'Calm yourself, child,' said Galina, licking Belka on her face. 'Come with me to the front of the sheds and tell me all your troubles.'

Away from the others, Belka lay on the paved ground while her mother tenderly cleaned the dust and grime of a long journey from off her coat.

'We suspected something like this resided in you,' said Galina. 'Just a new pup, you were. Your eyes had only just come open, yet you couldn't stop watching the runt of Oksana's litter. We tried to make you play with her, but you wouldn't go near. It was my grandmother who noticed it. "She sees sickness," she said, and confessed to me that all her life she'd been able to see certain kinds of illness in living things. I had no idea what she meant, and thought her mind might be beginning to slow. But then the runt died.'

'So you can't see it, mama?'

'It skipped me. And my mother, too. But it seems to have come through the line to you.'

'I see it on things that aren't alive, too,' whined Belka. 'On dead men and dead dogs. It's on the play equipment in the parks and on the tools left laying in the wheat fields. What about my great-grandmother? Did she see it clinging to things which never had life?'

Galina gave it a moment's thought. 'She never mentioned it. It might be that the perception is stronger in you.' She paused again. 'Or it's some new kind of sickness. But settle yourself, my daughter. Tell me, why do I not see any swelling in your belly? I know you're not yet fully grown, but I was already full with my second litter at your age.'

Belka's whining became uncontrollable. While her mother gave comforting licks, she looked for the right words, but each way she thought of expressing it merely added to her pain.

She turned to face her mother and ceased whimpering. Then, with a confidence that ensured Galina wouldn't challenge her, she finally imparted words she never dreamt she'd have to utter.

'We all know how the story goes, don't we, mama? Meet a dog. Make a bond. You have your pups and live happily for the rest of your life. But that's not the ending for me.'

Galina's head tilted. 'What are you saying to me, Belka?'

'I'm saying, mama, that my body will never be able to grow a litter.'

9

BALL BOY AND RED CROSS GIRL

ALL THROUGHOUT THE NIGHT, puttering engines pulled up at Archway and set people down. In the past, vehicles had never given Ony cause to worry, but ever since the explosion rattled the world and brought a new type of man to the region, each wheeled machine now made dread swell in the pit of his stomach.

Yesterday, barely any human folk were to be found in the Camp grounds. By this morning, however, their number had multiplied many times over, and as Ony skirted the tree line around the western edge of the site, it was apparent that groups were forming among the arrivals. Picking out the alphas, though, was a task which quickly defeated him.

Each of the newcomers took up a position in the line that led to the folding table. The girl with the frizzy hair and the red cross on her hat was nowhere to be seen today; in her place was a man with far more summers behind him, and while she had met yesterday's arrivals with a friendly but awkward smile, he greeted this morning's with an intimidating air.

The boy was absent, too. This was disappointing. Ony's nausea had persisted through the night, and he wondered if something warm in his belly might help settle it.

Although his energy was low, Ony moved away from Camp to map the area. Rejecting pack life in favour of ranging alone meant having to quickly rely only on himself for knowledge of local territory – a dog who was ignorant of shortcuts and bypasses was much weakened – and it was a task he prioritised wherever he went.

A natural trail led west through a grove. The woods here were dense with peeling birches, but soon began to thin out again, and after a short time running, the scent of minerals on the breeze told Ony a river was up ahead.

It appeared from the far side of Birch Grove on a north/south route. Sparkling beneath Sun's morning light, this wide waterway marked the western boundary. Ony locked this frontier in his mind's map.

On his way down the bank to the water, prickly grasses irritated his tender underside, but the moment the cool current washed under him, Ony's soreness melted away completely. Surrendering his weight to the water brought much pleasure.

Belka would be glad to know such a place existed. He looked ahead along the river's edge to see if there was a suitable oak which might replace the one she'd had to leave behind: finding a new den was essential for the litter they'd soon bring into the world.

With his sore underside now calmed, Ony pulled himself up onto the banks and shook the river out of his coat. Proceeding south, he noticed a figure up ahead, standing at the water's edge and, beyond, a second individual. When he was close enough, he recognised them as the boy and girl from the camp.

Standing apart, the young people were holding out lines into the fast-flowing river like the men in Belka's meadow. At the thought of a fish's succulent white flesh, Ony licked his chops and dropped down halfway between the pair.

A short time later, the frizzy-haired girl let out a guttural yell and began to furiously wind in a contraption. A fish surfaced with a flash of aggression, which sent Ony's tail into an excited swish. She whipped back her stick until it arched almost back on itself, then the boy, taking up the net that lay on the stones, ran across to her. But within moments the line snapped, sending the girl hurtling onto her bottom with a dull thump.

The boy held out his arm. The girl took it and hauled herself off the riverbank. Pointing at the net, she shook her head. 'That was a bit optimistic, don't you think?'

'I thought you had it for sure,' said the boy, and as she patted the dust off herself he went back to his own spot.

Ony edged closer and spoke to the boy with his eyes.

'Hungry are you, Foxy?' The boy fiddled around in his pocket and pulled out bread. He took a bite, then tossed the other half in Ony's direction. 'It's not much. The Party is supposed to be organising a food drop today.'

Grateful for the morsel, Ony lay down on the grass and let Sun seep into his damp fur. He was about to fall into a nap, when the girl made her way over.

'Excuse me, cadet. Did I hear you say they're bringing food today?'

The boy, pulling sporadically at his line, nodded. 'So the Colonel says. Have they placed you yet?'

The girl shook her frizzy hair from side to side. 'They want to assemble the main teams first. Then they'll decide where to put the medics. How about you?'

'I start with the mining team tomorrow. Medics? Aren't you fifteen? That's a little young for a nurse, no?'

'Of course it is!' laughed the girl. 'I haven't even finished my basic First Aid at cadet academy yet.'

A quizzical look spread across the boy's face, but before he could speak, his line suddenly shot off into the river. Ony watched fascinated at the explosion of tugging and winding that followed, and was amazed to see the fish now at the water's edge.

The boy bent down to lift up a net, but the girl was already holding it out. 'Keep winding!' she was calling. 'One more!' Giving his stick a final heave, the boy brought the catch close enough for the girl to scoop it into her net and, with a whoop of delight, he dropped to his knees.

Ony peered over the rim and wagged his tail at the sight of a plump and colourful trout. But since a third person was making his way over, he backed nervously away to watch the boy work the hook out of the animal's mouth while it thrashed against the damp soil in a pointless attempt to save its own life.

The girl cleared her throat. 'You know, that technically counts as my catch.'

'Because you landed it? I don't think so.'

'Not because I landed it – because that was the fish I had earlier.'

Ony observed the boy's face contort with disgust. 'That dirty old catfish that snapped your line?'

'Catfish! You're blind as well as pig-headed, then?'

'Listen, I may be pig-headed but at least I can bring a fish in.'

'So can I! I wore that trout out for you!'

'Ah yes, your incredible trout that can disguise itself as a greasy catfish.' The boy laughed. 'Foxy, why don't you put in a claim, too?'

The older fisherman, who'd sat watching the pair as they bickered, spoke up then. 'Good fish,' he said. 'But he's not for eating.'

The boy and girl looked at one other. 'This is prime for eating!'

'Before the accident, yes. But this is the Pripyat River. It flows right past the Chernobyl site.'

The man went back to his little stool. The boy, holding

his arms out at his sides, spoke with a lowered voice. 'What did he mean by that?'

The girl shrugged her shoulders then looked away, and when she spoke again the normal rise and fall of her speech was replaced with a curiously flattened tone. 'The guys from the Party who came to my school told us it was only a minor incident.'

'Same,' replied the boy, whose enthusiasm for their conversation seemed similarly absent. 'So did the lady on the news.'

Ony bristled as the atmosphere grew suddenly tense. The worry that descended upon the pair was almost visible to him, like a low fog coming down over pastureland in late summer. But he wanted nothing to do with people's mysterious anxieties, so stood to walk a circle around the fish and watch as it sucked down its last gasps.

The girl went back to her spot while the boy took the fish between his hands and submerged it into the river. 'Sorry, Foxy. We're not eating him today.' The animal's shiny body came back to life and it swam away, at which Ony offered a grunt of disapproval. Such a waste!

The boy plunged his arm deep into his bag, then brought it out again with a perfectly round object in his fingers. 'Do you like fetch?' he said, holding the thing out before him.

But Ony would never take anything directly from a human. He'd warned Belka often enough to be extremely cautious in this very situation, and would need to impress upon the pets back at Camp the same thing.

This, however, was not food. When the boy let the object drop onto the grass, it rolled away. Ony followed it with his muzzle but remained where he was, and the boy reached down to hold it aloft again. Ony's eyes blazed with concentration as he followed the boy's next action: first, his arm pivoted back. Then, it came quickly forward, then, finally, the ball went up into the air.

Ony's tail swung wildly from side to side as he shot off after it. He didn't even know why he wished to get the thing, but retrieving it seemed like a matter of life or death. As the ball bounced off the stubbly grass of the river bank and rolled away, Ony accelerated at full pace to catch it and in that moment neither his nausea nor his scorched underside troubled him. Between chasing it down, taking it up in his jaws and delivering it back to the boy, nothing existed at all.

'Good boy!'

Ony's heart warmed. Dada used to say that. The words were somehow soothing, and he wished to hear them again.

Again, the ball went up. And again, Ony fetched it.

'Good boy!'

They repeated the act many times over as Sun climbed higher into the morning sky, until eventually the boy and girl began to pack up. 'That'll have to do for one day I'm afraid,' said the boy, and he and his frizzy-haired companion scurried back up the bank.

As Ony followed them through Birch Grove towards Camp, with his eyes fixed hopefully on the boy's bag where the ball had been placed, a scent on a sapling made him suddenly halt – and just like that, the ball was the furthest thing from his mind.

Moving his nostrils right up to the spindly trunk, he knew now that there was a more pressing matter to attend to.

This tiny tree, swaying gently in the breeze, smelt just like Han.

Ony sprinted through the woods, so fast that fallen leaves swirled in his wake. If Han wanted to finish this now, he was ready.

But it wasn't Han he saw when he rounded a corner. It was the pets.

Panting and wheezing as they tried to catch their breath, the small group were huddled together. When they saw Ony charging at them with his teeth bared, their heads dropped.

'You think you can ambush me?' Ony growled, lashing at each of them with his fangs as they cowered low.

'We meant no harm! Don't hurt us, Ony!'

'Then what are you doing here?'

One of the terriers dared to bring his head up. 'You said people can't be trusted. You said we're not to seek their affection. But you were playing fetch with that one.'

The tension in Ony's body subsided. His ears came down and he sheathed his teeth back behind his lips. 'Get up, all of you.'

The dogs did as he commanded.

'I know how it looks to you. But things are different for a stray. Come back with me to Archway and I'll explain it to you all.'

Leading the animals on a run through Birch Grove, Ony considered how to make them see it. Until they themselves had experienced the violent side of peoplekind – the way men could inflict harm even while smiles lit up their faces – it simply wasn't safe for them to be near strangers. A stray learnt things a pet did not, and those lessons were taught by pain.

In other circumstances, Ony would have gladly stood aside and let them learn the hard way. What did it matter to him if they wished to make the kind of mistake that had cost his own mother her life? But these weren't ordinary times. Men, for reasons he himself didn't understand, were actively searching for dogs to destroy.

Life on the streets had helped Ony distinguish the harmless from the dangerous, but even with a stray's smarts, each and every encounter with a human was a risk. With time, the pets could understand. They, too, would be able to judge when the risk was worth taking, the way he had judged it this morning with Ball Boy. But that time wasn't now, and an error of judgement could see them all blasted with the men's awful killing tubes.

Coming now out of Birch Grove, Monument and its strange stone animals appeared, followed by the dwellings of Camp. Now back, the time had come to begin the task of educating the pets. The gap between what they understood and what he and Belka did was dangerously wide, and unless efforts were made to narrow it, tragedy was unavoidable.

The pets assembled with haste to hear what Ony had to say. But before he could speak, Jayla, the fluffy-haired female with short legs, interrupted him to draw attention to something: there were fewer pets here now than had been here before.

Ony glanced among them. Jayla was right.

He instructed the pets to remain where they were, then set off on a lap around the perimeter of the site. But no matter how thoroughly he looked, four of them were nowhere to be found, so he eventually returned to the waiting pets and began his explanation for his interactions with the Ball Boy.

The pets listened agreeably. He'd been ready to meet their protests with force, but they simply accepted what he told them in a way that Ony found unsettling. These animals were seeing in him a pack leader, when he wished to be seen in no such way.

The sooner these useless lapdogs were out of his life, the better. Beyond obeying his wish to refrain from attracting human attention, he expected nothing of these immature animals, and felt it unwise that they should expect anything of him. Once Belka was back from her visit to Creche, it was likely the pair would head further afield to start their family, and when they did, the rest were not welcome.

All throughout that evening, the pets followed close while Ony continued to search for the missing four. Then, as the forest began to shrink into darkness, he instructed them to go find their beds for the night.

It was as he was looking for his own sleeping spot that he picked up – faint, but unmistakable – a scent that put a bounce in his step and a thump in his chest:

Wolf.

He upped his pace. Nearby was a rocky slope rising from the forest's edge. Wolf-dogs were at their most dangerous when they worked to surround their target, so a hollow in a hillside offered much better protection. Before curling up, he briefly considered running back down to warn the pets. But as a long yawn escaped him, he changed his mind.

They had their own noses, after all.

~

As the first light of day found its way into the woods, the people of Camp began to rise. Soon, engines came to disturb the peace of the forest, and a line of vehicles was waiting near Archway.

When Ony came down from his hideout to start a new day's surveying, the pets followed him over to a paved hill at the northern perimeter. He'd made a note of this spot yesterday, fancying it as the premier location from which to see the whole site. As far as he could tell, there was no better vista in the area.

Once at the top, a spaniel plopped down beside him. 'What are those long machines?' he asked, but Ony, who couldn't possibly know the answer to that, remained silent.

'It's called a bus,' said a hound whose maleness had been mutilated.

Ony peered down at the floppy-eared fellow. 'Bus?'

The hound, cheered by Ony's attention, looked devotedly up. 'People can't run the way we can. So they ride buses. My master went on one everyday to go to Chernobyl.'

'What is *Chernobyl*?'

The pets began to snigger. 'It's the name of the power plant, Ony.'

Ony let out a grunt. These dim creatures knew more about peoplekind than they knew of their own nature.

From his vantage point, Ony watched as the humans shuffled towards the front of the buses. At the door of each, a man clutching a sheet of paper spoke to each person individually, until eventually they were all seated behind the vehicle's windows.

'Look, Ony,' said a terrier. 'The boy is talking with that soldier.'

'Soldier?'

'The men in the suits. They're called soldiers. My master was a soldier. That's your master down there with him.'

Ony lashed out – 'I serve no master, foolish animal!' – ensuring that the scolded terrier, who was now nursing a shallow but painful new wound on his breast, thought twice before remarking so clumsily again.

But it was, indeed, Ball Boy. Standing alone outside the vehicles, he spoke to a soldier through an open window, gesturing with his arms until the buses roared into life and began to roll away without him.

A herding dog grew excited. 'They left! They left!

Ony threw a glance his way. 'So?'

'You said we shouldn't go near the people,' said the herding dog. 'But the people are gone. Now we can go in to scavenge.'

The others liked this. 'Yes, Ony! We can scavenge now!' they yapped.

Ony stood with his head high. 'Go. But if the buses return, get out of there right away.'

With that, the dogs hurried down to Camp. But Ony,

troubled that the four vanished animals still hadn't returned, hung back on the hill.

There was no good reason for them to take off yesterday. Many dogs fell aside during the sprint away from their ruined home in the east, either too unfit to keep up or else breaking away by choice. But those that had made it had done well to reach a place of relative safety, where multiple groups of people meant decent pickings from the bins.

What other option was better than this presently?

As the pets vanished around the other side of the huts, a flash of colour on his right side caught his eye. Ball Boy, carrying the same apparatus as yesterday, was making his way to the path through Birch Grove, his head hanging forlornly. Resolving to catch up with him later, Ony first turned to the paved hill's other slope. This was one of the few parts of the local map he hadn't yet internalised.

Near the bottom was a circle of mossy boulders. Ideal for launching an ambush, these towering stones would offer shelter from Sun, too. He made his way to the nearest stone, but even before he got to it, a scent entered his nostrils.

He sniffed the line of pee on the rock's jagged edge. It was beyond doubt: Han had put this here very recently.

10

BLOODSHED AT CRECHE

BELKA'S JOURNEY to the fields of her birth had failed to adequately enlighten her.

Her mother, blind to the strange shimmer like all the others, was clueless as to how Belka might rid herself and Ony of its lingering effects. The older dams recalled certain dogs over the years who claimed to be able to detect things invisible to others, but they'd never heard of anything to equal Belka's odd talent. A sensitivity to vibrations in the earth before a weather event was one thing, but an ability to see a sickness that thrived after the life of its carrier ended was something else altogether. Belka was on her own with that one.

Still, keeping company with the girls of the Creche fields gave Belka a feeling of peace; as a new dawn broke, she felt little desire to hurry back west. Provided the winds didn't change, and if the people remained absent from the machines inside the buildings, she would recover here a while from the mayhem and trauma, letting the soft yips of the newborns in the sheds conjure bittersweet visions of the brood she longed for.

In the afternoon, when the females were coming back together after foraging for snacks in the nearby fields, Belka was laying with Lala, whose emotional state had by now improved. Although she would always grieve for the lost litter, Lala was cheered to know that soon another would be growing inside her, and this one, she proudly insisted, would flourish.

But such an assertion troubled Belka. It was wrong to go on this way, fancying that Plant's infected vapours would spare the dams of Creche. It was a matter of *when* the wind changed, not if.

'Listen to me,' she said, when all dogs had reassembled. 'You've got to pay attention to your senses all the time now.'

'But what are we looking for, Belka?'

'Different things. A bitter taste, that will prickle your tongues. An itch in your throat, like you swallowed thorny stems in the briar patches. Perhaps your eyes will begin to burn. The biggest thing though, is if you notice that everything loses its scent. When that happens, gather up your pups and leave. All of you.'

'Where shall we go?'

'West. It seems to be weaker there. When your scent comes back, then you can rest. But keep alert and be ready to move on again.'

As though her words caused their senses to sharpen presently, all nostrils began twitching.

'That's it, sisters. Stay attuned to your noses.'

'No,' said Galina. 'I'm picking something up right now. Engines.'

Belka stood with pointed ears.

'The people are back!' Lala called out.

Sure enough, a vehicle was approaching, and its shape sent a bolt of terror along the length of Belka's spine.

These were dog killers.

As loudly as she could, Belka barked out a warning. 'Bolt! Don't allow yourselves to be seen!'

With great urgency, the mothers dashed across the yard to the sheds where their distressed pups lay in a huddle. From the door, Belka kept watch, trying to keep her mind calm with memories of growing up in this very nursery.

The vehicle pulled to a stop. Two men emerged from inside, their heads covered like the honey harvester in the riverside meadow.

To Belka's relief, the arrivals held no weapons, only wide metal grates, like doors turned on their sides. These, the men fastened together around the buildings, until eventually something resembling a wall began to appear.

Lala, watching beside Belka, began to whine. 'What are they doing?'

'They're fencing off the buildings from the yards.'

'Are they going to kill us?

'Just stay still.'

'They are, aren't they?'

Belka gave Lala a comforting lick and kept her eyes trained on the men. There was nothing to fear if every dog stayed as they were, out of sight.

But Lala's state of agitation was getting worse. 'They're going to kill the pups, Belka.'

Reaching out, Belka placed her paw on Lala's backside where she sat. 'It's alright. We're alright.' The men, focused upon their task, took turns heading to and from the vehicle, each time bringing with them a new section of fence. For a moment, it seemed as though Lala might be finally calming, but she suddenly rose up onto her paws.

What happened next was so sudden Belka couldn't have hoped to keep it from happening. Lala, blinded by panic, ran straight out into the yard.

'No, Lala!' called Belka. But her distressed friend was deaf to her protests.

Lala darted at one of the men, who was kneeling at the join between two sections of the fence. She sunk her teeth into his calf, causing him to cry out with shock and pain.

The second individual took off running back to the vehicle, shouting and waving his arms. Belka's hackles stood on end: she knew exactly what he was going to fetch.

She made it to the sheds in no time at all. 'We need to run!' said Belka, panting heavily. 'All of us! Now!'

'But the pups, Belka. We can't leave them!'

'There's enough of us to take one each. Gather them up and run as fast as you can! Remember my warning – don't go where the air chokes you.'

She went forward and plucked away a pup nestling near Galina, feeling its tiny mass bounce from her teeth as she sidled through the others on her way back to the door. 'Come mama,' Belka whined. 'Come now!'

A terrible blast sounded from the yard. Belka, the folds of the pup's neck clamped tightly between her teeth as she peered around the edge of the shed, whimpered.

The man was now wearing a dog-face mask, and was holding aloft his metal stick. Smoke drifted from its end where flame had belched out. Lala was on the ground. Her rear legs were kicking as though she were in a dream.

But it wasn't sleep.

Certain that the dog killer wasn't looking, Belka made to dash. But the mothers in the shed were protesting. 'Don't take them! It's not safe! Keep the pups here!'

Belka was familiar with the speed of the people's lethal contraptions so, knowing how any delay could cost her life, she raced out across the yard as fast as her legs could take her.

When she was safely out of view behind a stack of boxes, she dropped the pup onto the dusty ground and dared a glimpse back towards the sheds. Where were the others? They hadn't followed!

The dog-mask man was striding towards the hut, his stick held out in front of him. His companion was following up behind.

Now! It had to be now! Why weren't they running?

Hoping to draw them away, Belka issued a bark, but the men didn't stray from their course. Then their devices were exploding with deafening eruptions, flashes of flame lighting up the dark nursery in which all the females – and all their litters – were trapped.

Belka's heart was a frozen rock on a river's bed. Too stunned at first to even breathe, the danger of the situation soon unleashed a flood of wild energy and roused her into sudden action. She took up the tiny creature once again.

There was nothing else she could do but flee from Creche.

But no matter how far away she got, the many, many blasts lost none of their terror, each one searing a deeper scar onto her already wounded heart.

~

Ony kept pace with Ball Boy as he marched through the birches towards the river.

Were this young man's words meant for a dog's ears? It seemed to Ony that he was really chattering away to himself. People did that, sometimes.

Perhaps there were human folk who stood apart from the rest of their kind, as some wolf-dogs tended to do. Given how these odd, upright creatures apparently *had* to speak their thoughts aloud, it was curious to think of them all alone in the wilds of the woods. How well could they fare, with nobody to talk to?

'Well, if the miners aren't ready I guess I'll just have to find a way to be useful around Fairytale,' the boy was saying, as he looked down at Ony trotting alongside him. Although he smiled, it was clear to Ony that he was sad.

A large white cloud moved in front of Sun, casting the open regions of the glade into welcome shade, but soon the breeze in the high skies shunted it along again, and just as the forest burst into dappled light, a voice called out from behind them. It was the girl, and she, too, appeared wrapped in an odd kind of sorrow.

They advanced wordlessly to the bank of the river where, to Ony's delight, the boy tossed the ball back and forth. He turned periodically to check the end of his line for a fish; today, though, Ony didn't care if he brought one in or not. He'd had no appetite at all since he woke up.

The fetching game came to an end, and Ony took a dip in the river. With the cool water soothing his underside, he began to wonder about Belka's voyage. Hopefully, she wouldn't delay much longer in getting back. Belka was as smart an animal as any he knew, and nearly as fast as him, but the times were strange and the safety of nothing could be assured. He wondered whether she might return with news of their old home. Perhaps all was safe there again, and they'd get another chance to raise a family in the nook of her splendid oak with its peaceful view down to the river. It was a happy thought.

When he pulled himself out of the water and onto the bank, Ony noticed that his legs felt heavy. It was odd: he hadn't played *that* many games of fetch. Fatigue like this seemed to be happening more regularly, it seemed. The preceding days, full of upheaval and uncertainty, must have taken it out of him.

He lay down to nap, coming-to again when Ball Boy and Red Cross Girl began packing up and, as a trio, they headed back through Birch Grove.

The conversation of the boy and girl came to a sudden halt after a time, and a long, tense silence hung between them which suited Ony just fine. On high alert for Han's ambush, he needed his ears, so when the boy and girl resumed their chatter, Ony dropped back.

'What made you want to volunteer for this, anyway?' he heard the girl say.

'I didn't volunteer. I was sent.'

'Either way, you're a true patriot, cadet.'

The boy, letting out a long breath, seemed to deflate. 'I don't know about that.' Ony recognised the look in his eye as one of shame, as though he'd done something wrong that he didn't want the girl to know about.

'You answered the call of your motherland in her hour of need. If that doesn't make you a patriot, I don't know what does. You'll have made the Party very proud.'

When they reached Archway, Ony deviated from the pair and ventured through Boulders to climb the far side of the bank. But before he reached the vantage point, his nostrils flared. That familiar scent filled his nose.

Han.

Here.

Right now.

Ony dropped onto his belly. As silently as possible, he edged down from the brow of the hill until he saw flashes of colour in a clearing below. Focusing his eyes, he was greeted by a most unexpected sight.

Han was addressing the pets. Gathered into an audience, they were listening attentively.

With a cat's stealth, Ony crept over to the rotten stump of a fallen larch, where Han's address became faintly audible.

'All of your woes are because of that animal,' he was saying. 'Ony destroyed our town, our lives, the lives of your masters, just so he could win more snacks from people. Pack with us, and we'll work to punish him for his deceit.'

One dog – Ony was quite sure it was Jayla – protested. 'But it was the dragon that caused all this turmoil.' The pained yelp that followed told Ony that Han had answered her offering with a swift nip.

Ony inched back from his hiding spot. If these animals turned against him in any significant number, he would need to be away from here as quickly as possible.

He turned for the hilltop, but just as he did the nausea that had hung dull in his core all day suddenly rolled up through his innards.

Was it the shock of what he'd just witnessed? Quite possibly. Or perhaps it was nothing more than the result of the deep tiredness that had been stalking him these past days. He began to silently retch; within seconds, a large pile of vomit lay on the leaf-strewn carpet of the forest.

Although he desired to know more of Han's plans, he was overcome by the need to rest. At this moment, no place on Earth appealed to him more than the quiet gloom of the rocky cave where he'd spent last night.

Belka's return from her traumatic journey to Creche caused quite a commotion among the pet dogs.

Their number seemed to her to be much diminished since she left Camp three dawns ago. Where was the terrier? There was at least one of that breed. And she was certain two hounds had followed them out of the old town, yet only one was to be found here now.

Conversely, the people's number had swelled. From out of the vehicles which were pulling up outside Archway, scores of them were emerging. They appeared tired and, in some cases, visibly distressed.

At the sight of them, Belka made a swift retreat behind a mound of clay bricks, from where she was just able to see the pets. Standing out in the open, they looked on as the humans first flung their bags and tools onto the road, then strode towards the dwellings beyond Archway and its glistening bell.

The pets' behaviour was a surprise. Ony had vowed to assert himself early on, yet their apparent fearlessness of the human folk told a different story: either he hadn't bothered, or they weren't willing to obey. Her heart fluttered for a brief moment at the possibility he'd taken his aggression too far and they'd overpowered him.

Discreetly, she walked around the full boundary, but found no fresh traces of Ony. There was so much she wished to tell him – including something that required immediate attention – but mostly Belka wanted simply to be near him a while. The horrors of yesterday couldn't be communicated, but he would know the moment he saw her eyes that pain of the very worst kind resided within her.

She let forth a bark. But the pets weren't interested. Most continued to watch as the engines burst back into life and the vehicles began to roll away, but after she called out to them a second time a couple broke off, dipping their heads as they approached her.

'Where's Ony?'

'He went to the river with the boy yesterday. But he never came back.'

Belka frowned. This would need to be followed up, but now wasn't the time. Fretting somewhat, she looked around. 'Are any of the females mothers?'

The pair looked at one another.

'Mothers,' repeated Belka. 'Have any of the female pets had pups?'

'Jayla had a litter before her master took her in.'

Craning around the brick pile, Belka called out to the short-legged female with her elegant snout and bright coat of the fluffiest fur.

Jayla ran across and sniffed at Belka. 'Did you see the dragon?'

'The what?'

'The dragon.' Jayla motioned over to one of Monument's stone statues. 'One of those things.'

Belka studied the figure behind her closely, but struggled to understand what she was looking at. Three snake-like heads appeared to come from out of the ground, with a single body set behind them.

Jayla plopped down onto the leaves. 'The explosion at the power plant. Ever since, a disease has been spreading across the land. Well, only dragons spread disease that way. Chernobyl must have been built on top of a dragon's lair, and the explosion must have woken him up. My masters used to read about things like that to Sofiy every night. Sofiy's my best friend in the whole world.'

This strange account intrigued Belka. With a brief ripple of her hackles, she briefly remembered back to when she'd stood in front of the burning wreckage and felt that something inside had come alive.

She let out a whine. 'Is it true you once had a litter?'

'A long time ago, yes. But then one day my masters took me to the vet and he put me to sleep, and when I woke up again a part of me was gone and I knew I'd never have another pup.'

Belka turned on the spot and took off at a trot. 'Follow me', she said, and led the pet away.

As the pair sprinted southward, Belka's mind was drawn back to what Jayla had said. Was this *dragon* the cause of the shimmer? If such a being possessed the ability to spread the sickness, it may also have the power to reverse it.

A feeling of hope began to warm Belka's innards. Perhaps if they paid this strange animal a visit, they could persuade it to find a better home and spare the rest of them from its destructive breath?

And if they couldn't persuade it, tough little Ony knew other ways to make a creature yield.

11

THE DRAGON OF CHERNOBYL

'You had a baby!'

Inside the concealed den, Jayla smiled widely as she looked upon the pup.

Belka, as weary in body as she was in spirit, felt no urge to correct the pet. A time would come when the awful circumstances of this creature's presence would need to be explained, but for now her only concern was getting food into the tiny thing. Whining, she nudged Jayla towards the sleeping animal with her snout.

Jayla cast a worried look back. 'What do you want me to do?'

'I don't know,' said Belka. 'It hasn't nursed since yesterday. You've got to give it milk.'

'But Belka, you're a stray. You're more complete than me. Why haven't you?'

Belka sighed, exhausted. 'It can't touch me.'

Yesterday, after she'd got far enough away from the horror at the Creche sheds, she stopped to examine the pup she'd plucked away. Instinctively, she'd laid on her side to allow it to suckle, and licked at its feeble form to clean away the grime of an escape it was lucky to survive. But just as the pup started shuffling towards her, she glimpsed the shimmery air around her own underside and pulled away.

To nourish a delicate new life with that alien force might have done it more harm than good. The nature of this vaporous sickness was unlike other kinds of ailment – it didn't cramp her innards the way spoilt food did, or swell her head as would an infected ear – but it was a sickness just the same. Ignoring the pup's whimpers had been upsetting, of course, but Belka had had no choice but to take the hungry pup by the folds of its neck and continue her dash west through the woods.

Jayla rose. Apprehensively, she inched closer to the snuffling infant, then flopped over onto her side. Belka stirred the pup into life with some tender licks, and they watched together as a mysterious natural force drove the pup towards the pet's underside.

'It's suckling,' confirmed Jayla, causing Belka to whine with relief. 'It doesn't mean there's milk, though. I've been a pet half my life. My body may not work this way anymore.'

Watching the pup nurse – its minute but sharp claws kneading into Jayla with desperation – brought an end to the fretting that had travelled with Belka all the way from Creche. Even if the pup was receiving no actual nourishment while it hungrily gulped at Jayla, it was comforted at least, for now.

Belka crawled out from the den, but Jayla, her eyes frantic as though being left alone with the pup were terrifying to her, called out. 'Where are you going?'

'I have to find Ony. Stay with her until I return.'

Outside in the stony undergrowth that hid the den, Belka got to sniffing. From the mightiest of oaks to the spindliest of saplings, she sought any sign at all of Ony's unique odour, eventually picking him up where the land sloped and the horizon was lost to rocky hills. But he'd left barely any pee anywhere; it was as though he were deliberately trying to conceal himself.

She ran until all paths were covered. Yet the trail led her nowhere. Not knowing what to do, and with the weight of fatigue crushing her, she could think of only a single way to proceed, and for the first time since before the frosts fell, she issued a call.

'Ony!' she howled. 'Ony!'

Silence.

'Ony!'

Distantly, a bark came back. 'Belka!'

She bolted. Navigating narrow strings of earth that snaked through the rocks, she ascended the slope. His scent was embedded on every surface now, and brought her to an opening in the hillside.

When she found him, he was laying on his side, panting heavily. The very sight of him iced her heart. 'What's wrong, Ony?'

Feebly, he said her name, as though disbelieving she were really here.

Was it the confined space that made his shimmer seem all the more severe? Before she'd left for Creche, a watery layer enveloped him like a thin skin, but now he was almost lost inside a vaporous cloak.

'Han.'

'No, Ony. Belka. Your Belka.'

'Han. The pets.'

'Lay down with me, Ony. You're in a fever.'

He'd spent a whole night and most of the day sheltered in this shallow cave without attracting attention to himself. Although he'd ceased vomiting, his energy remained so low that even walking in a straight line was beyond him.

During the few occasions when his mind stopped brooding, he found comfort in keeping perfectly still. But at times when the nausea pulsed inside him, his thoughts flashed with strange and disturbing images.

He saw Levka, his sweet mother, tongues of flame dancing in her eyes, and Pyotr, his father, the muscles of his upper torso rippling with tension as he advanced with his large fangs bared. All the things he saw in his mind's eye were hot and sharp and violent, and he wished that he could see instead the leaves of trees dancing in cool breezes, the brook of a forest washing over him, a bank of soft snow at the side of a hedge in whose powdery crunch he could lose himself.

If his body would only stop burning, his mind could rest and his stomach settle. He thought about the pit. What was in it that had set him aflame this way? He remembered the labouring people, tipping rocks with their peculiar black sheen into the smouldering, choking crater. Right before Han and Gleb ambushed him, he'd stood there wondering if something resided within it, and now that the pets told of such mysterious creatures, he wondered whether he'd been right all along.

Maybe some beast did dwell down there, some *dragon* that was nourished by chunks of scorched rock.

At times when his fever subsided, he turned his thoughts to a more earthly problem. The foolish pets were falling for the brutish Han's version of events. Ony had asked nothing of them beyond being careful, had shown them no ill, yet they had given in to his rival's will without any resistance at all, and now an attack pack had formed. They were out there: circling, sniffing, closing in.

Han, now their alpha, was convincing them of something that wasn't true: that Ony himself had destroyed Plant. And since no other truth existed for that stupid animal, a fight to the death was now unavoidable.

Ony went cold at the thought of it. How could he possibly hope to emerge victorious in his current state? All day, he'd done nothing but rest his head on his paws;

another bout of nausea was approaching even now. He closed his eyes. If he slept, he'd avoid the worst of it.

But just as he was crossing over to the dream state, he thought he heard a howling from outside floating into his ear. Could he trust his senses anymore?

It then sounded a second time. So, on unsteady legs, he rose and staggered across the dry cave floor. He poked his head out of the mouth, and let the howl flow into him like water. And just like water, it soothed him.

Ignoring his dizziness, he gave as loud a bark as he could muster until, a short while later, the red-gold coat of his beloved mate appeared over the hill's rocky face, and within seconds they were sleeping side by side.

When his eyes next opened, he discovered he was clear-headed. The infection had taken all the thoughts that lived inside his head and tangled them into a knotty mass, but in the moments that followed naps they unravelled just long enough to allow him to focus. Precious moments which couldn't be wasted, he used them to consider their future.

They should move on. As soon as they were able. Head west until they were clear of the wolf-wilds, to find a nice street corner some place where the territory was vast and the people friendly. Life was a battle for resources, and they'd soon be mature enough to fight it fiercely, sparing no mercy to any dog foolish enough to contest them. Then, with their environment healthy once again – when this *thing* ceased breathing poison far and wide – their pups could enjoy the kind of youth he'd only been able to imagine.

Aware that Belka was beside him, he remained still on the ground for fear of disturbing her. But he needn't have.

'Galina is dead,' she said, sensing that his eyes had opened.

Ony turned to face her. 'Was it the shimmer?'

'Men. They found us at Creche.'

Whining, Ony wriggled closer. He licked her muzzle. 'We're in danger. Han has found us. He's turning the pets against me. They're going to attack.'

'Ony, I have to tell you—'

'The boy. The one we saw at Camp. He's bonded with me.'

Belka looked at him, puzzled.

'The pets saw me playing with him. Now they think I tricked them to keep them away from the people and their food. I've lost their trust.'

They lay a while, letting the silence of the cave calm them, until Ony's vision began to blur at the edges again. Another bout of fever was on its way.

Belka, who must have noticed the change in his eyes, swallowed back the words he knew she wanted to speak.

'Sweet girl,' he said. 'I can see you're troubled. But we're in danger. Help me reach the river, or my thoughts are going to tangle up into madness again. Han won't attack me while the boy is near.'

Belka shunted him onto his paws, and the pair left the cave. After negotiating the rocky decline, they came to the forest floor, where Ony paced unsteadily to and fro. When he was cautiously confident he could make it the rest of the way to the river, he led Belka towards Birch Grove.

To reduce the crunching of leaves, they kept to the trails and walked with care; an ambush now could only end one way. Then, when the woods thinned out, they crouched to the height of the grass.

Discreetly, they sidled past the point nearest to Camp until they were surrounded by the peeling trunks of birches, and only there did he dare to speak again. 'The pets are stupid. But they know things about the world that are a mystery to us.'

'It's true, Ony. Jayla told me about some animal.'

'They're calling it a dragon,' nodded Ony. 'Do you

think it's true? Do you think one really woke up in our town?'

Belka let out a single, sharp whine. 'I don't know. But if these *dragons* breathe fire and disease, then that's what's out there. *Something* is in the sky, Ony. It's everywhere.'

'Will it reach us here?' asked Ony.

Momentarily, Belka paused. Her eyes contained a sorrow more abysmal than the deepest well. 'Here. There. All places.'

Ony, thinking again of the pit where the grasslands once lay, cast a sideways glance at his beloved mate. 'Don't you think it's strange that people have come here? If this creature is so dangerous, it would make them run away, not go to it.'

'Perhaps they know how to communicate with it,' said Belka.

'The black rocks you warned me about. It was those that made me sick. I watched the people dump them inside that pit. I think maybe that's what the people came here for: to help this dragon.'

Glistening water appeared through the trees, and a fresh current cooled the air. Ony huffed with relief: any farther and he would have had to rest. Already the heaviness was back in his legs; he could feel the blaze of his underparts radiating now into the rest of his body.

A jog brought them out of the woods, where a lone figure was visible on the banks of the river. The scent coming downwind informed them it was Ball Boy.

'Who's this then, Foxy? There's a pretty girl,' said the boy, reaching into a bag for a paper wrapper. 'I helped with the cooking last night,' he added, placing some pieces of potato in front of them. 'Haven't worked in a kitchen since my time at the orphanage. Saved this for you, boy. You'll have to make it stretch two ways now, though.'

But Ony hadn't seen the human eat any himself.

'Aren't you going to eat, boy? What's the matter, don't trust me?' He took a piece from the packet and popped it into his mouth. 'See. It's good.'

Both dogs went to eat, but Ony suddenly felt too queasy, and left his portion to Belka.

'Well, they still didn't send me off,' said Ball Boy. 'The miners are having real trouble by the sound of it. I wish somebody would tell me what's going on over there.'

A trembling worked its way up Ony's legs, and he staggered over on his side. Belka began to whimper.

'Foxy?' said Ball Boy, his brow furrowed. 'Are you alright?'

Ony's breathing had quickened. His chest heaved in and out as his tongue lolled over his teeth, and his eyes began to roll back into his head.

'Goodness me, you're so hot. I can feel you from here!' The boy looked at Belka. 'What's he been up to, huh? Have you taken some nasty viper from the forest?'

With a thin groan, Ony called Belka closer to where he lay. 'Ball Boy will help me. You go. Talk to the pets. You have to convince them we're not their enemy.'

Belka gave Ony an affectionate nudge and readied to leave, but just as she swivelled away to face the tree line, Ony's body seized up into a solid mass. With alarming suddenness, each of his limbs sprang out as though some great shock had fired within his body, and his neck craned back at an angle not at all natural for a dog. He began to shake, softly at first, then with a violence that made Belka yap with terror. A foamy spittle began to bubble up around his lips, and his tongue fell limply from his mouth. Then, when the shaking finally concluded, he went still.

Too still.

Ball Boy dropped to his knees beside him. 'Foxy!' He turned his ear to Ony's mouth and began to listen intensely. 'Oh my!' he gasped. 'He's not breathing.'

Belka began panting heavily with grief, and kept her

gaze fixed firmly on Ony's flank for any signs of life. But no movement – not a single rise, or a single fall – disturbed the stillness of his orange form. He was like a lump of stone.

The boy shook his head from side to side. 'Poor thing just died in front of my very eyes,' he said, and brought his hands up onto his head.

'Ony!' barked Belka.

'I'm sorry girl,' said Ball Boy. 'I think we've lost him.' He reached out and placed a hand on Ony's lifeless torso, staying very still, as though he were trying to detect something. He slid his palm from Ony's side onto his breastbone, beneath which was the heart Belka so cherished.

'Ony! Come back!'

The boy, with lines of concentration etched upon his face, leaned in closer. 'Is that a—? Yes, I think it is.'

He stood. Using his arms like shovels, the boy scooped Ony up. 'His heart's still beating. We've got to get him to Fairytale, now,' he yelled. And holding him close to his chest, he suddenly took off running for the woods.

Racing through Birch Grove towards Camp, Belka stayed with Ball Boy with every long stride he made along the forest path.

There were times in a dog's life, she supposed, when it wasn't really possible to know exactly how to feel. She understood well enough that she was suffering. This was a fresh wound over a barely-healed scar – trauma *upon* trauma, like a heavy downpour on pavements already deluged beneath flood water. But beyond the vague sense that her world was in turmoil, her mind flitted from worry to relief to fear to anger in a constantly churning cycle.

The boy meant well. Didn't he? What she was witnessing *had* to be an act of kindness, for what possible harm could he do to a thing no longer capable of experiencing cruelty? When Belka was able to see Ball Boy's eyes, it was clear that he too was overcome with feelings. But what he wanted with her mate's lifeless frame was a mystery to her. Why didn't he simply leave Ony's body where it lay?

As they reached the midway point between the river and the camp, she reminded herself to notice her surroundings and fronted her attention to her snout. Inhaling deeply, she searched for traces of Han; thankfully, she found only older scent markings.

When they rounded a bend on the path, they startled some of the pets who were foraging in the undergrowth. 'It's Belka!' barked one.

'The boy has Ony!' remarked another, and the clutch of confused dogs fell into step with them as they advanced closer to the dwelling huts.

Belka wouldn't be drawn in on what had happened. Now wasn't the time for explanation, and none was owed this bunch, anyway. But the dogs excitedly yammered between themselves while they ran alongside.

'Han got him!'

'He wasn't as tough as he thought he was!'

'He can't tell us what to do anymore!'

Soon they came to Archway, beneath which the boy sprinted. Belka paused at the threshold, but the pets wasted no time heading straight through and, to her shock and surprise, they scattered *into* the wooden dwellings. What were they thinking?

She walked in circles while she considered what to do next. A bark, of the playful kind, came from the other side of Archway, and Belka halted momentarily to look across. One of the pets was in the arms of a man, at ease as though this individual had always been his master.

That was it, then. Despite Ony's threats, the dogs that

had followed them from the chaos of their hometown just couldn't help themselves. In spite of how very dangerous people seemed to be during these frightening times, convincing the pets to keep their distance had been a lost cause.

Even more troubling was the thought that she, too, was going to have to do the same. She couldn't just leave Ony in their custody. A dog, whether he was alive or dead, belonged among trees, not walls.

Whimpering, she brought one paw off the ground in readiness of entering Camp. But before she moved forward, her eyes were drawn to the canopy, where a single patch of wavering vapour was hanging on the air.

The shimmer had arrived.

12

HOUSE OF BEDS

ONY, asleep in the corner, was too sick to pay any heed to it, but their present situation was so very dangerous that Belka was dizzy with distress.

Simply entering Camp had been risky enough. But carrying on past the huts – and actually coming into the room – made them vulnerable in a way that Ony, in his usual state of health, would never have tolerated.

Thankfully, though, the human folk had shown no ill feeling towards Belka as she approached. If anything, the presence of canines seemed to have softened them.

Whether or not the people of Camp were the hostile sort was simply impossible to determine – though exactly how a dog was ever supposed to know which of them to trust and which of them to stay clear of was becoming increasingly difficult to figure out. The pets, who'd wasted no time moving in the moment the'd learnt Ony was down, seemed to have a much deeper intuition. It was as though they saw things in people that weren't visible to strays; perhaps, when the time was right, they could teach free-ranging strays like them to spot the truth of a person's nature.

Belka looked up to where Ball Boy was perched glumly on the edge of his bed. As he fanned himself with the corner of his bed fabric, he spoke in a hushed voice. 'I'm beginning to think this might be more than just a case of food poisoning, boy'. Worry resided on the young man's face as it did a dog's, and Belka supposed this was one of the ways to really know if a person was being honest. Dada had worn the same expression when the dog-mask men first appeared in their vehicle outside her garden.

Ball Boy stood up and ruffled his hand through his hair. 'We're going to need medicine,' he said to the animals, then promptly exited the room.

Laying beside Ony, Belka whined. For just a moment, it seemed he was about to engage with her, but just as suddenly as his eyes had snapped her into focus, they once again rolled back into the quagmire of a fevered mind.

'Don't you leave me, too,' she cried.

But no. Thoughts like that weren't helpful. A mind that was too troubled had a way of sickening the body as well, and over the course of the day she'd felt queasy enough. Such fretting had to be pushed away. So, with her head on her paws, she forced herself into a deep stillness.

Pretending that the future and the past didn't exist at all, she brought her senses into harmony with the present moment. The walls were ablaze with the light of dusk, and crumbs of tree dander swirled in the beams of Sun as it poured in through the windows. Outside, birds were returning noisily to the treetops to roost, and on the porches the people were fighting away mosquitoes, their quarrelsome moods made worse by the hot air trapped beneath the forest canopy. Blankly, she observed the mad flitting of a bat that had flown in through the open door, and she let the scent of meat roasting on a nearby fire stream into her nostrils.

All the while, soft vibrations shook her body as people moved across the porch. But now the floorboards were beginning to rattle, and Ball Boy was suddenly back, this time with the girl whose hat was marked with a crimson cross.

The girl set down a large bag and came to the corner, where she studied Ony with an intense glare.

'Feel how hot he is,' said Ball Boy.

Red Cross Girl reached out her hand, but Ony didn't recoil – truly a sign he was sick. Holding it near his belly, she nodded grimly. 'It's like he's burned. What have you been up to, huh, pup?'

Turning to Belka, the girl let out a sigh. 'You're not looking great yourself, pretty girl.'

'Do you think they've been near the power plant?' asked Ball Boy. 'The soldiers are saying it's way worse over there than anyone was expecting.'

'The *soldiers* are saying? What do you think?'

Ball Boy shifted bashfully on his feet.

'You mean to tell me you've just been at Fairytale this whole time? You're not a liquidator, cadet. You're a tourist.'

'*Tourist?!* Where d'you think your meal came from tonight? And your packed lunches?'

'Relax,' laughed the girl. 'You wind up way too easily, Alek Vann. The nurses reckon the miners are having a tough old time of it. You're better off on catering for now. Speaking of which—' She tapped the empty bowls sitting on the floorboards.

The boy darted off, and when he came back he set down mashed bread in gravy. The girl, meanwhile, worked a small clear bottle between her fingers, from which a squishy black bulb stuck out at the top. This she lifted off, letting three drips fall into each bowl. 'Good thing we're not in the capital,' she said to the dogs. 'The Party are always looking for strays like you for those awful research labs of theirs.'

She then took out a second clear bottle, filled with deep blue disks. Crumbling these between her thumb and forefinger, she sprinkled one each into the food, then gave the bowls a stir, before muttering on her breath: 'Hell, if I'm caught giving away potassium iodide like this, I'll be caged up in one of them myself.'

Ony, perceiving the tension in the room, weakly lifted his head up from the floorboards.

'That's it, Foxy,' said Ball Boy. 'You're going to have some food. It'll make you all better.'

Ony began muttering, so quietly Belka had to move closer to hear him. 'Levka,' he was saying. 'Butcher.'

'Come on,' said Red Cross Girl, a wide crescent of a smile on her lips. 'Good pups.'

Belka began to whine. Ony's account of his mother's poisoning had haunted her ever since she'd heard it – not because of its brutality, nor its pointlessness, but because the man had killed her with a smile on his face. What kind of creature could do such a thing? And why would such deviousness be a part of its nature?

Ball Boy suddenly stood. 'I know!' he said, and made a snapping sound with his fingers. He ran to the corner of the room, and dived into a bag.

'Look,' he said to Ony, holding a ball in front of his face.

Ony made a single swish with his tail, causing a clean triangle to appear in the dust of the floorboards. At the sight of it, Belka's agonised heart felt the faintest flush of warmth.

'Eat your food up, then we can play ball again. You like ball, don't you boy? And you, Hazel Eyes. You'll like it too. But you need to eat first.'

When Ony's eyes found Belka, she lowered her head into the bowl and took a sniff.

It smelt fine.

She took a bite.

It tasted fine.

Before she knew it, the bowl was empty.

'Come, Ony,' she said. 'It's good. You must eat.'

Ony positioned his mouth over the rim of the bowl and, as his vacant eyes rolled, he took a mouthful.

Relief joined the jumble of emotions coursing through Belka. She stood, and went out onto the porch, leaving Ony in Bed House like he was one of their pets. Tempted as she was to curl up here on the threshold to keep watch over him, he wasn't her only concern right now, so she began the run back through the woods to Den.

Above, Moon hung in a single slice, its light too weak to find the forest floor. But this was a help as much as it was a hindrance: it concealed Belka from Han, but concealed Han from her.

With care, she moved through the trees. If Han was around, or any of the pets he'd enticed away with his mistaken account of the catastrophe at Plant, she needed to know. Traces of these rivals were perceptible here and there, but since they were so faint she allowed herself to calm. An ambush was going to happen, there was no doubt about it. But it wouldn't be tonight.

She looked all around her as she neared Den, making sure she hadn't been followed, then squeezed her body between the two stone lumps of its entrance. Inside, Jayla was laying on her paws. The pup barely pulsed with life.

'Belka. I'm so sorry. All day I've tried to feed her. But no milk will flow out of me.'

Slumping onto the ground, despair crushed Belka. It was too dreadful to bear. The pups of the poor dams in the nursery sheds never even got to taste life. In this one lowly creature, hope was alive; yet here it lay, starved, readying to make its journey to the peaceful meadows that waited beyond the final sleep.

She should have kept away from Creche. Then, the mothers would have let the people carry on with their business undisturbed. But as it was, Belka had caused Lala distress with her account of the dog-men, and the grief-sickened girl went on to imperil them all.

But no! Lala was agitated because Plant's vicious

shimmer took away her litter. Belka had been right to warn them. The sickness *was* creeping towards the nurseries of the Creche sheds, as it was advancing now here to the west.

'I'm sorry, Belka.'

'You tried, Jayla. That's all I wanted.'

'I was about to tell her a story. Should I go on?'

Belka thought back to the night of the explosion, at the people crowding on the paved avenues and the child crying, and Jayla sat happily in its lap. 'I don't know,' she said. 'What are they for?'

'Stories? They're not *for* anything. But they bring comfort to the young. They let them know everything will be alright in the end.'

Belka's head dropped. 'But what if everything won't be alright in the end? What if everything's going to be swallowed up by the poisoned air?'

Jayla blew air out from her nostrils. 'You strays are hard work. Just listen, will you?' The pet brought her head close to the tiny ears of the sleeping pup. 'Once upon a time,' she said, 'there was a man who had an old dog. All his life he'd been a good boy, but when his teeth didn't bite well anymore the man put the dog out and said, "Find another home, mangy mutt!" So the dog rested in the barns of a neighbour and made friends with a wolf who roamed the woods.'

'Excuse me? *Friends* with a wolf?'

'Belka!'

'Sorry.'

'One day, the wolf had an idea. "I'll go to your master's house," he said, "for the baby hasn't yet learnt to stand and so can't defend itself. When the master isn't looking, I'll take the baby lightly in my jaws and carry him away. Then you will come and bark, and with what remains of your old teeth you'll bite me and I'll run off back into the woods."

'So the wolf waited until the mistress set the baby

down beneath a wagon, and he snatched it away. And the dog made such a noise that everybody in the village came out to see what had happened. And they all saw that old dog strike the wolf and take up the baby and set it right back down beneath the wagon.

'And all the folk of the village yelled to make that old dog their own pet, but the dog's master insisted that he was his, and let him back into his home. And all of them lived happily forevermore.'

Belka's head tilted to the side. 'The wolf *gave up* the baby, just like that? Do you even know what a wolf is, Jayla?'

'Sure,' Jayla proudly said. 'Little Red-cap's false grandmother was a wolf. A big, bad one. That monster in the pigs' chimney, he was a wolf, too. But no, I've never seen a real one.'

'Well let me tell you, when a wolf has flesh in its teeth, nothing will persuade it to let go.'

'It's a story, Belka. It's not real.'

'Well,' huffed Belka. 'Stories aren't going to put milk in that puppy's belly.' She marched towards the tiny creature and took it up by the scruff – its weight now was even less than when she'd first travelled with it in her jaws – and, wasting no time, she took off at a gallop back to Camp, letting her previous cautiousness melt away.

Red Cross Girl was about to enter one of the smaller huts, so Belka set the pup down on the leaves and issued a bark the moment she saw her.

Red Cross Girl turned. 'Hazel Eyes? What have you got there?'

Belka barked again. 'Come!'

The girl made her way over; Belka took up the pup again.

'Is that a—? Oh!'

Belka turned and paced back towards Archway. The pets had a better understanding of humankind, so could stay within Camp all they wanted. But even if its people were a safer sort than the ones who wore dog masks and carried shooting sticks, this wasn't a place for strays.

Again, she barked. 'Follow!'

The girl came after her.

Outside Den, Belka dropped down the pup. The girl crouched, and her face flushed with sorrow: it was an honest emotion. 'This puppy needs milk,' she said. 'Wait here, Hazel Eyes. I'll be right back.'

Ony awoke from a tormented dream in which the forest was aflame and he was trapped in its centre.

The food in his belly had rid him of the worst of his nausea, but his energy was still low enough to make his movements sluggish. He strained his eyes to take in Bed House.

Ball Boy was sat on the bed closest to him, making marks in a book. Now occupying each of the other beds, many other men were present.

His first instinct was to panic, but Ony steadied himself. The last thing he wanted was for them to trap him inside the room, and while they appeared unaware of him, he felt it better to stay as he was. Listening to them chattering away, his chief concern was that more of them might soon enter.

Even if he were not sickened, Ony would still have had trouble deciding whether the folk on their beds were arguing or simply conversing. Either way, they went on in a heated manner, occasionally giving their mouths a rest just long enough to allow him to settle. But always, they found something else to discuss.

'Has anybody heard about this *sarcophagus*?' asked a man at the back of the room.

Somebody near the door spoke up. 'It's ridiculous. Imagine how big such a thing would have to be to cover

over the whole Chernobyl site. Those Party folk are off their heads.'

'Well,' replied the first man, 'what else can they do? They're saying the land here could be radioactive for 20,000 years.'

Ony felt Ball Boy bristle. The colour seemed to be draining from his face. 'Why?' the boy called out. 'The Army General who came to my school said it was just a mishap.'

A man in the corner with floppy blond hair, who was scraping the fur from his face as though he believed it oughtn't to be there, looked over at the boy with sympathetic eyes. 'I'm not sure it's wise to believe everything they tell you at school, young cadet.'

An older man in the next bed reached across and placed the palm of his hand on the boy's leg. He, too, seemed suddenly sad. 'Why do you think the mining teams haven't started their work yet?' he said. 'How do you even start to tunnel beneath something as deadly as that?'

As if Ball Boy couldn't stand to be part of their conversation anymore, he shimmied down to the edge of the bed and peered down where Ony lay. 'Feeling better yet?' he whispered, before the walls of the room began to suddenly shake: heavy footfall outside signalled the arrival of more people.

'Better change the subject, boys,' said the floppy-haired man, and the atmosphere in the room went instantly tense. Perhaps they, too, were afraid that the dog-mask men were about to show up with their violent sticks of steel.

But it wasn't a dog man whose body swung around the door, just one of the ones the pets called *soldier*. Ony's thundering heart calmed.

'Alek Vann here?'

Ball Boy rose swiftly and held his hand beside his head in an oddly stiff pose. 'Yes, sir.'

'Good news, young comrade. The miners are starting their work tonight. Take bus number four in the morning. 0700 hours sharp.'

Ony rested his head on the floorboards. The boy's fretting, which by now seemed to have engulfed him entirely, was discomforting. He pined for Belka, but was glad really that she wasn't here. This was no place for dogs, even if the people appeared to be agreeable.

Poor, brave Belka. How lucky he was to have her. Certainly, it was lucky that hers was the face he'd first seen when he emerged from a dreamless sleep in this confined human space, or it was possible the shock would have finished him off. But even though her eyes had blazed with relief, he saw in them a familiar torment.

One thing and one thing only instilled her eyes with such a specific anguish: this wretched thing she called *the shimmer*.

And the thought of *that* was more than he could bear in his current state.

13

FALSE PEAKS

AT THE END of each day, Belka went to the road to meet Red Cross Girl off the bus.

Bus. That was what they called a long vehicle that carried many people. It was different to the box-shaped one in which the dog killers journeyed – this they called *van*. And the smaller, lower one: *car*.

Standing beside Belka this evening was Jayla. Jayla was the first pet she'd ever really known, and over the five twilights they'd shared in Den watching over the pup, a companionship had begun to develop. Wherever Belka roamed, Jayla tended to follow.

Although they were different, they shared much that was common – stray or pet, they were still dogs – and as Moon came and went over successive nights, Belka realised that there were a lot of ways they could help each other.

Though it remained a mystery to her how the pets came to know the human tongue, Belka absorbed all Jayla told her of the many terms the people had for things. She found her stories strangely appealing, too, and each dusk, when the shadows stretched long in the forest and she left Ony to rest for the night in the sanctuary of Bed House, she walked with a spring in her step, excited at the thought of the tale her short-legged friend would tell the pup later.

During the daytime, when Red Cross Girl went away, Belka caught herself thinking about the stories. There were ones with *heroes* – folk with swords who fought off the wolves in the forests. And there were ones with wicked mothers who were cruel to their daughters in a way she could never imagine Galina being to her. But the stories she especially liked were those where dragons were slain. It gave her a feeling of hope, even if – as Jayla always reminded her – they were just stories, and not real life. Would tonight's story feature one of the many-headed beasts?

With a juddering of engines, the buses began to arrive. Camp's weary residents were soon stepping down onto the forest road; keeping watch for a mass of frizzy ringlets, Belka, with Jayla close behind, went forward to greet Red Cross Girl with a wag of her tail.

'Hello ladies,' the girl said. 'Let's do our thing, shall we?'

The other folks filed through Archway on their way to the huts, but Red Cross Girl, with her bulky bag slung over her shoulder, tramped away from Camp with the two dogs until they reached the rocky scrubland that hid Den.

Slumping down in front of the lively pup, the girl took out a bottle like the one she used in the mornings to put drips into their food. With remarkable nimbleness – Belka was frequently astonished by how humans could put their hands to such delicate tasks – the girl poured in milk from another bottle and fastened the rubber bulb onto the top.

'Goodness me, you're growing so fast,' she said, as the pup gulped mouthfuls from the rubber teat. 'You'll be ready for solid food in no time.'

When the bottle was empty, the girl packed up and readied to return to Camp. Before she turned to leave, she let air out of her mouth in a steady stream. 'I think I might be homesick,' she said. 'I don't suppose dogs know anything about that kind of thing, though.'

~

As time went on and the white heat of fever cooled, Ony began to wonder whether Ball Boy may have saved his life by bringing him into Bed House. Left to heal in the wilds beyond Camp, he would have had no defence against a Han assault, let alone a pack of marauding wolves.

Because of his illness, Ony hadn't paid much regard to Belka on any of the five nights she'd been in to visit him. But her lingering sorrow was unmistakable. He wondered if the absence of a litter in her belly explained the gloominess of his cherished mate. A time was coming when they would be free to resume their lives. They'd move off and find a new home, and the family they craved would finally come into the world, and when it did, her sadness was sure to be healed.

Ball Boy, too, seemed increasingly downcast these days, a shadow following him wherever he went. Since Ony felt quite a bit better this evening, he glanced up to see if the boy might fancy a few rounds of fetch. The young human was covering his head, though, as though pretending he wasn't really there, so Ony snooped around in the open bag until he found what he was looking for.

A soft growl convinced Ball Boy to look up; he peered curiously over the papers he was studying. Then something unusual happened: for the first time in a long while, he smiled. 'I guess the medicine's working, huh, Foxy?'

With the ball in his mouth, Ony walked out into the clearing; when the boy followed, his tail began to wag with vigour.

The boy launched the ball. Ony, faltering at first for legs weakened by underuse, went after it.

'I just can't understand why they've banned *all* outward telephone calls,' the boy said, sending the ball up high. Ony, already finding strength in his haunches, sprang into the air to catch it before it hit the forest bed.

'I just want my foster parents to know I'm safe. Even if it's not true.'

Chasing down the ball as it rolled off along the track, bursts of acceleration filled Ony with joy. Of all the things he'd missed while infirm in the corner, running took top spot. Nothing in this world was better than feeling the air stream across a dog's fur.

After a few rounds of fetching, the girl appeared with her bag, followed closely behind by Belka, whose anguish wasn't quite as stark as usual. The look she gave Ony was somehow different this evening, and she came and licked his muzzle. 'I think it's happening to you, too,' she said, absentmindedly.

Ony's head tilted. 'What is?'

But instead of answering, Belka simply stayed close and rested her muzzle upon Ony's own.

Ball Boy set down the food bowls. 'How much more medicine do they need?'

Red Cross Girl puffed out air. 'The nurses say it takes about a week. A couple more days should do it.'

While Ony and Belka ate, the boy went and sat at the bench. Running his finger along the cracks in the wooden tabletop with a glowering expression, he spoke sadly. 'This must have been a really nice place to grow up. Far nicer than my orphanage, anyway. But Pripyat is really just a ghost town now.'

The girl let out a long sigh. 'Just one day, and the happy life you knew is all gone.' And when she said that, Ony saw the most unusual look on their faces, a kind of pained wisdom that only came from those who knew deep hurt.

As the evening darkened into night and the chirruping of crickets was joined by the hooting of owls, Ony and Belka lay together on the leaves until Belka gave a yawn and turned back for Den. But before she made her way back to Jayla and the pup, she gave another lingering look in Ony's direction, and this time her tail began to wag.

'What is it, Belka?' Ony asked.

'It's your shimmer.'

'What about it?'

'It's vanishing, Ony.'

~

The loosening of the vaporous cloak that had shrouded Ony so tightly brought both cheer and woe to Belka's heart. Being well again was something she'd barely dared to hope for, but a return to health meant a return to strife, and trouble was stalking them from many directions.

Keeping watch outside Den, Belka's brow withered. Each time her mind settled on one worry, another waited just beyond it, like a journey uphill when a new peak appeared over one freshly conquered.

Of least concern was that, before the end of tomorrow, Ony would flee the sanctuary of Bed House. His illness had subdued his spirit for a time, but it was unlikely to have dulled his temper.

She let out a grunt. Was there anything in this world that could cool the fire of that boy's temperament? Faced with threat of any kind, he simply couldn't help himself. Upon seeing how the pets had ignored his warning to seek new masters among the people of Camp, a scrap was unavoidable.

Then there was the matter of Han. With Ony out in the woods again, it was only a matter of time before his foe emerged from the shadows with his new pack – and two more pets had bolted over the course of Ony's illness. The murderous instincts fuelled by Han's hatred towards Ony assured violence.

A chill ran down Belka's spine. Why did violence have to always be so near? Brutality was as much a part of a stray's existence as eating and breeding, yet was never a thing to be hoped for. For so young a life, her mind was seared with such terrible images: the gaping throat of Feliks and his blood stained upon Ony's white breast; the incinerated muzzles of the old alphas as they lay limply across the vegetable patches; men in dog-like masks who used their fearsome devices – *guns,* Jayla called them – to senselessly blast holes into the dams and their broods.

These masked men overshadowed her worries about Han. Their guns hadn't sounded for some days, but little comfort was to be found in their silence, since those terrible blasts seemed always present in her ears. Their van could come by at any time; while she and Ony had wisdom enough to retreat, the trusting nature of the pets, however, would lead to their demise.

To top off all this worry – the very summit of the mountain – was Plant itself. Ony could end the pets. Han could end Ony. The exterminators could end dogs everywhere.

But Plant could bring an end to all things.

Nervously, she sniffed the air. An earthy, fungal scent seeped into her nostrils, and she felt glad. For a brief moment outside Den yesterday, when Sun was at its highest point in the bright blue sky, an odd metallic odour seemed to overpower the fragrance of the natural world. Thankfully, though, it drifted away again just as quickly as it had fouled the air.

She turned and squeezed through the stones into the makeshift nursery. At the sight of Jayla laying beside the pup, she felt suddenly shamed.

Jayla stretched out her paws and let out a long yawn.

Noticing Belka's head was drooping, the pet snuffled softly. 'What is it?'

'I've ignored my duties.'

'You've been sick in your bowels, girl.'

Whining, Belka's eyes watered. 'I used my illness to hide from our real problems. I'm going to call the pets to Monument. Round up any who resist. I just hope I haven't left it too late.'

By the time they'd managed to gather the pets together, Belka's sense of shame had twisted into one of anger. As she looked upon them now, she silently seethed.

If she had hidden from her problems this past week, it was only while she recovered from her shimmer. But this lot were more than happy to go on pretending forever that no threat existed at all, that so long as some fuss was given and snacks shared, nothing in the world would ever turn up to disrupt their cosy little lives.

They were alive by sheer luck. Jayla had told her many interesting things about the ways pets can read people, but there was no way they *knew* that the folk of Camp were the safe sort. No creature had lived through a time like this, when a creeping death was spreading as fast as the wind could travel through the skies.

'We've all suffered a great shock,' she barked. 'And in some ways, it's worse for you pets. The lives you knew were taken from you, your beloved masters moved away. I understand how tempting it must be to soothe your hearts with new masters. But you're wrong to think you're safe here. Terror is coming. I've tried telling myself it isn't, but Plant's disease is in the air even now. Dogs, we must work to find a way to better understand one another.'

Belka motioned for Jayla to step forward, and the short-legged pet began to speak. 'Comprehending the tongue of men, hearing their stories – those are things we can do that strays like Belka can't. But displaying caution around those we don't know is a talent of theirs that we mostly lack.'

Belka barked again. 'By helping each other, it's possible we can survive this death that's infecting our world. I know many of you thought that Ony was simply making a play at domination. And I know Han has been able to convince some of you that Ony merely tricked us so that he could claim more of the people's resources. But Ony's warning then, as ours is now, is meant to help you.'

A muscular pet with a flat snout stepped forward. 'The evil in the air, how did it get there? Han said Ony caused it.'

'Han believes Ony caused it,' said Belka. 'But he's wrong.'

'Then what is it?' asked a retrieving dog.

Jayla and Belka looked at one another with worry. 'It's a dragon,' said the pet.

The dogs of the assembly began to canter with fret as they looked towards the stone shape behind them with its three snake-like heads.

'But if it's spreading poison across all the land,' said the shallow-snouted bull baiter, 'then why should we run? Couldn't we do something else?'

'Yes,' said a voice not heard in these parts for some days. 'There is something else we can do. We can try to kill it.'

A great commotion broke out among the pets as Ony entered their assembly from around the corner. How long he had been there, no dog knew. But all watched nervously as the recovered stray moved along the line, with many – though not all – dipping in reverence.

'Bring up your heads,' Ony said. 'I don't wish to lead any pack, let alone you.'

Belka stepped across to Ony's side. 'But how, Ony? How can we kill the dragon?'

'In the grasslands around Plant, the men have dug a

deep pit,' said Ony to the hushed audience. 'The dragon lives at the bottom of it. It's getting the people to bring the blackened rocks that were scorched in the explosion, which it needs to fuel the shimmering air Belka sees. And because its work is so exhausting, it requires a constant supply of meat.'

'Dogs!' said Belka, with a terrified whimper.

'If we're to get back to the pit, we can't attract the attention of the dog-mask men, or any one of us might be the dragon's next meal.'

'But what are we supposed to do about the infectious air?' asked Belka.

'Humans know how to take away the shimmer – Ball Boy and Red Cross Girl just did it right here. Pets, with your special gift of bonding with people, you can make these folk help us when we grow feverish and weak.'

A din rose among the pets, but Ony continued. 'We all want a safe place where our pups can thrive.' The animals glanced awkwardly at one another, as though Ony had said something that reminded them of an uncomfortable truth. Ony, though, continued. 'This menacing dragon is going to drive us closer and closer to the wolf-wilds, and if that happens we stand no chance of bringing the families we crave into the world.'

The tension seemed to loosen. For the first time, the eyes of the pets weren't marked by a fear he was about to rip at them with his fangs.

'Soon,' said Ony, as softly as he'd ever addressed this odd assortment, 'I'm going to go east again.'

Belka yipped with shock. '*East?!*'

'My first encounter with it almost killed me, but now I know what it is, I have to face the dragon again. I hope you will come with me.' And with that, he turned and made his way back towards Camp, leaving the dogs of the assembly with their heads tilted far to the side in deepest confusion.

Belka ran up to him and began to lick his muzzle.

'Just wait,' she said. 'There's something I've been wanting to show you for some time.'

Ony turned and followed Belka through the forest until they came to a heavily sheltered row of rocks in which a small opening sat. Ony's tail swished with excitement at the smell of young life: this appeared to be a nursery.

Belka vanished inside, then returned a moment later with a fat pup between her teeth which she dropped onto the ground.

Ony shuffled on his front paws with excitement. 'We have a daughter!'

'Ony,' whimpered Belka. 'This is the only survivor of the massacre at Creche. The dog-mask men killed all the females and the litters. They killed Galina.'

Nudging Belka's neck, he began to whine. 'But this pup. She came from you? This child is ours?'

'We'll never know whose child this is. But she wasn't gifted by you, nor grown by me.'

Ony took a step backwards and felt his heart blacken with an emotion that was unfamiliar to him. By a tiny amount, his lips rolled back, revealing the very points of his fangs.

Belka looked suddenly fearful. 'Ony?'

'I'm going to Bed House now for one final night,' he said, turning away. 'Rest well. Tomorrow we'll begin our journey to face the dragon.'

But Belka didn't rest well.

After Ony left, she stayed with Jayla and the pup awhile before heading into the forest to wander.

Alone in the dark, the warnings of her old friends played over in her mind. Had she been wrong about him all along? So many times, she'd challenged their claims that Ony was a devil dog. He was just wounded, she'd said. Her belief had always been strong: a safe home, with a new family and a mate who properly understood him and encouraged his better nature, was all he needed to heal.

But something in the way he'd looked at the pup tonight made her innards feel watery. If such terrible menace truly did reside within Ony's spirit, how could she possibly go on defending him?

14

ENEMIES OLD AND NEW

IN THE SHRUBS outside the wooden walls of Bed House, Ony was having a bad dream.

'Nothing matters more, little one.'

He was picturing his mother. In her mouth, frothy blood was bubbling, and shadow was consuming the life in her eyes like it did at the end of a day when the warmth and light of one horizon is conquered by the fear and blindness of the other. She was spluttering as she spoke; communicating with him was almost too great a pain for her to bear.

'Your children come first. Never let them come to any harm.'

Watching from behind the doorway was the laughing man, his overalls stained with blood. He was holding out a chunk of fresh meat. *'Does puppy want a bite?'*

Drool was pooling in Ony's chops as he pondered the offering. He stepped closer to the door of the butcher's shop.

'That's a good little puppy.'

The meat was close enough that its minerals overcame his nostrils. He opened his jaws wide.

Then Levka wasn't dying on the hard ground anymore. Now, no spume sullied her muzzle. Her eyes were raging with life, and in her bared teeth there was a fury he never imagined existed inside his dear, gentle mother.

She was biting into the fatty folds of his tiny neck. His spine was a twig on the forest floor, ready to snap at the merest degree of increased pressure. Too shocked to protest, too utterly tiny to resist, his life was about to end before it had even begun.

But Levka let go.

'Listen to me, Ony. You must do whatever it takes to spare your babies from harm.'

The world was coming awake around Ony. In the canopy, birds chirruped their morning song, and as the light of day kissed the tall poplars with flame, the first of the human risers began making their way to the water rooms.

Soon, Camp exploded with activity, and the pets came down from the porches. In the clearing where the people burned foraged boughs – the stoutest of which were still glowing from last night – they sat together, moving into a tighter pack when Ony went and joined them.

They were afraid of him. And why shouldn't they be? They wouldn't know of the savage fates of Starla and Feliks, but a life marked by aggression was visible in the scars he bore. A stray male, especially one who had shunned pack life in favour of ranging alone, was volatile.

Then again, they outnumbered Ony, so what exactly was there to fear? As pets, they were softer animals, but they still had teeth in their mouths. At least six dogs had refused to dip for him last night. It was only a passive challenge, but it was enough to make clear that they'd battle him if the time came.

But if it wasn't fear that kept them away from him,

then what? Perhaps they were repelled by his sickness. It was unusual for a strong young dog like Ony, approaching the first of his peak years, to be so heavily enfeebled. Of course they would keep their distance if they thought some horrid disease might jump from him to them. He *said* he was feeling better, but how could they be sure?

But he wasn't a threat, and he wasn't diseased, and it was time they understood that; bad blood between them was uncalled for.

Casually, he went across and sniffed at them, then sat just beyond their circle. They tolerated his greeting, but they remained aloof.

Then, for the briefest instant, he caught the eye of one of them, and in that moment all became clear. This wasn't fear, and it wasn't disgust.

It was shame.

The cowardly creatures were thinking only of themselves. He and Belka had tried their best to convince them of the peril, but the pets were choosing not to journey with them to help rid the world of the dragon.

Rising, Ony held them steadily in his gaze. Their ears dropped and they looked sadly at the ground. He considered seizing one, but he thought better of it and instead let the weight of their own shame pull them right down to the leafy carpet.

Finally, a shaggy-haired mongrel known as Tuzik spoke. 'You said we should think about the world we want for our pups. But we can't have them, so why should we put ourselves in harm's way?'

These words flummoxed Ony. It was the sort of thing he might say himself; voiced by another dog, however, it sounded so very callous. Ony searched for a way to respond, but could find nothing, so simply turned and sped away.

By this time of morning, Camp was usually empty, but now people were gathered in every corner of the site.

The spluttering engines of the buses hadn't sounded yet, either.

Approaching Den, Ony heard a familiar voice, and veered off the path to find Ball Boy communicating with the soldiers.

The boy's face was unexpectedly cheery. 'Foxy!' he said, when the people's discussion came to an end. 'How about this for good luck. A lorry has turned over. The buses can't get to us. I'm going to the shed to pick up a rod, then I'm off to the river for a bit.'

Since the boy offered no snacks, Ony proceeded as before to the rocky foliage that hid Den, noticing that the same brooding air that overcame him last night was surfacing in him once again. It was a mood so unfamiliar to him in its darkness that it made him feel almost like a different dog. A thought shoved itself to the forefront of his mind but, discomforted by it, he quickly pushed it back down.

Outside Den, Belka was standing in a guarding stance. The sight of her initially startled him, then made pride swell in his heart. She looked so very fierce. Soon she would be keeping watch over their own, and every living thing had better beware.

Although Belka went to sniff at Ony, she was curiously unsociable. 'What are you doing here?'

'These good-for-nothing pets are going to stay.'

'Then they're wiser than you.'

Ony let out a growl. 'We can't run forever, Belka. If they're not going to help us, what right do they have to live?'

'Don't say such things, Ony.'

Shifting his weight over to one side, he strained to see around Belka to where the pup was hidden. 'In there, is it?'

'Her name's Sofiy,' said Belka, studying Ony's face intensely. 'Jayla named her after the daughter of her master.'

'It's going to be hard for you and me, you know.'

'It's going to be hard for us all, Ony.'

He scraped the claws of one paw along the pebbly forest bed. 'That's why we need any advantage we can get. Do you know what my mother told me before the meat she ate poisoned her?'

Belka's head tilted.

'She said, "Do whatever it takes to protect your children". Other dogs' pups aren't the neighbours of our future children, Belka. They're their rivals.'

Belka, keeping her eyes fronted on him, remained silent.

'Levka took the meat to spare my life. That was her lesson. We've got to do whatever is necessary to ensure our own children are safe.' His lip suddenly rippled and peeled ever so slightly away from his fangs. 'Even things that seem appalling to us.'

Belka began to growl. 'Go.'

As Ony's hackles stood on end, he allowed his teeth to be fully visible now. But before he could advance, Belka darted at him first.

Her attack was fast; she jumped at his head, grazing him beneath the ear, then quickly twisted around his other side to land a heavier blow on his rear.

Jayla appeared with a startled outburst of barks. 'What's happening here?'

'Guard the den,' sneered Belka, tumbling as Ony leapt onto her.

The pair rolled away along the line of rocks, biting and clawing. When a turn brought Belka upright, she disengaged and sprang away, and stood panting before Ony with her ears pinned back. 'Go, Ony!' she yowled. 'Before we hurt each other!'

Ony stood back. His chest heaved in and out. The blood from his head wound, which had run down in a thin trickle into the side of his mouth, made him think of Starla and Feliks.

Belka was right: they were going to hurt each other. And for what?

Unsure what had happened here, Ony paced away, leaving Belka baying at the entrance to the nursery with her lip curled into a snarl.

When the rush of fiery energy had cooled inside him, he trotted through the woods to the river, where he found, perched on the banks, Ball Boy and Red Cross Girl.

He sat near them, trying his best to ignore the sting of his wound; this wasn't a good time for pain. The eyes of Red Cross Girl were discoloured and puffy, and deep sadness caused her body to shake as she sobbed. Wiping her face with the backs of her hands, Ony was put in mind of a cat washing itself.

With great patience, he waited for the ball to appear. Surely the boy was going to get it out soon? Ony stole a glance towards his bag, but a brief flash of white from the edge of the birches pulled his gaze away. With ears pricked, he kept his eyes fixed on the grove.

After some time, Red Cross Girl, her eyes now dry again, spoke. 'Do you think the Party would ever lie to us?'

The boy's chest puffed slowly out, then in again. 'If it was for the greater good, maybe.'

A long silence dragged on before the girl spoke again. 'Say there was an accident. Like, a *really* bad one. And the Party urgently needed people's help, but since it might make the motherland look bad, they downplayed just how bad it really was. Would that be for the greater good?'

The boy's mood, which had darkened in an instant, caused Ony to look up. 'I guess so, yes,' Ball Boy said, and although Ony couldn't possibly understand what the boy was saying, he suspected that his words were not coming from his heart.

The girl began to trace her finger around the big red cross on her hat.

'Come on, Narmin,' said the boy. 'Out with it.'

'What if the accident could have been avoided?'

'You mean, like if somebody knew that they were doing something dangerous but did it anyway?'

'Right. Do you still think it would be okay to hide the real truth from people?'

But the boy didn't say anything else.

Fatigue descended on Ony, as it always did after a scrap. Hopeful that a nap would take away the burn of the slashes Belka had ripped into his side, he let his eyes blink shut. But before his lids could fasten, another blur of white suddenly flashed from the trees.

Ony sprang up onto his paws. That was no rabbit.

With his ears pinned back against his head, he took off running for the forest.

Han was launching his ambush.

As Ony bolted through Birch Grove, dogs chased him on each side of the trail. With the river acting as an impassable boundary, his rival had enclosed him on three fronts. At some point ahead, Han himself was no doubt waiting for just the right moment to pounce.

As well as he could, Ony sized up the animals flanking him. On his left was a large guard dog, a pet who'd never had to scavenge for his meal but who lacked the pampering of most at Camp. The guard dog had wolfish eyes and pointed ears; Ony's sole advantage against such size and strength was that this foe had never known the frenzy of a true tussle and was therefore likely to fluster quickly. To his right was a pair of smaller dogs, both descendants of hunters. Sleeker and shorter than the other pursuer, they were fast, and their heritage meant they'd be both clever and scrappy.

Ony swung to the left.

Launching himself into the guard dog, he slashed with his teeth across the pet's side. The animal toppled with an agonised whelp, and cowered upon landing, tucking his bushy tail between his rear legs to immediately concede the fight. It was more than enough for Ony, who left the whimpering dog behind and proceeded through the birches with lightning speed.

The hunters peeled apart, with one now taking up the left side where the defeated animal had previously given chase. Ony, looking between the two, saw no obvious advantage in either, so veered again to the left and ran head-on into the second of the three pursuers.

The woolly-eared hunter sprang with impressive height into the air, evading Ony's assault. Landing with a deft turn, Han's boy was already waiting for the follow-up. Wasting no time, Ony darted at him again, and this time the pair fused in a grappling rage. As they tumbled along the soft foliage, Ony used his experience to pin the hunter to the ground at the first opportunity and plunged into his breast with a deep bite. The ample force of the strike was enough to make his opponent yield.

But the third animal made the most of the situation and ripped across Ony's rear with three claws, right where Belka had caught him, a proper blow he was lucky not to have taken sooner. The other hunter was back up now, too, leaving Ony with just one option: he had to keep running.

Close enough to Camp to hear that the buses had now arrived, Ony headed towards the hill on the north side, its higher ground giving him the best possible defence against multiple assailants. But looking around, he realised that he wasn't being pursued any more.

Everything, suddenly, was still. Ony planted his paws into the soil. At the first sign of movement, he was ready to spring away. But no threat appeared to be around him.

And then a very different threat was.

New noises now filled the woods, their pops sending him cowering behind the nearest tree. Those were guns, and they were coming from Camp. Somehow less violent than the other killing sticks he'd encountered, they were nevertheless a clear sign that the dog-mask men had found the canines.

Blood sounded in his ears as it rushed around inside him. He dropped onto the ground. Skulking low through a hedge of young trees, he advanced until the road pulled into view.

Vans, of the type they'd first seen on the grassy tracks outside Dada's garden, were parked outside Archway.

His mind quickly turned to Belka. She, among all others, would have acted the very moment the first blast sounded, but he wished to take nothing for granted. He turned back to the trail that led off into the denser part of the forest where Den was hidden.

Staying low, he aimed for the circle of boulders at the foot of the hill, but had to hold back his sprint when a man emerged around the side of a dwelling hut. In his hand was a cage, and inside the cage was one of the pets, and a hair-raising image appeared in Ony's mind of the dog-mask men lowering these captured canines into the dragon's dreadful pit. Another man came, and another, both with animals laying lifeless inside their metal boxes.

When he was sure the men were far enough away, Ony sprang from his spot and ran into the space between the boulders, scanning for his next hiding place. Near the tall stones, a piece of meat lay on the grass. There was no question it had been poisoned: the pets had failed to heed his warning.

As he readied to sprint, a sudden movement struck fear into Ony's heart: hurtling right towards the very shelter he was aiming for was Han.

Ony pivoted back into the boulders. Sneaking a look past one, then two, then three of the stones, he saw that dogs were approaching on all sides.

He was trapped.

He looked to the crest of the boulder. Not even a cat could make such a leap.

What was coming now was the fight of his life. Even if he survived, which was extremely unlikely, he was going to be a much-changed animal.

He went back to Han's side in time for the volley of pops that rang out. So similar to the sound of guns, but somehow *thinner*.

Laying low amid the boulders, Ony peered around to a most surprising sight. Han and his advancing pack were on the ground now. Sticking out of each of their bodies was a curious tube with a vibrant bird's plumage at its back end.

Four men approached the bodies, placing each into its own cage. They scanned the forest, but their eyes flicked straight across the boulders. Ony's presence remained concealed from them.

As still as the very stone he leant against, Ony's eyes tracked the men as they carried their cages back to the vans. A further stack was positioned near the rear of the vehicle, whose open doors were ready for loading.

He strained to get a better look at the creatures in the cages, and shock iced his innards to see, lifeless on a cage floor, a female of slight build with red-gold fur.

The men spoke, then hauled the cages into the vehicle. Upon lifting the last one, it span, revealing to Ony the creature inside.

It was Belka.

15

COLLECTING THE CANARIES

THE DOORS of the van slammed shut with such force that an echo bounced through the trees. Then the engines roared into life and the vans rolled away, and Ony could do nothing but lay in the shade of the boulders, where the tingle of a familiar emotion moved through him.

It began in his neck, just behind the ears: a prickling, needling sensation like his blood had come alive with a warm fizz. Spreading down his head, it moved into the sockets of his eyes and along the snout to the tip of his nose, bringing a flush to his face, before making its way to the underside of his mouth where his top and bottom jaws met.

From experience, he knew what was happening to him. This was the physical form of grief. The tingling glow that warmed his neck and face was a wave of pain and, like water lapping against a lake's shore, it would ebb and flow with its own rhythm as time moved forwards. And he understood that while no wave would be more powerful than this one, it was only the first of many more to come.

Seeing Belka tossed into their vehicle the way men in the old city tossed bins into their truck was a shock that rooted him to the spot. He couldn't have fled, not even if it was to save his own life. It was just like after Levka died, when the laughing butcher made his way over to the pavement where his mother lay, sweeping a fat hand below the car that sheltered Ony's trembling little frame. Frozen with terror, it was only luck that saved him that day from the grasping fingers of that monster.

Overcome, Ony flopped now onto the soil. He fell into a sleep that was more of a trance than a nap, and for a few lovely moments he forgot all about the death of Belka until, some time later, voices drifted across from Camp. At this, the next wave rolled in. But this one brought anger as well as grief.

His ears rose, and his lips drew tight. The pupils of his eyes hardened into dark disks, as though the very soul behind them were bruising. Roused into action, he stood stiff in a baying stance.

Images of the pets danced in his mind. He pictured them carelessly cavorting around Camp, worshipping for attention and treats as though in the homes of their masters. Stupid, selfish creatures. This was their doing. The danger had been obvious the moment he and Belka realised they'd reached human dwellings. Hardly the blink of an eye passed before he'd said it: the pets who'd followed them must be warned not to befriend its inhabitants.

If not for his fever, he would have made good on his threat and killed the first of them to cross beneath Archway. What terrible luck! Without his aggression to discourage their sociable instincts, they'd ignored his warning. And in doing so, the pets did exactly as he'd forecast: they alerted the dragon's masked soldiers to their presence.

The beast hadn't even needed to leave its scolding crater to score this most dreadful victory. There were now even fewer dogs around to help in the fight against it.

Over the din of voices, Ball Boy's suddenly stood out, and a growl rattled Ony's teeth.

As he knew they would, the people had betrayed the dogs.

He went down closer to the dwelling huts. Concealed behind a shed, Ony watched, and waited. The blood that pulsed through his body was charged with an anger so powerful now that vengeance was all he desired. But at whom was he supposed to direct his fury?

A large group of people, in a state of agitation, were crowded around the soldier who'd replaced Red Cross Girl at the table that first morning. In his tight clothes and dark hat, the man stood so stiffly he was almost leaning back. All humans were upright, but the most sinister of them exaggerated their height by pulling back their shoulders and puffing out their chests. It was meant as a clear signal to others that *he* was the dominant one. But as every dog knew, dominance was established by what you did, not how you looked.

'They were harmless creatures,' one of the men from Bed House was saying.

'Calm yourselves, comrades,' the soldier called out. 'They're just dogs. Think about your countrymen.'

Turning to each other, the people shrugged. They shook their heads, and scowled. Ball Boy and Red Cross Girl seemed especially enraged.

'Comrades,' continued the soldier. 'What us liquidators are doing over at the Chernobyl plant is vital for the protection of the Soviet Union's people. I understand those dogs were your companions, but I hardly need to remind you that a person's life is worth so much more than a dog's.'

Ball Boy, rising on his heels to be heard, spoke up. 'I don't get it. If dogs are now so useful, why were exterminators brought in in the first place?'

'The answer is in your question, young cadet. A

present need has been identified. You know yourself how much trouble the miners are having installing their heat exchange unit below the ground. A lot of the tunnels they dig are blocked by underground pipes, and alternative routes are proving far too radioactive. Smaller animals like dogs are helpful in both regards.'

Red Cross Girl held her head in her hands, as though the words the man spoke had caused her physical pain.

The soldier went on like this for some time, until eventually the group broke apart and made their way to the buses waiting for them on the road beyond Archway. The boy and girl stayed where they were, however. Downcast, they slumped onto the benches and sat in silence.

As Ony's heart ached, his eyes blazed into the pair. Why did people have to be such enigmas? The rest of nature was simple. When Sun rose high, the land bloomed, and when it rose low, the same land frosted. Creatures sought meals and mates, and the pups they bore, if they survived, went on to have pups of their own. There was nothing to it, really.

But *people*. What dog could hope to know the workings of a person's mind? Their teeth weren't sharp and their claws were blunt. They weren't fast, or strong, and were heavy on their feet. Yet they ate when they wanted. They sheltered from the elements in heated rooms. And nothing was *ever* enough. Nature, for them, was a thing to be controlled, not experienced, which was why they did such thoughtless, reckless, cruel things.

In spite of his young age, Ony had already experienced human folk at their extreme ends. At one side there was kind old Dada, who shared what little she had and asked for nothing in return. And at the other side was the butcher, who murdered while he grinned. Where did Ball Boy and Red Cross Girl fit on the scale? Was it these two who brought the men and their cages to

Camp? If so, they stood even further along the scale than the blood-stained man who destroyed his mother. As brutal and senseless as that was, it resulted from a fleeting moment. But these two, they had shared their time with he and Belka. Comfort, from each to the other, had lessened their respective woes. If this bond had been forged merely to trick them, they were callous in a way that was inconceivable.

Still hidden, Ony watched as the girl gave a long sigh. 'I suppose this is what we're meant to call "the greater good",' she said.

Ball Boy wasn't listening though, apparently. He kept his focus on the wall behind her, as though something of great interest resided within it. 'Look at that mural,' he said, pointing. Ony followed the boy's finger but saw nothing of note, only angular shards stuck together on the wall.

The boy's eyes narrowed in concentration as he stared harder at it. 'I'm growing tired of these things. Everybody always looks so happy in them. Sometimes I wonder if it's all just make believe.'

The girl peered round to face the wall, then nodded sharply. 'Have you noticed how the colour is always the same? Why are the tiles always that same shade of red?'

'Not sure,' said the boy. 'But what I do know is it's the exact same red as spilt blood.'

At that, Ony stepped forward.

The eyes of the young humans lit up with joy. 'Good boy! You escaped the catchers! Oh, but he's hurt, Alek. Look at his back.'

Ony pulled back his lips to reveal his fangs – and suddenly neither of the pair seemed quite so pleased to see him.

Only once had Ony gone for an actual person, when he finally went back to the butcher to gave him the bite he deserved. But the man who'd killed his mother was slow and heavy, and Ony had taken him by surprise. This pair were young, and lithe – and prepared for an assault. Attacking the boy and girl might cause more harm to him than them.

His nose wrinkled and his ears came back. He gave a growl, but remained distant, for now.

The boy held out his arm and pointed away. 'You've got to go! You hear me? It's not safe for you here!'

Ony gave a loud bark.

From around the corner, the soldier called out. 'A dog!'

The pair looked at each other, distressed. 'Go!' they shouted, just before the soldier arrived from around the edge of the hut.

Lifting a contraption to his mouth, the soldier yelled into it with such force that flecks of spittle fired from his mouth. 'Tranquilliser team to headquarters!'

Now facing three of them, Ony remained in his baying stance. He wanted to pounce, but at the same time, he didn't. He just couldn't tell whether Ball Boy and Red Cross Girl were more sad, angry or afraid.

Without warning, the soldier lunged forward and kicked out, his boot barely missing Ony's mouth. The boy and girl reached out at the man's arms to pull him back.

'Are you crazy?' screamed the soldier, shoving their hands away from him. 'Do you have any idea what happens to silly little children who defy the wishes of the Party?'

The man sprang forward again. 'Tranquilliser team to headquarters, this instant!' he blurted into the box, and kicked out a second time.

Ony hopped back, then turned and bounded away. As he'd planned with Han and Gleb, the only way he'd be able to get at this pair again was while they were apart.

As he sprinted from Camp, the soldier's voice boomed out through the trees. 'Contact General Drozdov at the miners' camp! We've got one more canary for him!'

~

The moment she heard gunfire, Belka fled from the men.

The pops from their weapons began ricocheting from the trunks of the horse-chestnuts, bewildering her sense of direction. All around, the pets were running away, looking to each other for reassurance, but finding none. In their confusion, they went backward and forward, round and round, as hopeless an attempt to save themselves as she could possibly imagine.

Bolting away from Camp, she was on the verge of evading the people when, up ahead in a wide half-circle, she noticed more approaching. The men, clever creatures that they were, had enclosed them.

A sting pricked her side. Was that all their guns did? She expected it to hurt a lot more. At the end of a tube that now stuck out from her torso, a colourful, feather-like tail flapped in her airstream. She scanned the forest, desperate for a hiding spot, but saw only the rotten stump of a long-fallen poplar.

She lay on the leaves in the shade of the stump, investigating the damage. Guns put holes through dogs, but no cavity marked her torso where the tube had struck. It was as though she hadn't been shot at all. Where was the blood, the screaming, searing violence of a body torn by the cruel inventions of humankind?

Everywhere, men were shouting. Cages swung in their hands as they dashed around the trees. The first of the dogs hit with the weapons were now limp on the ground, splayed out in whatever position they'd landed. The men were scooping their lifeless bodies into the cages. And one was making his way to her.

She felt her lids grow heavy. It surprised her to discover that dying felt just like going to sleep. Her heart rate was slowing. The man was just a single tree's height away, but she couldn't move to evade him. Death was seeping into every bit of her. Although her eyes remained open, she could only look in a single direction. She understood that, within moments, her vision would fade away and she would see nothing else again.

Had there been clues these men were coming? If she hadn't been so agitated, she may have spotted something which could have spared her – and the others – from this fate. She'd let them down.

The man, now half a tree away, was advancing in slow motion, his limbs leaving trails through the air.

A long sigh – or perhaps it was short; time had ceased functioning normally – escaped her nostrils at the thought of Ony. His rage was expected. Of course the pets would refuse to go with him on his terrifying journey back to Plant. But his fury with them was uncalled for, and was making him wild. Before she even knew it, he was going on about Levka, about the need to defend a brood that didn't yet exist – and never would – from outside threats, about how appalling things had to be done if they wanted to protect themselves.

She'd seen many signs of the torment within Ony in the time they'd ranged together. There was no doubt about it: he was a hurt animal, wounded by insecurity, by grief, by a lack of trust in others so deep that the very idea of belonging to a pack was inconceivable to him. But she'd never before seen so dark a face to his torment. He was suggesting that taking the life of a helpless creature, one who was innocent and pure, was the right thing to do. And at the sight of the menace in his eye, something stronger than she'd ever felt before – stronger even than her devotion to him – awoke within her, and she was suddenly lashing out and tearing into him with her teeth.

As she realised just how much that vicious fight had compromised her alertness, she was gripped by remorse.

With her lids drooping even lower, a bright light found its way into her eyes: this was one of Sun's beams reflecting off the metal bars. The man was moving near, his cage swinging as he approached. His footsteps were now audible as he trampled down the dry grass.

Her memories were beginning to fade, her mind growing more befuddled by the second. Now, nothing existed in there beyond the very recent past. She remembered how she wanted to chase after Ony as he ran away injured towards the river. It was better to let the beating of her heart steady, though, she'd supposed. Then, just as she was able to convince Jayla to step back into the shelter of the nursery, the pets had all come bounding along, yipping excitedly about meat scattered on the forest floor.

To these animals, who'd been given every meal, meat may as well have been something that grew out of the ground, but she of course knew otherwise. She took off after them, urging them not to eat anything they found.

Most of it was gone by the time she reached them, though more was waiting in the woods. The pets had begun spreading out, unable to believe their luck, their tails wagging and their faces wide with smiles. They bounced happily around, incapable of suspicion and deaf to Belka's barks.

Charged from the thrill of her fight, she nipped at them, ever more desperate for them to heed her warning. Then, across a clearing, she'd seen Han.

The battle had come.

She left the pets; if the meat was poisoned it was too late anyway. She turned to the river. Ony had to be warned.

But there was no time, for right at that moment the first of the guns sounded. The men were sweeping the forest towards Archway. The pets, insensible creatures that they were, saw nothing of danger in the advancing folk; they didn't scatter, as any stray would instantly have done – they went *to* them.

And then the men had got her, too.

No. There were no clues that this was going to happen. There was just Ony's warning.

He'd been right about the people all along.

Presently, the man was crouching beside her. As her lids flickered, he set down his cage.

Feeling warm human hands hoist her from off the soil, all went dark and silent.

16

BREATH OF THE BEAST

THE SLASHES on his rump blazed where Belka and the hound had got him, but since it was an inconvenient time to hurt, Ony had allowed himself a mere dip in the river. Standing idle now in the shade of rich-scented berry blooms, waiting for his coat to dry, his dazed mind worked to establish his next move.

The earlier cacophony of explosive pops, yelling men and panicking dogs made the peace of the late morning seem that bit quieter. In fact, the land had grown silent in a way that was almost unnatural. Where was the chatter of birds? The mad barking of squirrels? Even the smaller creatures had gone shy: no roaches clicked, and the chirping rattle of crickets, a sound so common as to be almost unnoticeable, was absent from the trees.

The only noise at all came from high up in the bright blue sky: a *helicopter*, Jayla called it, which whirred east through wispy clouds on business Ony couldn't possibly understand.

When the fog of emotion lifted from his mind, he made his way back through Birch Grove. Expecting more chaos, he proceeded in bursts, concealing himself behind one shrub before darting on to the next. All around him was the legacy of violent chaos: bloody streaks on the leaves of saplings where dogs were hit by the men's blasting sticks; chunks of half-chewed meat, scattered by the human folk to bait the foolish pets out from Camp the way Ball Boy brought sparkling fish to the river's shore. He saw on the slope of the glade the spilt blood from the earlier scrap with Han's pack dogs, though no other traces of the animals themselves were to be found. These, too – and Han himself – must have been taken in cages.

The eventful morning had left Ony famished. He'd watched the residents of Camp leave on the buses earlier, but he was unwilling to take even a slight risk, so waited on the hill until he was sure not a soul was down in the huts. One thing was certain, though: he wouldn't eat anything left by Ball Boy and Red Cross Girl.

In the hut where the people kept their food waste, Ony found a sealed bag from which the scent of cooked meat was drifting. He slashed it with a claw, and dragged the contents over the floor until he was faced with strands of fat and a few picked bones. Unconcerned with whether or not the food might be harmful – what did it matter if it was? – Ony gulped down the lot, then went and toured the perimeter of the site.

Eventually, he found himself back at Monument, where he slumped down at the edge of Round Pond. He fixed his eyes on the stone beast, whose three heads came out of the forest floor like giant snakes. Did the dragon of Chernobyl have as many faces? He snorted a burst of air at the thought of the creature.

Once, in the yard at the foot of Wheel, he saw a man whose leashed dog was performing for a crowd of onlookers. It was the oddest thing: each time the man issued a command, the dog made a particular action. It stood on its hind legs and began walking like a person. It climbed into a little chair and sat at a desk like the children Ony saw through the windows of School. On one instruction, it even rocked itself forward onto its front paws and walked upside down. Fascinated, Ony held back after the crowd broke apart, to see the man feeding treats to the peculiar pet.

The people were just pets of the dragon, he supposed. They did as it commanded, and it fed them snacks. Every one of the dogs had been taken from Camp because human folk knew some sort of reward awaited them if they obeyed their master. What did it matter to people to snatch away some dog's beloved mate? So long as they got their treat, they would do anything it asked of them.

In the still, silent air of the forest, Ony lay with his head flat against the soil while grief crept around his heart like ivy up a wall. His sorrow ran even deeper now: Belka was just one dog, but their entire kind had been scorched by the beast from its flaming den beneath the grasslands of Plant. If Ony was now the last canine ranging the earth, what difference would it make if he did defeat the dragon? Who would be there to share his victory with him?

A snapping twig sounded in the trees behind him; in the stillness of the morning, it rang out like the blast from a human's exploding stick. Without a moment's delay, Ony leapt off behind a nearby mound.

The assailant, realising its mistake, made no more movements. Ony wondered if he should strike first; he sniffed for clues as to the nature of the foe, though, curiously, the air smelt of nothing.

A faint noise sounded from its direction. Straining to hear, Ony thought it sounded like whimpering. He let out a bark. 'Who's there?'

The whimpering got louder.

Ony broke cover to investigate. There, beside the soft spikes of an immature fir, was Jayla.

Why he growled he wasn't sure, but the pet wasted no time dropping onto her back in total submission. He stood above her, teeth bared, the heat of rage flushing him while he searched for a good reason to savage her by the throat.

Then, sheathing his teeth, he stood back. This animal had done no wrong. 'Get up,' he said.

With her head bowed low, Jayla resumed her earlier cries. 'Belka set out at dawn to gather food for the pup. When she didn't return to Den I started to worry. Now I find that all the dogs are gone and Belka is nowhere to be seen. And you, Ony, you're wounded.'

'The men killed them. They're all gone.'

Looking up with sad eyes, Jayla said nothing while she considered his news. Then, when the true weight of it seemed to settle within her, pain replaced the sorrow that moistened her eyes. 'It was as you said, Ony. The humans were not to be trusted.'

They stood, alone in a hushed wood bereft of life, until Jayla eventually turned. 'Sofiy is hungry. I'll go to her.'

At the mention of the pup's name, Ony's heart tightened. Watching Jayla pace away, he called out. 'If you see meat, leave it. That's how the men got the pets into their cages.'

Jayla paused, and turned back. 'Cages?'

Ony's head fell at the memory of Belka's limp body splayed on the bars.

'Are you sure the men *killed* the dogs?' said Jayla.

'They carried away their bodies in cages and put them into their vans.'

A sudden burst of energy seemed to liven Jayla's spirits. 'You watched them drive away?'

'Yes. Then I went into Camp. I wanted to hurt something. So I found the boy and girl. I'm so confused about them, though. Are they our friends or our enemies?'

'They were still here?'

'The soldier was talking to them, yes.'

'What was he saying?'

'Jayla, you know I don't know the human tongue.'

'Think, Ony. Think of the terms I taught Belka. Were there any at all you recognised?'

As the incident had been so charged with distress, it was hard to remember. One word did stick out, though.

'*Chernobyl.*'

The pet's tail began to wag.

'What are you thinking, Jayla?'

'People use cages to take dogs to the vet.'

'What's *vet*?'

'It's a doctor for animals.'

Ony's head tilted.

'Doctors fix our masters when they get sick. If the men who came here killed Belka and the others, why would they put them in cages? When the exterminators killed the strays back home, they left them where they lay. Ony, I don't think the people came to kill them.'

'But they used their horrid metal contraptions.'

'They fired guns? But Ony, I was napping at the mouth of Den. I would have heard blasts. Are you sure it wasn't a different sort of weapon?'

Ony thought carefully. The devices looked exactly like the other "guns" he'd seen people wield. Yet he recalled how the explosions seemed *thinner* than before, somehow less violent.

Becoming increasingly impatient, Ony gave a snarl. 'Are you saying Belka could still be alive?'

'I don't know, Ony. None of this makes any sense.'

Just then a loud thump interrupted the pair, followed right away by another, then another.

Jayla began to whine. 'What's that?'

They ran for shelter beneath Archway. Standing in its shadow, they watched as objects too numerous to count dropped out of the sky with a dull thudding.

'They're birds,' said Ony, sniffing at one when the very peculiar downpour had concluded. 'It's raining birds. They're all dead.'

Without a single breeze to rattle the boughs, Ony was beginning to feel that time had stopped. But when the buses returned to Camp in the golden glow of evening, he was reassured that life had gone on as normal.

Waiting on the hilltop – the safest place to be if gunmen showed up again – he was working through the best route to get him back to Plant when he heard their voices. Ball Boy and Red Cross Girl had, at last, returned.

Keeping low, Ony sidled down the hill to the edge of the huts. As earlier, the people were brimming with angst. Their faces were worn with fatigue and emotion, and their sunken eyes were ringed with dark circles, and now they were getting scrappy, too: two men were shoving each other, while the others scrambled to keep them apart.

Red Cross Girl seemed especially fraught. Water pooled at the bridge of her nose, streaming down her cheeks while she yelled.

While Ony waited for his opportunity to confront them, his eye picked up a flash of white through the log pile on the other side of Archway. He let loose a growl; in spite of his caution to stay well away from the returning residents, Jayla had come anyway.

Bristling, he crept around the buses and accosted her. 'You pets have got short memories. Have you forgotten already what happened to the others who ignored my warnings?'

'Ony, you don't understand what they're saying. But I do. Let me listen. Perhaps we'll learn more about where Belka and the others were taken.'

'Shut up! All of you!' the soldier was yelling. 'The deadly material that's leaking into the ground has to be cooled. All teams are being redeployed to the miners' camp – that's a direct order from the Party. And yes, Narmin, that includes the medics.'

Red Cross Girl sniffed and wiped her eyes. 'But the evacuation squads brought so many sick villagers today,' she said. 'The nurses are relying on me to assist. I don't want to let them down.'

'Let them down?' snapped the soldier. 'Do you understand, Cadet Narmin, that we are at war?'

Jayla's eyes widened. 'Listen,' she muttered on her breath.

'Our enemy may not be a man—'

The pet jolted with shock.

'—but that doesn't mean the motherland isn't facing the most serious threat in her history.'

'What's he saying?' said Ony.

Jayla turned to face him. 'There is a dragon. And they're just as terrified of it as we are.'

The people began to disperse, but Ball Boy and Red Cross Girl stayed where they were. The empty buses pulled away; black clouds belched into the forest with a roar of engines. This usually made the forest smell foul with a chemical, pungent odour, but Ony couldn't detect any scent at all right now.

'I don't want to do this anymore,' the girl said to the boy. 'I just want to go home and see my mother and sister. They depend on me, Alek.'

'We just have to hold on a little longer, Narmin. You've seen it yourself. The miners are finding their way through. And the dogs are helping to keep them safe. The sooner they sort out the situation there, the sooner we can go home.'

The girl made fists. 'But it's not right! They're just innocent creatures! That level of exposure will kill them!'

'Then you'll have to find a way to get medicine to them as you did Foxy and Hazel Eyes.'

Jayla, who'd been listening intently, brought her rear paw up to scratch behind her ear. 'I know what the people did here today is beyond our understanding, Ony. But these young ones had nothing to do with it.

They're upset that the dogs were taken. Anger towards them is unwarranted.' She began to move slowly away from the log pile. 'Remember, they showed you kindness,' she added, and vanished into the cover of the bushes.

But Ony stayed where he was. The time had come to begin the journey to the dragon's pit, so if he was going to hurt these humans who'd caused him so much pain, it would have to be now.

The eyes of the pair contained such sorrow, though. Why were they so much younger than the other folk at Camp? They seemed barely of an age to be out of their own creches. Perhaps Jayla was right. Over the course of his illness, they *had* shown him much kindness, and had sought nothing in return. Not once did they try to make him sit at a little desk like the children at School or walk upside-down on his forepaws.

Letting out a tiny whimper, Ony backed away. Attacking them solved nothing.

He found Jayla among the shrubs, and they ran together until the voices at Camp dimmed to silence. Then, where the woods sloped down toward a brook, the pair stopped and Ony went down to drink.

The water level was low; Sun was really beginning to send its most scorching rays. This summer, if it came, would be his third. How very excited he'd been about the prospect of his early adulthood, of siring a family with Belka and ranging around the fields with pups in tow in search of treats and adventure.

But the dragon had ruined everything.

He couldn't even drink properly; the wound on his rear made it too difficult to lap at the river. It was making him limp, too. He let out a grumble: the journey to Plant would take even longer now. For some scraps with Belka and Han's pets, he'd lost his lightning speed.

After a few mouthfuls of water, he hobbled up onto the bank and faced Jayla. 'I'm leaving now.'

Jayla gave a swish of her tail. 'I want to come with you.'

'As you wish. But you'll need to keep up.'

'I will. Just let me get Sofiy first.'

Ony began to growl.

'I can't leave her, Ony! She's barely eating solid food yet. She's still way too young to survive by herself. It won't take me long to get her.'

'The pup is not coming.'

'But—'

Ony made his feelings even clearer by wrinkling his nose and setting back his ears. When Jayla failed to roll over for him this time, he went to her and gave her a nip. But still the pet wouldn't submit.

She was playing a very risky game. 'What good are you to the pup if I tear your throat, foolish pet?'

'Ony, smell the air.'

'What?'

'Smell the air.'

Ony focused on the tip of his nose and gave a sniff.

'Do you smell the moss of the rocks?' asked Jayla. 'The minerals in the brook?'

'I don't smell anything.'

'The birds dropped out of the sky on the day when things lost their odour. What do you think Belka would have to say about that?'

Picturing his beloved mate in his mind, Ony saw all the times when her eye settled fearfully on some patch up ahead where nothing at all appeared to him to reside. Plant's shimmering sickness was here. Camp, whether its human residents knew it or not, was spoilt now.

'Please, Ony. We can't stay here. Let us go with you. I can help. I can teach you all I know about the human tongue. It'll serve you when you go to the dragon.'

'I won't be responsible for another dog's pup, Jayla. Join me if you have to, but come alone or not at all.'

Jayla yipped with annoyance. 'Goodbye then. I wish

you luck. For all our sakes.' And with that, the pet took off into the trees.

Ony inhaled another breath of the air. Not only was it unusual in its scentlessness, a metallic taste dwelt upon it as it had back in their hometown. The dragon's diseased breath had found him.

Turning away from the woods into which Jayla had vanished, Ony set off with a hobble, his tender rear leg pulsing with pain each time his paw made contact with the ground. He cast a last glance through Archway, into the clearing where people were lighting a fire in readiness for their evening meal.

Eventually, he came to Monument with its stone fish – *dolphin*, the pets called it – and the three-headed beast, at which he fixed an intense glare. Within a few dawns he'd be standing before the real thing, sickened and scorched and trying desperately to get at one of its scaly throats. But for now, it was enough to lift up his leg and spray the middle head with a blast of hot pee.

He moved further from Camp's southern edge, hearing, faintly, a voice calling out.

'Foxy! Foxy! Where are you boy? Come and get some dinner!'

But it didn't matter what Ball Boy was saying. There was nothing any human could offer him now that would ever be of interest to Ony again.

17

ZONE OF ALIENATION

BELKA'S EYELIDS were the first part of her to wake up. Against incredible resistance, they came ajar to bring to an end a dark and dreamless sleep.

Her tongue was next. Oversized in her dry mouth, she dragged it over her teeth, pressing it into the points of her fangs to check she could still feel.

With her head flat against the floor of her cage, she let her eyes roll up to begin the process of making sense of her surroundings. Beside her, in another cage, was a dog she didn't know, and in the one beyond that was Tuzik, one of the pets from Camp.

Although she wished to crane around to see more – was Ony here, too? – the weight of her head was too great, so she concentrated instead on her other senses, hoping to gather as much information as she could.

All around, a chorus was blaring: 'Let me out! Let me out! Let me out!' Her ears were working fine, then. Her nose, however, was useless. Either it hadn't yet woken up, or else nothing in this space smelt of anything. A faintly metallic taste resided in her mouth, deepening her longing for a drink of water.

Expanding and collapsing with each of her laboured

breaths, her torso slowly heaved. She sent a message to her paws. They twitched: a promising sign she wasn't broken completely. Attempting the same process with her tail, though, was less successful. Not the faintest swish disturbed it – but then, how was a dog's tail supposed to wag in a situation like this?

As her brain adjusted to consciousness, she was perplexed by the lack of trees. Where were they all? At the time she'd been shot, a sea of green and gold had enclosed her. She had no recollection of moving, so just how was it that she now found herself surrounded by plain fabric walls?

In a voice so thin and strained she didn't even recognise it as her own, she groaned: 'Where am I?' She longed for a single lap of water, to give power to her barks as much as to slake her thirst. 'Tuzik,' she wheezed. 'Where am I?'

'They're calling it the Zone of Alienation,' returned a croaky, disembodied voice.

From nowhere at all – had her eyes closed for a time? – a man was suddenly beside her, unclasping the lock from the cage door. Hands came in, working in that endlessly fascinating way, to fasten a collar around her neck. The suggestion of a growl formed in her throat, convincing nobody.

'Belka!'

She focussed on her paws once again. This time, she was able to rock them this way and that with some control. Still, though, her tail remained inanimate.

'Belka!'

The man was clipping some sort of tether to the collar and fastening the other end to a spike in the ground outside the cage. Pain would be coming soon, perhaps, but for now, at least, he wasn't hurting her.

'Belka!'

Somebody was calling her name. How long had they

been doing that? The voice was familiar, but she couldn't place it among the foggy landscape of her memory. She made to question who had spoken, but again a mere rasp formed in her throat – now, though, her powerlessness enraged her, and she came suddenly to life.

Springing up onto her paws, Belka barked in full voice. 'Who's there?'

'Belka! It's Han!'

She whipped her head to the left to face him. Though she'd thought of Han as an enemy right up until her capture, none of that seemed to matter given their current plight. 'Han,' she said. 'Where are we?'

'Plant.'

An ill-tempered bark was enough to express how she felt to hear that dreadful name.

'They brought us right back to the grasslands, Belka.'

Fully restored to her usual state of vigilance, she surveyed their environment. This soft dwelling was at least as big as Bed House. On all sides, tables skirted the fabric walls, with cages placed on top and below. Some dogs were still down; among those who stood, she recognised several as pets from Camp, as well as the few who'd broken away from the main group to join Han. Most, though, were strangers.

None of the animals wore the same orange hue as Ony. That smart boy! It didn't matter how he'd managed to evade the men and their feathered pipes, it was enough for now to simply know he had.

She looked around the room for signs of an infant or a well-groomed white coat, but neither was present. Jayla and the pup must have been inside Den when the men struck: a piece of good fortune that had spared them from this fate.

But just what was this fate? Why were dogs here?

An image appeared in her mind of Monument and its three-headed beast, and an icy surge rippled through her body.

What was it Ony had said? Dogs were the meat that gave the dragon its strength, so it had set the human folk the task of gathering its meals. But here was a multitude of living canines. The terrible beast must have eaten its fill for the day. Or else, it had found a new use for dogs.

Through the entrance to the fabric enclosure, a large group of people began filing in, none recognisable from Camp. In the corner nearest to the entrance, men were taking hold of the dogs' tethers and tugging the conscious ones down from their cages, then leading them outside.

Even in heat this stifling, Belka was in no hurry to be taken anywhere. The last time she'd laid eyes on Plant, it was a vision of something beyond nature, pulsing with the watery shimmer of a force not meant for living things. What possible state was the place in now? Too dreadful to even consider, Belka curled up into the cage and tried her best to shut out the world beyond the fabric walls.

A short time later, another pair of people came in – one tall, with floppy curls of blond hair, the other short, with no hair at all – and stood beside her cage. The floppy-haired one was familiar: he slept on a bed near Ball Boy. Belka watched as they conversed in hushed voices. The nervous energy which crackled between them made her wonder if they were talking about something they knew they oughtn't to be.

Startlingly, the voice of the shorter man grew louder. '*100,000* deaths?!'

'Shhh! That's what they're saying, yeah. And that's just the Ukrainian side.'

'The radiation has spread, then?'

'Thousands of miles.'

A soldier entered the tent behind them at that moment, causing the two individuals to jump with shock and peel apart. The familiar of the pair went straight across to Han; the other clumsily fumbled with Belka's tether.

Unclasping the leash from the spike in the ground, the bald-headed man issued a light tug on Belka's collar to pull her down from the cage. On trembling legs, she moved closer to the open flap of the tent's entrance.

Sun's brightness forced shut her eyelids, which only served to draw out the fear of what she was about to see. But when she opened them again, she was surprised by the scene before her. Almost everything she looked at was affected by the shimmer – men and trucks and tools bore fuzzy boundaries where their edges should be solid – but the most vaporous of the stuff, which at one time seemed angry enough to swallow everything, was less severe now. Perhaps the awful beast beneath them had done all the damage it wished to do already?

On an open stretch of land which stood a short distance away from the tent, Belka could see many dogs tethered to posts. A film of saliva coated her tongue to see bowls of water set down beside them. Craning her neck to see all around her on the way to this yard, she looked over to where the skeleton of Plant jutted out from the landscape.

Wood, steel and brick, and gadgets of all shapes and sizes, had been carefully gathered into a huge pile of rubble that towered almost to the height of the ruined building itself. On all levels of the horizon, people were busily conducting themselves: on the tops of nearby buildings, on upper-storey floors exposed to the summer sky, on the yards surrounding the buildings. They were even engaged in tasks below the ground, she observed, as the shiny-headed man fastened her leash around a spike.

After lapping up the water from her bowl, Belka surveyed the scene again. How to make sense of the peculiar work she was witnessing? Wheeled crates were rumbling along rail tracks, like miniature versions of the ones that carried trains to and from the city through the countryside north of Stadium. The soil was ramped, allowing the crates to descend beneath the level of the ground to where an opening had been hollowed out like a cave's mouth. The carts went in empty, but came out again filled to the brim with earth sullied with a hot and hazy shimmer. In some of the crates there were people, their papery gowns and hats stained with soil, and in others there were dogs. No kind of creature appeared especially glad to be involved in this mysterious business.

Shovelling the soil out from the crates was a different team of men. Ball Boy was among them. She watched him fill up a barrow and wheel it over to where the ground dropped away on a shelf. The rumble of engines came from over the edge: trucks were catching what the men dumped, before driving away with a deafening roar.

On the other side of the yard were more tents. One bore a red cross similar to the one on the girl's hat. In fact, Belka thought she saw Red Cross Girl herself among the folk inside, though it was possible it was just another young person with saddened eyes and masses of frizzy hair.

With every drop of water gone from her bowl, she thirsted for more. The dog nearest Belka was led away into one of the crates and pushed along the tracks into the tunnel entrance; she tried to get at the contents of his bowl, but her tether fell tantalisingly short.

Shyly, she turned to the other animals, longing for any kind of reassurance. 'What do they want with us in there?'

'Nothing,' replied a tall retrieving dog marked by patches of shimmering air. 'We're just the canaries.'

'The what?'

'That's what they call the dogs in our tent. It's good being a canary, because we get to come out again. It's *that* one you don't want to be in,' he said, looking at the fabric structure nearby.

Belka's head tilted. 'Why? What's in there?'

'The blasters. Those dogs go into the tunnels, but they never come out again.'

A shrill noise whistled out from the cave's mouth, and a man with a bright red face approached Belka to untether her. He took her over to a crate that had arrived with a rattle and a squeak, and commanded her to jump up inside.

Before the crate moved off on the tracks and went inside the ground, a second man came across. This one clipped a curious yellow box to Belka's collar. He fiddled with it for a moment, then yelled over to the other people.

'Bloody dosimeter's bust! Chuck us another one, pal.'

The man attached a second box to Belka's neck. Again, he worked its controls, and this time an erratic, insect-like clicking sounded. The man slapped the side of the cart three times, then Belka felt a pull. Slowly, the crate began to descend, and then the ground was above her head.

While her eyes adjusted to the darkness, she was surprised to see a whole world here where tunnels, lit by electric light, forked off in many different directions. It put her in mind of a badger set she'd once squeezed herself into when she first ranged away from Creche with Laika and Lyuba. Although it appeared to her like a maze, the men knew well enough where they wanted her, and directed her cart as they saw fit.

And as she went deeper into the ground, she noticed a very odd relationship between the environment and the box on her neck: the more the air shimmered with the infected energy of Plant, the more intensely the machine chirruped.

~

By the time Sun made it to the lower horizon, Ony was exhausted.

Between the bout of sickness and the wound on his flank, his stamina was much reduced. It was a good job he wasn't in a rush; a mood made sour might have cost him his alertness.

As it was, though, there was no urgency to this journey. Was there even such a thing, any more? Out here in the dog-less wilds of a blighted land, where all things were simply waiting to end, there was little, if anything, worth hurrying for.

He longed for a body of water to appear somewhere on his route, and tasted the hot evening sky for traces of salt as he went. A dip would make a refreshing end to an afternoon's walking – the transition of seasons had happened so quickly that he'd not yet adjusted to the heat – but none of the usual minerals of a river or lake were detectable. His best bet now was a stream inside the woods themselves.

As he was focussing on his tongue, however, a different kind of taste made itself known. Vaguely organic, it put him in mind of flesh.

Given the lingering presence of Belka's invisible menace, he had to work twice as hard to find the source of it, but after a few careful moments spent weaving among the columns of aspens, Ony's eye was attracted to a glistening splotch on the soil up ahead.

Where the wall of aspens ended and a patch of heathland stretched away to the next copse, the remains of an animal lay splayed on the scrub. It was the biggest carcass he'd ever seen, of a creature that he'd heard about but never actually encountered. Large antlers protruded from what remained of the animal's head: broader and flatter than the type sported by deer, with stubbier branches. Its entire torso was nothing more than a cavity now, though, its white ribs exposed to the elements with its innards nowhere to be found.

Ony licked his chops.

Then he stood back.

On a day when the pets had quite probably lost their lives for not showing enough suspicion of treats left laying on the forest floor, it would be an act of utmost stupidity to begin feasting now.

He lowered his body. Hopefully he hadn't already drawn something to him. The scrubland encircling him was just about the worst of all terrain to ward of a threat – at his height, it was difficult to see in any direction over the tops of the spiky bushes – so he hastily darted back into the gloom of the aspen shade and waited.

If it was a trap, it wasn't one set by the human folk. No people had traversed these deep woods recently, if ever. Most likely, the carcass was evidence of a hunt. But no single thing could bring down an animal of that size.

Ony bristled at the thought.

This was the work of multiple predators. And the only creatures that worked these lands aroused a fear in him so primal he turned on the spot and went back to a sheltered area where a tall trunk had long ago collapsed.

Upon a soft bed of pinefall, Ony closed his eyes and tried not to think about wolves. But in dwelling upon Belka, they quickly sprang open again.

Had she thought about him, when the hot metal they fired from their horrid gun went into her? He hoped the memory of him brought comfort to Belka in the moments before the lids of her pretty eyes closed for the final time. A tiny whine escaped him; given how he'd behaved the last time they were together, it was likely that if she'd considered him at all, it wouldn't have been in a favourable light.

Sweet Belka had always defended him, but not even she would tolerate the aggressive intent he showed towards the little one. Yet all he wanted was a pack of his own flesh and blood. That really wasn't so much to hope for, was it? He'd imagined it again and again in his mind's eye when he'd been most wretched with loneliness: a call howled into the yonder, answered with glee by his own brood, his own family who would never plot to hurt him or cast him out. How could some other dog's pup be expected to behave in such a way? It was sure to strike out against him the moment it saw in him frailty or weakness.

Shame needled his heart. The presence of the pup hadn't even been a threat. It wasn't as though it was an additional mouth to feed, another competitor for the limited resources available to his own brood. He had no brood! To act so jealously over an imagined concern was a test too far for his beloved girl. She was right to stand up to him the way she did. The hot pain across his rear – a wound that had turned what should have been an unremarkable journey into this laboured trek – was much less than he'd deserved.

In this way, scolding himself for his many wrongdoings, he spent the dusk, eventually showing himself just enough mercy that he was able to get to sleep.

But sleeping with fresh meat so nearby was a mistake; dreams of food disturbed the peace of his night's rest. Mostly, these involved he and Belka feasting on the tastiest of treats, playing happily with bellies full by the banks of a shallow river. But in another, he *was* the meat. A piece of flesh on a line, there only to entice a larger carnivore – one which screamed flame from out of its mouth and belched poison that sailed away on every breeze that blew.

He woke, his heart beating fast. Of course the pets refused to go with him. He was heading to his death. Whether the dragon had three heads or one; no matter if it flew, as some said, or crawled, as claimed by others; whether its breath killed a creature on the spot or made it suffer in drawn-out agony – it was unbeatable.

When enough time had passed, Ony felt it was safe to take a nibble of the carcass he'd discovered. He rose, and in the blackness of night, had just begun to wander over to the ravaged animal when a sudden snapping of twigs sounded close by.

He froze, and sniffed the air.

Something was upon him, and it was unmistakably canine.

18

FOREST OF DEATH

FROM THE TIPS of his claws to the points of his upright ears, not a single part of Ony was untouched by the ice of fear. It was in his loins and his belly, along his spine and in the lungs that gasped fast, shallow breaths. It was in his constricted throat and in the sockets of his wild, staring eyes: a mortal terror, keeping him rooted to the soft forest floor.

Where there was one wolf-dog, there were more. And when such a predator had manoeuvred to get just close enough that its scent could be faintly whiffed, it was already too late: whichever direction Ony now chose to flee, it would be into the path of another, and from there, the final thing an ensnared stray could look forward to was the blissful oblivion of death.

Another branch cracked as the animal edged closer; Ony fought to suppress a whine from escaping him. Then its movement changed. Scurrying paws suggested a skittish – and small – creature.

Ony gave a cautionary growl. If this wasn't a wolf-dog, he had a fighting chance.

To his surprise, the faint form of a regular dog emerged out of the trees. A second, tiny, individual was tottering beside it.

'Ony,' a voice said, as Jayla orbited his body with a waltz of sniffing.

As the frosty grip of fright loosened, the beating of his heart calmed. Full breaths brought steadiness to a body that had been on the verge of collapse. His hackles, and his ears, came down.

The pup, clambering over the fallen log and chewing at seedlings, made Jayla's already strained face flush with exasperation; without taking her eyes from Sofiy, she slumped down onto the earth.

'I must sleep now,' she said. She summoned the pup with a commanding yip, pulling it tight into her spreadeagled body, and before Ony could even think about protesting, she was fast asleep.

It wasn't long after that he fell into dreams, too, and when he awoke, the day had already dawned. Panting with the heat – even in the shade, it was stifling – he stretched out his rear leg. Though it was still tender, it was lithe: it wouldn't slow him today.

And neither would this pair.

Ony looked across at Jayla. The pup had crawled beneath the narrow arch between the log and the ground, and Jayla was trying to catch her. He barked a simple farewell, and ambled off.

The decision to follow him here had been theirs. If they wished, they could follow him further – they could follow him all the way to the searing teeth of the dragon itself if they really wanted to – but he was not going to allow them to walk with him.

'Please wait!' yelled Jayla. The pet crouched to the pup and licked its small head, muttering something softly on her breath, and with this, the pup straightened itself into an upright position and bowed its neck. It was as though Jayla had told it that for the next few moments it was to be on its best behaviour.

When Jayla stood before Ony, the pup held its

respectful stance. 'Look at the colour of her fur,' Jayla said.

In the soft light of the rays spilling into the copse, the pup's coat was coming through in a reddish shade of gold. Ony lamented the sight of it; given a chance to age, the lowly creature would have been very pretty, but living things everywhere were soon to be robbed of their chance to grow old.

'The colour of her eyes has come out. Look at them, Ony.'

A rich brown, the colour of a hazel's seed, sparkled in the blush of daybreak.

Ony titled his head, confused by their similarity to other eyes he had once known.

'You see it, don't you?' said the pet.

'There's no time, Jayla. The dragon's infection is spreading further from Plant every day. If it isn't stopped soon, there won't be anywhere left for living creatures. You understand that, don't you?'

'It's you that doesn't understand, Ony. Listen to what I'm trying to tell you. Not long after you left yesterday, Sofiy began barking. These were her first real calls. I wondered if she'd heard the people return with their cages, but no vehicles had been at Camp since the buses left with the residents. She became so distressed. I knew it wasn't hunger, because she ate what I scavenged from the porches, and it couldn't be fear, because no other animals were near – not even birds. Do you see, Ony? Not even birds.'

Ony looked on, blankly.

'I didn't know how to calm her, so I moved her away. She fell silent for a short time, then carried on yipping again right as a metallic taste settled on my tongue. Each time I moved her, she'd settle, until something seemed to catch her eye and then off she'd go again. I studied our surroundings as carefully as I could, but nothing at all was approaching. But then my eyes began to burn the way they do when the flowers of rye grass brush against your face.'

Ony felt the roots of his hackles tingle on his neck.

'Eventually, there wasn't a single spot anywhere around Camp where Sofiy would settle and where the air wasn't spoiled. So we picked up your trail and left. I'd have caught you much sooner than I did last night, were it not for Sofiy. Not because she's slow – she'll keep up fine with enough encouragement – but because every time we narrowed your lead she'd begin to bark fiercely at nothing at all and we'd have to change course.'

'She sees it,' said Ony, his eyes widening. 'The shimmer.'

Jayla's mouth rose at the sides into smile. 'She has the same coat, the same eyes, and the same strange gift. We can be sure of it. Sofiy is Belka's sister.'

As gently as he could, Ony leaned forward to lick the pup around her neck and ears, sending her little tail quivering back and forth.

'Alright,' he said. 'We can go together. She can help us find a safe path through to the city. But once we get close, you'll need to keep back. There's too much open space around Plant, and the dog-mask men will have an easy job of firing holes through you both. Now come, we have a long walk ahead of us, and the heat will make the distance seem twice as far.'

Turning to lead them away, he began to ascend the dell when a sight made him fall to the ground with terror.

This time, he really had been caught.

Towering right above him was the most enormous animal he had ever seen:

A grey-maned wolf.

A canine couldn't even hope to understand the ways of humankind. What drove them further into the ground beneath Plant was a total mystery – not only to Belka, but to all the dogs she encountered during her first voyage into Tunnel.

The humans' business appeared exhausting. Hacking into rocky soil to scrape it away and load it into the carts was slow work, made all the more tedious because each time they stumbled on a patch of rippling air – when the box around her neck spluttered with its mad crackle – the team downed their equipment and took off along the tracks back towards the entrance.

The first time that happened, they came back into Tunnel some time later wearing dog masks, causing Belka to fret so heavily that one of the men gave her a swift crack across the back with the handle of a tool.

Although the sight of them behind their round panes of glass always made her mindful of the exterminators, her whimpering began to lessen with each new incident. Eventually, with the day dragging on and on, their odd, elongated faces became so commonplace that she ceased to even notice them.

When they finally put her into a cart and sent her back along the tracks to the outside world, she was confused by the lack of darkness. It ought to be night by now, surely? Granted, the dreamless sleep she'd had between leaving the camp and arriving at the tent had made time run strangely, but she knew from Sun's position when she'd come underground today that it should have fallen over the horizon already.

Back in her cage, the permanent electric light made her confusion and bewilderment all the more unbearable. The thin lids of her eyes couldn't shield the hot glow, so even her dreams seemed to be bathed in its harsh tones. The perpetual light affected her body too. There are rhythms she supposed were common to all creatures: hunger, excretion, play, investigation. In here, such rhythms ceased to exist. While the spirit was beset with woe, the body that held it was in a constant state of discomfort.

When the electric glow was finally switched off, the natural light of dawn was a most welcome sight. Further relief followed soon after when Sun began to bake the tent and a familiar face appeared inside: Red Cross Girl. It was clear, though, that the girl was agitated.

'Why must we do it, huh?' she sighed. 'Cage souls against their will?' She threw a nervous glance over her shoulder in both directions, then pushed a piece of bread in through the bars of the cage. 'Sorry it's not much, but it's good for you,' she whispered.

Belka ate, noticing the familiar bitterness of the Bed House bowls. The girl, meanwhile, went around the other dogs, slipping bread in through their cages and speaking as she would to her own kind. 'The fallout has spread west. It's at Fairytale already. I guess they'll be moving us to new accommodation soon.'

Belka pleaded with her eyes to be let out of this awful place, but Red Cross Girl, seemingly unable to bear looking at her, turned with a deep sigh to look out of Tent's front side, where noisy vehicles were pulling away.

The secretive pair from yesterday entered. Glancing over to the corner, the one with the floppy hair called over to Belka's cage. 'What's a medic doing in the canary tent?'

'Must think she's a vet,' laughed the bare-headed one. 'Where's the young lad you bus in with?'

She gave a flick of her head towards the outside. 'You know the ditches where they dump those black rocks?'

'The graphite pits?'

'Yeah, those. They're filling them in with all the mined soil today. Alek's pretty happy about it – that's him now driving one of the trucks.'

'Lucky boy,' said the floppy-haired boy. 'Well, come away now comrade. Shift change for the canaries.'

Red Cross Girl stepped aside, and the pair began

taking dogs from their cages. As they unfastened Belka, she felt sorrow of the heaviest sort envelop the girl. 'Stay safe, pup,' she said, as the man in the white suit took hold of Belka's leash and led her towards the tracks of Tunnel.

~

While Ony and Jayla lay trembling at the sight of the wolf-dog, Sofiy wasted no time lolloping over to say hello.

Side by side, it was like looking at an acorn at the foot of an oak tree. The wolf, bigger than the biggest dog Ony had ever seen, appeared almost as wide as it was tall. While the animal paid no heed to the pup and kept its pale eyes fixed on him, Ony wondered just when the rest of its pack would tighten the circle no doubt around them this very instant.

The wolf lowered its trunk of a neck to the pup, and Ony braced for an appalling scene. But the animal merely gave her a sniff and nudged her with the end of its snout.

Still no pack appeared. Ony began to breathe again. Perhaps he might survive if he fled now? No dog in the old city was faster than him, but what good was pace against a creature like the one now towering above him? This wolf had more strength in one paw than he possessed in his entire body. Besides, Jayla deserved better than to be left like that. She had put herself at risk to help him. When the wolf finally struck, he could take all three of them together.

But the wolf didn't strike. In fact, the huge canine didn't seem to be moving very much at all. Remembering the stone figures of Monument, Ony felt it was more like an impression of a living thing than an actual breathing creature.

Taking utmost care to keep his movement as fluid as possible, Ony stood and bowed almost to the ground. The wolf responded with total blankness, so Ony began to pace forwards, ensuring his hackles stayed down and his teeth remained hidden behind his lips; the slightest hint of aggression from him, and he was wolf food. Slowly, tiny step by tiny step, Ony went to Sofiy, instructing her to return to Jayla with the softest of commands.

Ony was so seized with fear that he couldn't know for sure whether this was really happening or if he were experiencing another of the fevered dreams that had plagued him for so many nights. Standing directly beneath the wolf, he trembled as he spoke. 'I am Ony.'

The wolf lowered its neck to sniff him. 'I am Volya. Follow me, Ony.'

Ony remained frozen to the spot until the animal had moved several paces ahead. He looked across at Jayla, whose eyes were still wide with terror. Wordlessly, he told her to remain where she was, then proceeded onward.

What to the wolf was a steady walk was to Ony more of a canter. As he followed the animal across a wide expanse of scrubby vegetation to a gentle slope lit by Sun's streaming beams, he maintained a respectful distance.

At the foot of the slope was a glade, walled by a bank of fir trees. Into this, the wolf vanished. No denser forest had Ony ever seen – in places, the trunks were packed so tightly he wondered how the wolf even managed to squeeze its broad body through.

When Sun's light finally found the pine-strewn carpet once again, it was on a basin that ran down on both sides to a stream. The tinkling of water brought just a touch of comfort to Ony's fraught mood, but the colour of the trees – they'd taken on an odd, reddish hue – did little to lessen his distress.

The wolf came to a stop; Ony stood beside him and peered up for a clue as to what had caught its attention. Down in the brook, splayed out on a nest of rocks, was something that looked like an animal, but since it was the size of one of the people's cars, it couldn't be. Brown fur coated the thing, and what looked like claws stuck out from the ends of its lifeless limbs.

'What's that, Volya?'

The wolf remained still as stone. 'That is a bear.'

Although he'd never seen one, Ony knew of such creatures. These mountain animals came down to the lower forests in the warmer months for fish. Their strength and speed was unmatched: it was said they could climb trees faster than most dogs could run down a hill.

'What's it doing?'

'It is dead,' said Volya, and much to Ony's surprise the fearsome wolf let out a whimper.

As they moved off, Ony found it impossible to look away from the bear below. He doubted that even a pack of wolves could take on something of such an enormous size. So what animal had killed it? He thought of the dragon – the very creature he was journeying to face – and his heart trembled beneath his ribs.

After they traversed a rocky copse, birds in the treetops began a commotion that carried far through the forests. Ony balked at the sight of vultures. Boorish, bullying birds, he was glad to have had only limited encounters with them. They longed for meat, and even though they were too lazy to hunt for it they staked a claim wherever it lay. Another fallen bear was ahead, perhaps, on which they were readying to feast.

The smell of rot appeared on the air. The wolf, still several paces ahead, stopped. The ground before him dropped away; over this shelf, the wolf's head went down, sadly.

Underneath the unpleasant stench of decay, Ony detected strong canine odours. He approached the edge, and peered over. Shock made him recoil. But Volya's wretchedness was causing his own heart to ache, so he stood close by his formidable companion.

Below, several wolves lay across the brush. Too many to count – were there six? Ten? Twelve? – only a pair showed signs of life, such as it was. Suffering of the sort they were now experiencing was worse than death. Mercifully, that would arrive very soon.

'This is my pack.'

Ony made no sound. What was there to say? Such a sight would strike terror into the marrow of anything that drew breath, but he felt only sorrow.

Eventually, he turned to his grieving companion. 'What happened here, Volya?'

The wolf began to cough, and soon these became whimpers. 'We were ranging across lowland, where the river pools upon the banks. Many dead animals were scattered there. We feasted on them until no more would fit in our bellies. But we grew sick. I watched my brothers and sisters fall into fever, and now they run forever in the meadows that lay beyond our final sleep. What could have done this to us? We were in our prime. Now we are nothing. Can you help us, Ony?'

Even though the grief-sickened wolf would probably tear out his throat for speaking of such fanciful things, Ony would tell Volya what he knew about the dragon. But not now. At this moment, all Ony could offer was silence.

They stood together for some time surveying the harrowing scene when Volya leaned close to lick Ony's neck. 'Forgive me for taking you away from your own business.'

Ony looked up, his spirit darkened with pity. 'Why did you, Volya? I'm just a little stray.'

'Because,' said Volya, walking back into the shade of the pines, 'you're the only living thing I've encountered in days.'

19

MINERS' BEST FRIEND

EVERY STEP EAST took Ony and his two companions nearer to the dragon's fiery pit, and the weight of the coming battle was growing so very heavy that by the time Sun vanished, he felt almost crushed by it.

Of course, they nearly hadn't set off at all. Walking was fine while his shadow fell on his left side or his right, but when Ony got back from Volya's desolate forest, it lingered directly beneath him. It was unreasonable, he convinced himself, for one as small as Sofiy to be expected to journey when Sun was so high in the sky. But as the afternoon turned to evening and the shade beneath the trees began to deepen, a thought nagged at Ony: the longer he delayed, the further the infection spread. So, upon legs which felt curiously reluctant, he'd managed to spring into action to lead his unlikely party on through the woods.

Twilight seemed to stretch on almost as long as the day itself, and made for such pleasant walking that Ony was tempted to carry on through the night. The pup, though, was beginning to lag, and Jayla was fretting about moving closer to the terrible beast, so he decided rest was probably the smart choice.

Where a section of old wall lay crumbled upon the

forest floor, they stopped. Jayla and the pup curled up and went straight to sleep, but Ony's eyes, tired though they were, refused to close. Sleep seemed so wasteful now; whether he made it to the dreadful pit tomorrow or the next day, a slumber was coming that for him would never end.

Resting his chin on his paws, Ony watched as bats gleaned mealworms from the underside of leaves, and listened to the mellow hoo-ing of owls. The world beyond the reach of humankind was so peaceful. Without people's chaos, their incomprehensible desire to organise nature, everywhere could be like this. Still, how they'd lived in the time before the dragon woke was their business; they were just as defenceless as everything else now.

At some point in the darkest depth of night, Jayla, who must have sensed Ony's worry, came and sat by him. 'Your meeting with the wolf-dog has made you troubled,' she said.

Ony shuffled onto his side. 'There's no way I can defeat this thing.'

Jayla yawned. 'That's what every hero says.'

'*Hero?* What is Hero?'

'The one in the stories who saves the day. The one who slays the dragon and rescues the princess, like you're going to do. The one who does the right thing, even when it causes them to suffer.'

Ony's spirits dipped. How fanciful this pet dog was. 'Does Hero always save the day?'

'Of course.'

'And does Hero always survive?'

'Always.'

He sank into the soft needles of his forest bed. Though Jayla knew much of people's ways and of the odd untruths with which they entertained each other, something had gone wrong in her mind. A creature that had killed wolves and bears without even leaving the comfort of its own bed didn't allow for Hero – not his victory, nor his survival.

The dreams that awaited him when he finally fell asleep were tormented, and when he next opened his eyes he didn't feel at all rested. But the first hint of blue was warming the sky, and no more time could be lost to idleness.

Jayla and Sofiy kept pace well while the woods were dense, but when the trees thinned into open tracts, clear walking meant Ony naturally moved off too far ahead. He stopped to let them catch up, then to have a rest, and in this way most of the morning passed without disturbance, not by a living creature nor a filthy pocket of toxic sky.

As Sun was ascending to its highest position, Ony began to recognise the land beneath his paws. He'd ranged these parts as a grieving pup throughout his first solitary nights outside Creche. He recalled men working on the road near here, pouring a foul-smelling, steaming substance across gravel and driving across it with a huge metal wheel. They left behind crusts of bread and sausage ends, which he'd gobbled down without even having to think about some pack brute coming and taking it from him – a rare meal enjoyed in peace. He wondered whether such treats may lay in wait here now, but quickly pushed the thought out of his mind: people were not a source of food, however tempting it was to believe it.

When they eventually came to the road, he showed Jayla and Sofiy how to look in both directions before walking out. As the pup was bounding across, however, she stopped and began to bark.

Jayla called out. 'What did Ony say, pup? Never stop in the middle!' But the infant was disturbed by something up ahead, and would advance no further.

Ony surveyed the landscape before them: no visible threat awaited them. He looked from north to south for indications of where the terrain better suited inexperienced paws, then turned back to the road. 'We'll have to go around,' he said.

But which way? The north was a more direct route to the city, but it was also – in less extraordinary times – busier with people. Numerous small villages awaited on the south route, but these tended to be quiet places where elderly folk like Dada resided. They'd get to the river faster that way, too, and from there he'd be able to use its high banks to make his way up to Plant – a safer approach than the paved avenues. That settled it.

Sofiy journeyed in a state of distress. With the shimmer's edge lingering wide on their left side, she yipped all the way across the southern fields to the grain barns, only settling when they came to the ramshackle dwellings of the first village.

The place was recently deserted. On a fast tour around its streets, Ony found a chicken's carcass in a festering trash pile, which he took to the tool shed where he'd left his travel companions sheltering from Sun. Although the meal offered little nutrition to the older pair, the pup was so enraptured by it that Jayla had to keep close watch, intervening when Sofiy went for a piece of bone far too big for her little chops.

Ony marvelled at Jayla's parenting. 'Belka said you had your own brood once.'

'Before my master took me in, yes. A litter of three.'

'How do you know what to do?'

Jayla smiled. 'You just know.'

'My mother told me, before she died, that the survival of your pups is the most important thing, that you have to do whatever it takes to protect them.'

'They're helpless without their parents, Ony.'

'And that means you must be willing to die for them. Even kill for them.'

Jayla, crunching through a piece of neck bone, blew air from her nostrils. 'Some dogs would say so.'

'Don't you?'

'The trouble with killing, Ony, is that it causes so much hurt. And in my experience, hurt dogs just hurt other dogs.'

At these words he fell silent, overcome with a curious kind of pain. In part, he was cross; it felt like an accusation. But as he watched the pup happily snacking away, he felt shamed by those horrid thoughts he'd harboured towards her.

Still, this wasn't the time for pain. He pushed back his behind with a long stretch, and stood. 'Will I leave you here?'

Jayla looked at the pup. 'You say there are more villages before the river? In that case, we'll come further. If infection blights the sky ahead, Sofiy will help you avoid it.'

Indeed, Sofiy began barking not far from the village's eastern boundary. This time, coaxing her on wasn't as straightforward, since all directions they faced seemed equally distressing to the pup. A zigzag trail, at times feeling more like a circle than a line, provided just enough reassurance for Sofiy to proceed. It was as though they were negotiating a forest of trunks where no trees actually stood.

In this slow, inefficient way, they progressed across pastureland until the pup eventually calmed.

When they made it to the next dwellings without once having to stop, they were all relieved. As before, this place was deserted; it wasn't, however, silent. Ony's ears pricked, while Jayla stiffened with alertness. But whatever was making that soft mewling fell suddenly silent.

When they came to a road that bent through the centre of the village, they halted. Up ahead, laying in a pool of blood in the middle of the road, was a dog. Her neck was clearly broken. A numbing sense of desolation washed over Ony – here was another victim of the dragon's cowardly violence.

Jayla motioned toward two blackened streaks of rubber that marked the road in a half-circle. 'Tire tracks.'

The poor girl had been hit by a vehicle, then.

Soft mewls began to sound again. Ony looked around: they were coming from the verge that fringed the road. His heart quickened. It was clear what waited in that long grass.

Sure enough, Jayla discovered eight tiny pups, shivering together as they huddled. Their eyes still blind, they were spared from the sight of the awful scene in the middle of the road.

Jayla took up one of the wretched things and ran with it into the nearest shelter – a donkey barn whose resident was gone. She repeated the process seven more times, and when the motherless infants were snuggled safely altogether, Ony went to look at them as they whimpered on a piece of old cloth sack.

Yip yip yip, they went.

Turning from the pups to Sofiy, his head drooped.

Why did Levka have to leave him when he was still so small? Every dog needed their mother's care and guidance to understand the world; how could he be expected to follow her lesson while he was watching her gasp her final breaths? Of course he'd misinterpreted her words: he was hurting.

The pups now in front of him were even younger than Sofiy, not yet at the stage when they wanted to explore every insect that crawled and every leaf animated by the breeze. But they would grow. They would be ranging strays, just like him, striving for a meal and battling to keep a hold of a prime patch of turf. It didn't mean they were a threat to him, though. Nor to the pups he himself might sire.

Hurt. That was what did this to him. Hurt had made him think of the litters of others as his enemies.

Looking down at these helpless animals, no growls rattled his throat now. His nose didn't wrinkle, and his hackles stayed down. His fangs remained behind his lips. These were living creatures, just as he was. They hadn't asked to come into this hard world, and wanted only what was available to all dogs: love and care and a mouthful of milk.

He watched while Sofiy tried to get the snuffling brood to play with her and while Jayla brought them in to suckle. Though she had no milk to share, it was clear the pups were finding comfort through simply being next to her body. Jayla was doing this only for them, not for herself.

He went over to the pure-white pet and gave her muzzle a lick. 'Your children were lucky to have you,' he said, and he walked to the barn door.

Taking one last look at them all, he ached for Belka. The last time she'd seen him, he was at his very worst. If she could see him now, know the truth of his heart as it beat in this moment, she might say this was him at his best. All he longed for presently was for an end to the suffering. Not his own – though that, too, would be welcome – but an end to the suffering of these poor pups, and to that of all creatures everywhere.

'Hero always survives the battle,' he whined. 'But I'm not Hero.'

And with that, he sped away with a flash of orange.

All day – if daytime was what this was – the machine around Belka's neck had failed to function as it normally did. Before, it reliably crackled wherever the air in Tunnel grew dense with infection, yet since she was brought in today, its cricket-like clicks had barely sounded at all, even when the men moved into violently shimmering pockets.

Confusingly, it was silent now, despite the way the air ahead appeared. Rippling with a vapour so watery it was like staring through a fire, the men were simply crawling on towards the worst patch she'd yet encountered.

With eyes burning and throat parched, Belka barked loudly to them. 'Stop! If you keep going, you'll reach the den of the dragon itself!'

But they advanced anyway.

A short while later, after they'd put down another piece of track for their cart, she barked again, this time as fiercely as she could. To her relief, this time they came backing out from the dark.

But the men, with faces blackened by grime and dripping with sweat, were glowering down at her. Why didn't they appreciate the help she was offering? 'Stupid mutt!' one of them was yelling. 'What's wrong with you?'

One of the men came closer to her neck, straining to focus his eyes on the box hanging from her neck. 'Is that —? How did this get turned off?!' he said, tetchily. Working the device with his nimble fingers, he let out a loud tut and unfastened it from the collar. 'Lads!' he called, tossing it over to his workmates. 'Another dodgy dosimeter. Chuck me a working one!'

A second box came hurtling out of the darkness. The man gave its buttons a squeeze, then, with a chaos of clicking, the thing burst into life.

The man's eyes widened. '400 sieverts an hour! Boys, we need to move back now! Go! Go! Go!'

'We'll have to blast instead!' called out another.

Bemused, Belka observed how the chittering box caused a quarrel. The men tossed words back and forth, becoming ever more irritated with each other.

'We should waste no time blowing it up,' went the one.

'And risk drawing in the very waste we're trying to divert?' went the other.

Then speech was no longer adequate to express their

thoughts and they started hitting each other, rolling across the mucky gravel of Tunnel's floor in a violent embrace while they shouted about "the obstruction".

Eventually, after they'd tired themselves out, the men all vanished to join another team farther back, leaving Belka alone in the dark. She longed to be outside, somewhere free from this hot and choking air where the dreadful clicking of the machine around her neck didn't hurt her ears quite so much. But if she tried to move away – as she had once before when a sudden slackening in her bowels made her instinctively want to seek out a patch of grass – they were sure to whip her again with her tether.

The longer the men of her group were gone, though, the more her courage began to grow. With no dawn, noon, dusk or night, time ran like a single moment stretching on and on, so she couldn't be sure just how long she'd been alone. But when she established they weren't coming back anytime soon, she made the decision to leave her spot and go find another dog.

With her leash trailing behind her, she veered sharply into a left branch of this hollowed-out underground world. As she had done, several other dogs stayed where they'd been ordered, similarly fearful of a crack across the flank.

An older female was up ahead, looking around aimlessly. 'Why did they leave me? Why did they leave me?'

Belka went near. The animal's misty eyes were struggling to focus, the way Ony's had been when she found him in his cave near Camp.

'What's your name?'

'Darya. Please, bring them back here to me.'

'Listen to me, Darya. You're sick. When they take you back to the tent, look for the girl with the frizzy hair and the red cross on her hat. When you see her, call her. She has bread that will make you better.'

'I'm not going back to the canaries.'

Belka shuffled on the dry earth. The tracks were rattling; soon work would be resuming. 'What do you mean? Why aren't you?'

'The men said so. They sent me to the other tent. The blasters.'

The intensity of the vibrations within the tracks was increasing. The screeching of metal wheels – distant still, but moving closer – was reverberating along the walls of the long passageway.

'What does it mean?' yapped Belka. 'What are blasters?'

But Darya merely resorted to her earlier distress. 'Why did they leave me? Why did they leave me?'

Belka turned and sprinted back to her abandoned station in time to see the people returning. Their cart swerved away to the right, revealing another cart directly behind them. This, too, went into the right fork. The third headed left, down towards Darya.

Inside the fourth cart was Tuzik. She'd been thinking about him a lot. When the people brought him back to the tent earlier, it was clear he was unwell. Belka had studied him, wondering if the shimmering cloak that stuck to his shaggy coat only looked severe because of the harsh electric light shining in from outside, but when he vomited repeatedly in his cage, it confirmed the worst. The poor creature was indeed suffering from a special kind of sickness.

The cart housing Tuzik pulled to a stop and for a short time the immediate area went quiet. Distantly, the boxes of other dogs' collars chirruped.

Among the returning men was a new member of their team. He wore a cumbersome outfit made entirely of metal, and struggled at first to get Tuzik out of his crate. The metal man took hold of a darkly coloured garment and strapped it around the confused dog's torso. Belka had seen pets wearing clothing while she'd scavenged among the avenues in the winter months. This garment was different, though, since it had peculiar red tubes all the way around it.

What happened next was all so stressful and confusing that it was only after, when the dust settled down and the screaming in her ears faded to a mere hum, that Belka was able to piece the sequence of events together.

First, the metal man crawled away, trailing a wire that was connected to the red tubes around Tuzik's body.

Then, following the shrill whistle meant for her, Belka came away from the patch of vaporous air. She passed Tuzik on her way back to the men huddling in their chamber, and took care not to look at either the dressed dog nor the man in the metal suit. The men of her team made a fuss the instant she reached them. 'Here she is!' they said, patting her on the head. 'What a good girl! Our own living radiation detector!'

'Shame to think you'll be in a vest of your own soon,' said another, stroking the fur along her back.

While this confusing display of affection was carrying on, a lump of meat appeared, which she thought might be for her. But the men placed it inside the smallest vehicle she'd ever seen, a miniature version of the truck outside that Ball Boy was driving earlier.

The little car drove on down the tracks to Tuzik. He sniffed at the flesh, and his tail began to wag, but before he could take a bite the tiny truck sped further along the tracks to the dark end of Tunnel, where the worst of the shimmering air lingered.

Tuzik followed it.

The miniature vehicle tipped the meat onto the ground. Then it came speeding back towards the chamber.

Tuzik leaned in for a good sniff.

Belka barked. 'No, Tuzik! That's not safe!'

But he was already tearing at the edge of it.

The men suddenly hunched away, turning their backs to the animal up ahead whose tail swished with delight as he gulped down the tasty treat.

Then a massive blast sounded and a shower of rocks scattered along the tunnel floor and, when the dust had finally cleared, Tuzik wasn't there anymore.

20

INTO THE LAIR

ONCE, long before the dragon awoke beneath Plant, Ony crossed into Bimka's patch.

It was an honest enough mistake. That alpha's most loyal dogs liked to bed down beyond the lawns in an alley, and since none were there on the grass that day, Ony decided he'd cut across. Yet three males had been tussling unseen in a trench on the lawn's far side and, happening upon an invader, they quickly gave chase.

Ony bolted, but it was clear right away that his immature legs – it was coming up on the first anniversary of his birth – were no match for these fully grown brutes. Within moments he was ripped by fangs.

His lesson learnt, he shuffled sadly onto the road when he saw the golden coat of his free-ranging companion up ahead. He spent most days on the streets with her, but since Belka always went back to the Creche sheds at dusk, it was a surprise to see her still roaming here.

She licked at his scratches and sat with him while his fretting heart calmed, then a playful smile spread across her slender snout.

'What is it?'

'Want to see something?'

Ony, his spirits already cheered for a bit of company, wasted no time following Belka across the town.

Grassy fields took them to the yards at the foot of Wheel. They darted up the steps and passed through the flower gardens until they reached another road. Wide but quiet, this man-made boundary marked the edge of town. Jumping up onto the verge, they were soon in a meadow that rolled down to the river.

An ocean of tall grass rippled on the breeze, its delicate rattle at once peaceful and soothing. At the head of the meadow, in its centre, was a wide oak tree to which Belka led Ony with a jaunty bounce.

'Like it?' she said, nestling into the hollow of a protruding root.

Curled up against a curved wooden wall, facing down to the river upon which the last sparkling flecks of sunlight were fading away, Ony opened out into a long stretch. 'It's the best bed in the whole city. But what about Creche? Won't Galina be expecting you back?'

'Creche is for pups,' she yawned.

As the summer stretched on and the leaves began to harden, something happened. Was it her scent that changed? Or just that, as her body grew into itself, she appeared suddenly more athletic: a spring in her legs that gave her a speed almost as great as his own? Whatever it was, he found himself thinking about her more and more until, by the time the pavements crinkled with a carpet shed from the boughs above, he lost the appetite for solo ranging altogether.

Eventually, whether he'd been roaming in the bustling centre or the open yards of Park, he always went back to Belka's tree. How very comforting it was to know that, no matter if some bigger, tougher dog struck him or took away a treat scavenged fairly, he always got to sleep beside his friend.

Presently arriving at this very tree, Ony's heart ached to find her gone. Beyond a mere trace, not even her scent was detectable. In her place was a dead crow, broken and flimsy like an old umbrella left beside a bin after a storm. He wanted to lay down – forever and ever if he could have – but Belka's voice sounded in his mind. Were she here with him, she'd be bristling at unseen invaders aswarm in the branches above and urging him to advance on.

He got back up onto his paws. It was time to face his doom.

As he pushed eastward, Belka remained in his mind. How pretty she'd grown to be. But Ony hadn't been alone in noticing the change in his sweet girl; soon, it became common for other males to follow her around, too. One night, beneath Moon's pale glow, Feliks arrived at the oak with his pack mates, each of them as lofty and bitter as the other.

'This isn't pack territory,' Ony barked.

Feliks stepped forward. 'It's whatever we say it is, Lonely Ony,' he sneered. 'Now stand aside and let Belka see what a real dog looks like.'

It was the first of their many scraps. Accustomed to violence, Ony was able to hold his own for the most part, so gradually the boys from Sergei's pack began to lose interest. They'd have kept away altogether, perhaps, but then he bit the butcher man. And when that terrible human took his fury out on the rest of the city's dogs, Ony, once again, became a target.

Coming now to the river, Ony let out a bark of relief. He'd made it through the town without attracting attention to himself, and felt good about his decision to use the cover of night to get here.

Cantering along the bank, his nostrils twitched. He looked down: the grass beneath his paws was stained with Starla's blood. This was the very spot he'd agreed to meet Sergei's boys that day, and where their foolish attempt to muscle him out of town ended with such terrible consequences.

How very, very, long ago that was. Every part of his life had changed in the time since he'd last stood here. Yet barely half of Moon's cycle had passed.

As he'd done when Sergei's pack was chasing him, he scanned across the pine tops to the chimneys of Plant, lit up in the night sky by electric light. As ever, the main building was blanketed beneath a fog of smoke, but no flames now raged as they had when he'd last seen it.

His mind turned to the frightful black rocks. How many had been dropped into the dragon's pit in this time? The beast's power was already great enough then to make his eyes burn and his throat prickle; by now it seemed likely that a dog would light up in flames as soon as he broke cover from the forest.

Taking a deep breath of fresh air into his lungs, he ran down the bank and into the maze of pines. Although the light of day was absent, he was able to tell by the colour of their trunks that the trees here were somehow different. Daybreak, in the unlikely event he'd live long enough to experience it, would no doubt confirm their colour to be the same odd shade of red as the trees in Volya's deep woods, where the bears lay dead.

At the far edge of the forest, Ony came at last to Plant. The scene was so unfamiliar he began to wonder if he'd taken a wrong turn. Before, squat buildings were dotted around the landscape here, but now only a few structures could be seen. Even though it was late into the night, newly razed tracts swarmed with busy human folk.

Like miniature villages, clusters of vehicles in circular formations marked an otherwise empty landscape. Luckily, the soldiers were having their discussions in the centre of these clusters, giving Ony a chance to sneak across to the pit undetected. Still, though, he wasn't going to take anything for granted. To be seen now would almost certainly result in a hot hole through his head.

From one makeshift village to the next, Ony crept as carefully as he could until he reached the central formation, but the sound of an explosion coming from Plant meant bad news, and made him reluctant to proceed. So he waited, listening to the tense chatter of the men at the circle's centre.

'Forgive me, comrade,' a weary-looking soldier was saying. 'But even with a million men working a million days, we'll never liquidate these levels of radiation.'

The other man nodded his shiny hat up and down. 'Which is why my Party comrades keep pressing for the sarcophagus. It'll be thousands of lifetimes before this place is habitable again.'

More booms sounded. When Ony was sure these were far enough away, he dashed to the next circle of vehicles, and from there onto the next where military dogs lay tethered to a truck. He was glad to see some of his kind, but rather than risk them alerting their masters, he proceeded to the final cluster without saying hello.

A huge vehicle with chains for wheels stood solidly on the ground. Beneath this, Ony dropped onto his belly. He glanced around to the land ahead of him, which sloped up. This was the embankment on which the pit was located. The shelter of this towering machine was welcome: it was a fine spot from which to launch his surprise assault on the dragon.

But looking more closely at the hill, it was different from the memory seared into his thoughts.

The same metal walkways surrounded the slope, and the road at its top edge was there, too. But it seemed somehow less *open* than before. The large trucks they used to tip the poisonous black stones into the dragon's belly were no longer at the site, either. Straining his eyes, he could just make out those particular vehicles in the adjoining fields, where several large tents also stood, illuminated beneath harsh white light.

Steadying his nerves before making the final dash to face the enemy of all enemies, he let the voices of the soldiers calm him. Even though Ball Boy and Red Cross Girl had allowed the dog-mask men to capture Belka, he missed the sound of their words.

Distantly, another boom sounded.

'Hear that?' said one of the soldiers. 'The miners are really going for it now.'

'The first teams have got beneath the reactor hall at last. They'll have the heat exchange installed soon. I'm amazed they've got this far, to be honest. I never thought we'd pull it off.'

'Good thing we had the dogs.'

'Poor things.'

'Greater good, comrade. Greater good.'

Ony took a big breath of air into his lungs. Not even three summers lived, and the end was upon him.

What the dragon was planning to do next, he'd never know, and there was a certain comfort to be found in that. Would it leave its den to take flight, and rain its fiery disease on any land not yet cloaked in its infectious rot? Would it await another challenger, some other stupid little Ony, to jump into its pit and wage hopeless war against it? Or would it stay exactly as it was, keeping human folk in a state of fear, having them do whatever it wanted without ever rearing one of its three horrible heads?

It was time to find out.

He bolted.

No shots rang out, as they'd done when his paws last touched this patch of dry earth. He'd feared he would never even get this close, so was buoyed by the victory, such as it was.

Up the hill he went.

Just as expected, the air was foul. That familiar,

metallic taste settled on his tongue, and all scent disappeared.

The muscles in his hind quarters rippled in readiness. Should he peer over the rim? No. The choking fumes would only blind his eyes and dry his mouth.

The best thing was to leap right in.

His claws clinked against the metal bars of the walkway, as Han and Gleb's had done.

He closed his eyes.

In his mind, Belka was resting in the nook of the oak tree's roots, and he was beside her. A faint smile curled his lip. None of this had ever happened.

He sprang.

And dropped.

But the fall was much shorter than he'd anticipated.

Opening his eyes again, he saw the familiar landscape of Plant tumbling around him.

He hit earth, then scrambled onto his paws, frantically.

Staggering through his dizziness, he leapt back to the top of the dragon's pit. And, with his eyes now able to focus, he saw there was no pit to vanish into: his fall had been broken by a hard grey expanse which sent him tumbling.

The crater's mouth was now a solid block.

What lay beneath his paws was warm, and had a slight tackiness, like mud in a bog baked by Sun. The air felt oppressive as it did before a storm, and was charged with a similar, though undeniably more hazardous, energy.

Ony sprinted across to the other side. Did the dragon have a hidden door in case it wished to come and go in secret? No: on all sides of what had been an open cavity, the edges were fused to the platforms.

As his eyes began to burn, he dashed back down the hillside, lowering himself once again behind the chains of the vast metal vehicle. His mind raced so fast that he couldn't hear a single thought, but the sound of canine grunts nearby helped him compose himself again. Did the military animals know what had happened here?

He bolted across to the next cluster of vehicles where the dogs were tethered. Sidling up on his belly inch by inch, Ony braced himself.

The military dogs let forth a cacophony of barking, which their master brought to a swift halt with a sharp command. Nevertheless, the ears of the animals remained erect as they fixed their gaze on him.

From beneath the vehicle, Ony kept his head on the ground to show he meant no harm. 'Where are you from?'

The pair looked at each other, then the tan dog spoke. 'Capital.'

'What is *capital*?'

'What do you want, stray?'

'The dragon. Did it fly away, or is it still down there?'

'What are you on about, cur dog?'

'At the top of that mound, there was a crater full of dark rocks. Now there's a hard cap over the top. How did it happen?'

The black dog looked at his companion. 'Does he mean the cement trucks? What do you care if our masters filled in the graphite pits?'

'It was filled in? Did a creature fly out first? A beast with three heads and a tongue of fire?'

The tan dog huffed. 'These country dogs truly are a mystery to me,' he said. 'Listen, mongrel. They've been tipping earth into that hole for days. Then they poured cement over the top to seal it up.'

'What does that mean?'

'It means that anything that was down there is staying down there. Run along now, orange fur. Can't you see we're military dogs? We have far more important things to do than stand around talking to the likes of you.'

~

Belka stood a long while staring into the space where Tuzik had been.

The wall which had blocked the tracks was now rubble on Tunnel's floor. The men threw their muddy white caps into the air with a cheer when it had first exploded, but their lightened mood quickly dimmed and they started to bicker once again.

'How can our team still be forty metres away?'

'Because the others haven't had to dig around these damn pipes, that's why,' snapped a second man. 'It's a struggle to even get the dogs through, the spaces are so tight.'

A third man joined in with the quarrel. 'Why don't they install the heat exchange unit now if they're already in place?'

'You saw the plans, comrades! Any one of these tunnels could fall in. Drowning in radioactive lava might not bother you, but I've got three kids at home. Yavorsky, go fetch another dog. A small one, if you please.'

'There's not a lot of choice left, to be honest captain.'

'Just get me a dog! I'll radio for Zlenko to prep a detonation vest. The rest of you, take twenty minutes outside. Find something to eat and drink if you can. We're going to have to tunnel through the night.' He looked down at Belka, who was trembling still from the shock of the blast. 'And switch this one for another canary. She's earned a rest.'

Hoisting Belka up into her own crate, the men followed behind while she was winched along the tracks and out into the open air. Just the sight of Sun dropping in the west was enough to improve her wretched spirit.

Inside Tent, a man gave Belka a drink of water and some tasteless food from a tin can. The awful glare of white light made being asleep and awake equally unappealing, but allowed her at least to see the other dogs. Newcomers – snatched no doubt by the masked men with their feathery darts – occupied a few of the cages, but each time the men had brought her back here, she observed how Tent hosted ever fewer canine residents.

Dropping in and out of naps, Belka grew more worried. Mostly, she fretted about Jayla. Ony would be alright – he simply wouldn't let them take him – but Jayla was like the other pets: trusting and easily duped.

How long had Jayla waited after Belka failed to show up at Den? At some point, she would have had to go scavenge for the pup – would the meat on the forest floor have tempted her? Surely not; Belka, who'd tried her very best to share with Jayla what little she understood about the ways of humankind, warned her again and again about their many tricks.

The possibility that Sofiy was all alone now made Belka feel hollow inside. The poor little thing would starve if Jayla had indeed been snatched. The only chance the pup had was if Red Cross Girl could get in through Den's narrow entrance. But that was a squeeze even for a dog.

The cooling of the tent suggested Sun had now departed for the day. Belka's mind had just begun to quiet by then, so when a commotion sounded, she was annoyed to be roused back to wakefulness.

A dog was yapping her name. She looked around to see Han. Staggering and drowsy, he was being reluctantly led by a man out towards Tunnel. 'Belka,' he said, weakly. 'I was wrong about Ony. I see it now.' He gave a few feeble.barks, which soon became coughs. 'Please!' he spluttered at the men. 'Don't send me back down there again! Help me, Belka!'

But all Belka could do was watch from behind the bars of her cage, and listen as his fit of coughing moved across to the neighbouring tent where the so-called blasters were kept.

When Red Cross Girl came in a short while later with Ball Boy, Belka was glad to see them and, as always, whined for the pair to let her out.

'Goodness,' said the frizzy-haired girl, looking around at the empty cages. 'Where've they all gone?'

Ball Boy shrugged.

The girl poked crusts of bread into Belka's cage. 'How long until the bus?'

'Ten minutes.'

Red Cross Girl grew quiet as she softly ran her finger over Belka's eyebrow. 'They're going ahead with the sarcophagus.'

The boy gave a nod. 'Planning starts next week, I heard.'

'And did you hear how long it'll take them to build?'

A fraught energy now came from Ball Boy. 'Come on,' he said. 'If we miss the bus back to Fairytale, we'll be sleeping here.'

'Six months, Alek.'

The boy's mouth fell open. Water began to quiver on the lids of his eyes, then the girl started to sob.

'You know what this means, don't you, Alek?' she sniffed. 'We'll be here until winter.'

21

LEAP OF FAITH

As the first rays of dawn shone in the pines around Plant, Ony woke up. The forest's edge had indeed taken on a red hue, and many of the limbs had fallen away, leaving trunks bare all the way up to the crowns.

Such an alien landscape ought to have repelled him, but he was experiencing something like excitement, and wasn't yet ready to run back to the donkey shed where Jayla was waiting with the motherless brood.

With the dragon buried, there was hope. Still, though, he had to show maximum caution. That beast had awoken once beneath firmer earth than the grey cap of the pit, so there was no reason to think it wouldn't rise again. And in the meantime, its ghastly emissions were still out in the world, a creeping, clinging force that observed none of the usual respect for territorial boundaries.

His energy now restored, Ony stretched out his paws, and was just about to set off west when the sound of barking carried on the wind caught his ear.

Instantly alert, he turned back to face Plant. The commotion was coming from the illuminated tents he'd seen last night. While faint, the distress was obvious and caused a fresh wave of grief to lap against his heart. This one wasn't only for Belka, however. It was for all the animals, dead and living, that had endured such awful pain.

Keeping low, he ran out from the trees and headed back in the direction of the pit. He fringed the vehicle clusters, then crept around the foot of the mound in which the dragon was sealed, until an open expanse brought him to the back side of the first of the tents.

As its walls were merely fabric, Ony was able to get his snout underneath. With his face now poking through, he saw cages like those the men used to take away Belka. In two of these there stood clearly sickened dogs; all the rest were empty.

Ony shimmied back out again. Across the yard was a second tent, from which a chorus of confused and frightened yelps was spilling out. He ran to the rear of this one and, as before, nudged his nose through the flap of fabric at its rear.

His head titled in confusion. Calculating just how many animals were caged in the tent wasn't possible, but it was certainly a greater number than were in the other one: as many, perhaps, as the pets who'd followed them to Camp.

Faced with such deep distress – even the humans were in a state of heightened agitation – he began to whine.

Exhausted from days of anxiety, Ony's mind struggled to make connections, but he did his best to piece together the mystery of just what had gone on at Plant. The human folk had turned against the dragon. Exactly why, he couldn't possibly know, but what was clear was that the people had sealed the creature under cement before feeding the last of the dogs to it – meaning the animals in these cages had been spared.

So why didn't the soldiers simply release them?

'The canaries have served their purpose!' a man in a

stiff suit was shouting. 'All dogs are now needed for blasting. These are Party orders, comrades!'

Ony tried hard to focus on the cages, but this was made difficult by the many legs that shuffled around in the tent's centre. When the people started to exit through its front side, however, he was able to get a better look. The metal bars of the cages were flimsy: surely such things could be prized open by a dog of his strength?

As he pondered it, he remembered Jayla and her account of the one who killed the dragon and rescued the princess. The one who *always* saved the day. It had to be worth a try.

He flexed, ready to push himself through the fabric wall, but a flash of red-gold fur near the front suddenly stole away his attention.

His tail began to wag vigorously.

He was looking at Belka.

Standing next to her cage was Ball Boy and Red Cross Girl. The pair looked even sadder than they had back at Camp; the girl's sunken eyes were pooling with sorrow, and the boy bristled with distress.

'Belka!' Ony called out, adding his own barks to the many others which pierced the air. 'Belka!'

The pretty girl turned his way.

'Belka! Here! It's Ony! Your Ony!'

Seeing him, Belka rose to her feet and began spinning tight circles within the confines of her cage. 'Ony!' she called back. 'Let me out! Quickly! They're going to put me in with the blasters!'

His tail flicked up stiffly. The moment was here.

With a burst, Ony sprang forward. But the moment he left the ground and passed through the flap, a hoop tightened around his neck, and he was pulled back outside into the open air where a man clutching a pole shoved his head into the ground.

Ony wriggled with as much strength as he could

muster, but with his neck pinned firmly down there was nothing he could do to free himself.

The man looked upon him with a confused frown. 'How did you manage to get out? Come on,' he said, shoving him back to the first tent to join the two sickened dogs in their cages. 'The dynamite crew is ready for you.'

~

As the night had stretched endlessly on, two different types of disturbance wrenched Belka from her shallow sleep.

First were the booms that echoed out from Tunnel's mouth. These deep, rumbling blasts made her think of Tuzik, who'd so mysteriously ceased to exist right in front of her eyes. The second was the chatter of the men in their white suits, who tonight came to get dogs with unusual frequency. Strangely, the men didn't return the ones already taken: not her neighbour, nor the pets, nor Han. She tried her best not to wonder about the dragon, and whether its appetite had suddenly increased.

The dreams she'd endured only served to strengthen her weariness. Pups featured prominently in these: either herself, lost in the woods as a tiny infant; or Ony, cowering beside his mother's stiffened body; or the babies from the Creche shed, nuzzling so peacefully one moment, suffering so incomprehensibly the next. She also saw what might have been one of her own broods from some future time: a litter of six. Crouching to clean them, her tongue seemed to pass right through, as though her children were reflections on a pond rather than the solid things they were meant to be.

That one had made her come awake with a start. Ever since she'd first detected the shimmer on her own underside, back at the tree she missed so much with its long view down to the meandering river, something had felt wrong. The drops in her food had worked well to rid her of the weakness and nausea, but did nothing to take away the emptiness she felt in her heart.

Until recently, Belka had thought all the time about the brood that Ony would one day give her. In some ways, it felt to her to be the only thing in the whole world that truly mattered. Raising pups to be big and strong, passing on the wisdom she'd gained from a life on the streets to her own flesh and blood, seemed to be the very reason she walked the earth. But that had changed. What had always existed somewhere in the background of her mind, like a faintly distracting hum, ceased to bother her anymore.

Jayla had said a similar thing. After her master carried her off in a cage to visit the doctor, she felt like a piece of her was gone. As a pet, Jayla never again had the chance to receive the gift of a litter from a dog. Curiously, though, she never again felt the urge to seek that gift, either.

Now, the same thing was happening to Belka, too.

It was Ony's sickness, perhaps. In his weakened state, worry had prevented her from thinking about him as a father of pups. The shock of the massacre at Creche, too, had dampened her desires. And, on top of it all, there was the beast in its white-hot pit, a foe who favoured frailty over health, decay over blossom, still and silent death over joyful good cheer. It sought more territory not because it wished for tastier snacks or cleaner water or safer turf on which its young could play, but because it wanted to see all things scarred with rank, shimmering cloaks. Who would wish to bring pups into such a world?

Not that any of it mattered anymore. Now, this was her lot. Day upon day, her sole task was to lead the people ever deeper into the fiery air below Plant, closer and closer to the dragon itself whose three horrid heads would be the last thing she ever saw.

On and on like this her thoughts had swirled,

torturing her with all that might have been and all that was soon coming to an end.

Eventually, the blinding lights blinked off to reveal the pale light of morning. She let out a whimper. Another day was beginning. Tunnel was waiting.

Voices outside signalled the arrival of the workforce, and a group of people, quarrelsome as ever, came filing into Tent.

A man in a white paper hat was especially lively. 'You weren't supposed to use the entire supply!' he yelled.

'What's the big deal? This is Ukraine. There are strays everywhere!'

'*Were*, Yuri! *Were!* What do you think the exterminator teams have been out there doing? Picnicking on the River Dneiper?! Why did you blow up so many, man?'

Over the shoulders of the squabbling soldiers, Belka noticed Ball Boy and Red Cross Girl come wandering in. With their round eyes as wide as their open mouths, their faces were pained with horror, and the girl let out a scream which sent a spasm of horror through Belka's body; in all her life, she'd never heard a person make a sound like this one, or imagined such a thing to be possible. Red Cross Girl sounded like a fox.

'What did you do!'

Ball Boy's voice was more recognisably human but it, too, was filled with violent rage. 'Not in my name! Not in my name!'

The men began to yell at the pair, and Belka, turning away in the hope of blocking out their angst, was about to curl up into a tight coil when, from the back of Tent, a different noise caught her ear.

'Belka! Belka!'

It was such a familiar bark.

'Here, Belka! It's Ony! Your Ony!'

At the sight of him, she span in circles. He'd made it here! Was the dragon dead?

'Let me out!' she called. 'Please, Ony, let me out!'

She watched as he first sprang forward, his white breast and orange coat glimmering, then as a hooked pole came in behind him. It went over his head and snapped back over his neck and, as quickly as he'd burst in, he was hoisted out again into the yard beyond the fabric, and taken across to the other tent, where the blasters were kept.

Ony's cage was slammed shut, and a metal bar was slid across its door. With barely enough room to look around this tented space, he felt glad he wasn't a bigger dog.

Processing what was happening was impossible. The raw emotion of the bickering people went right into him, and more were arriving all the time, arranging themselves instantly into two separate factions. Each side was facing off against the other, their tempers high and their hands clenched into tight balls, a stance Ony recognised as being like the hackles on a dog's neck. This looked like a pack brawl; if Ony had learnt anything about the nature of conflict, scrapping was going to commence any time now.

While the argument continued, a man in a white cap extracted one of the two sickened dogs from a cage and began strapping a curious garment around its torso. With a shove, he lead the dog towards the world outside, when Ball Boy suddenly appeared in the entrance.

The young man stood in the older man's way. The dog, confused and afraid, barked.

'Mind yourself, cadet.'

'Where are you taking that animal?' asked Ball Boy.

'I'm obeying my orders, comrade. I suggest you do, too. Now step aside.'

Ball Boy folded his arms in front of his chest and shifted his weight to root himself heavily to the spot. Red

Cross Girl, watching on from the frame of the tent's wide mouth, was biting her lips with anxious anticipation.

An arm was swung. With his open palm, the man in the white cap hit Ball Boy's face, causing him to fold at the waist.

The sight of it made Ony furious. He barked for the man to leave him alone; confined to his cage, however, he was powerless to protect the boy.

The man in the white cap leaned over and shouted into Ball Boy's ear. 'You'll get back to your dump truck if you know what's good for you!' Then he walked away with the dog.

Red Cross Girl put an arm around the boy's shoulder and aided him back upright. A trickle of blood was running from his nose. Ony was about to begin pleading for the pair to let him out, but more white-capped men entered at that moment with the dogs from the neighbouring tent. Among them were some of the Camp pets, but Ony paid no mind to them since Belka had arrived too with the newcomers.

'What kind of place is this?' he yapped, as Belka was shut into the cage beside him.

'The worst kind, Ony,' cried Belka, whose eyes appeared to him to be fixed upon the pile of odd-looking garments strewn on the ground.

A man came forward and began to fasten one of these strange items around the body of the second of the sick dogs.

Belka let forth a distressed cry, startling Ony. 'Don't let them put that thing on you!' she yowled. But the animal was clipped into the garment nevertheless, its strings pulled tight to hold it snug against him, and the man began to lead him away.

Belka was looking at him with desperation, but he didn't know what she wanted him to do. 'They're going to take us all into Tunnel,' she said. 'Then they'll make us disappear forever.'

Ony let out a whine. He wished to know more, but before he could communicate with Belka any further, a large figure suddenly appeared in the entrance, blocking out most of the morning light. It was a soldier, and the voice that thundered out of him brought the commotion of shouting and barking to a sudden halt.

'Right! Everybody outside, now!'

With fearful expressions, the people brought up a hand to the side of their heads and held it sturdily in position. 'Yes, Comrade Drozdov!'

In a line, the people hastily shuffled out of the broad door. Once outside, the large man continued to yell with his ear-splitting voice. 'Calm yourselves, comrades! Get a drink and take ten, then I want to see the rest of those dogs in their vests. Am I clear?'

'Yes, Comrade Drozdov!'

To Ony's relief, all became quiet again then, except for the hushed voices of Red Cross Girl and Ball Boy. Somewhere around the side of the tent, they were having their own little meeting.

Finally able to greet her properly, Ony brought his nose close to Belka's through the bars between them, and inhaled deep sniffs of her. 'When the dog-mask men came,' he cried, 'I thought the worst had happened.'

'Did they capture the pup, Ony?'

'Jayla kept her hidden in the den. Belka, the pup. I don't know why I behaved like that.'

'It's because of your wounds,' said Belka, licking his muzzle clean as best she could. 'They run so deep. You'll tackle any foe, won't you, Ony? Any at all, except the foe that is your own pain. But Ony, the dragon. Did you face it?'

Ony fell into whining. 'I tried to. Men sealed it inside the pit. It's weakened now.'

'In the sky, maybe,' whimpered Belka. 'But under the ground, the shimmer's still very powerful.'

Casting his eyes down to his own white feet, Ony

puffed air from his nostrils. 'That might be the best we can hope for.'

With sorrow weighing him down, he kept his damp nose against Belka's. 'So many creatures are suffering out there, Belka. I'm scared many are going to be struck down by the sickness in the air. But there's still new life in our world, and at least it has a chance to grow now that the dragon is in its own cage.'

Belka's head tilted to the side, as though she didn't believe such words could come from him.

His head dropped in shame. 'My wounds *are* deep, Belka. But if we ever get out of here, I'll—'

Ony wasn't able to finish, though, because at that moment, Red Cross Girl came marching back into the tent. Something was different about the way she carried herself. She was more upright than usual, her head high and chest inflated. But there was a change in her face, too. She didn't look quite so young anymore.

With a calmness that was almost unnerving, the girl began to slide across the locks on each of the dogs' cages. She then pulled wide every door, and slapped her palms against her legs. 'Come!' she said.

Belka jumped down first, followed immediately by Ony; they spun in a waltz of sniffing while the other dogs exited their own cages. Looking up to Red Cross Girl for a cue, a moment of intense stillness filled the tent. If the girl's heart was fretting, she was doing very well to hide it.

'Ready?' said Red Cross Girl, and turned to the outside. 'Stay with me.' With that, she strode purposefully away across the yard.

While Belka led the dogs in pursuit, Ony fell back to the rear, nudging the sicker and more confused among them ahead until all animals were keeping pace with the frizzy-haired human at the front, who by now was running across the open tracts.

'Keep up!' she called.

Ahead, the earth appeared to fall away over a ledge, but Red Cross Girl obviously wasn't concerned. Charging on as quickly as she could, she tossed her head back over her shoulder. 'Good! Good! Come on! Keep going!'

An engine's roar suddenly sounded as they sprinted closer and closer to the edge of the shelf.

Red Cross Girl leapt. With her arms out wide, she vanished down over the side. One by one, the other dogs jumped after her. Not Belka, though: she was perched on the very cusp, waiting.

Stood beside each other, Ony and Belka peered over. Red Cross Girl was splayed out on a mound of soil that was piled high in the steel trough of a truck's rear. Dogs, panting and bewildered, surrounded her.

'Come on!' she shouted up. 'Jump now!'

A voice yelled from the front of the truck. It was Ball Boy. 'Narmin! Are we good?'

'Come on, Hazel Eyes! Come on, Foxy!'

The pair looked at one another, intensely nervous.

Angry voices were approaching from behind. Ony and Belka turned to see soldiers and men in dirty white caps hurtling along the dusty ground towards them. There was no choice; simultaneously, they leapt.

The moment the pair landed on the mound, the girl slapped the side of the trough with three heavy blows. 'Now, Alek!' The truck roared into forward motion; as it weaved to and fro on the road that stretched away from Plant, the travellers tumbled from side to side.

Red Cross Girl kept her gaze on the site behind them, her eyes widening when she noticed something beyond the trough's wall. Crawling on all fours to get through the soil to the truck's front side, she rapped on the roof above Ball Boy's head.

'What is it?' he called out.

'They're following!'

The truck screeched to a halt. Then, something

curious began to happen. It was as though the world beneath them were suddenly tipping up.

The girl fumbled with some chains, and the whole of the trough's rear wall swung open. The soil beneath Ony's belly began to drop off the back, spilling all across the road's width and tipping the dogs closer to the edge. When the base beneath them was as steep as a valley's side, they followed the girl's lead and leapt down.

'Quickly!' yelled the boy, now standing in the open door of the carriage. 'Get up here!'

The dogs rolled down the tumbled soil and fell onto the road.

The desolate landscape of Plant's outskirts stretched all around them. It took Ony mere moments to work out that if they tried running from here, they'd be easily brought down by the men's terrible weapons. Two of the other dogs weren't so worried about that, however, and took off into the open in spite of his warning.

'Up! Up!' yelled the boy and girl as the dogs jumped onto a step and into the carriage.

But once again, Ony and Belka stood apart from the rest.

'Should we trust them?' said Belka.

A very faint smile rose on Ony's lips. 'People are more dangerous than we can possibly understand,' he said. 'But not these ones.' And with that, Ony took the leap.

Belka let out a whine. 'How can you be sure, Ony?'

'It's like us dogs and our tails. They always give away how we're truly feeling. With people, it's their eyes. They can trick us with their faces and their actions and the words they use. But their eyes tell the truth.' He motioned towards Ball Boy and Red Cross Girl. 'Look at them.'

Belka craned her neck to observe the frantic faces of this young pair of humans, and her tail began to vigorously wag. 'They're our friends,' she said, and jumped behind Ony into the vehicle.

The doors slammed shut and the engine rumbled. The boy turned to the girl. 'This is it,' he said. 'We'll be branded traitors.'

The girl let out an odd laugh as the vehicle lurched forwards.

Soon, the boy was laughing beside her. 'They can't get through! I blocked the road!'

And with a sharp lurch, the truck pulled noisily away.

22

CALL OF A LEADER

THEIR LAUGHTER DIDN'T last long.

Soon, the atmosphere between Ball Boy and Red Cross Girl changed into something neither Ony or Belka had ever encountered. The joy they were feeling was unmistakable, as was the sorrow. The difficulty for the dogs was that these young humans were feeling both emotions *at the same time*. It was like the song Ony heard Dada singing the day he took down Starla and Feliks.

The truck juddered around the bend, causing Belka to fall into Ony. Righting herself, she quietly muttered: 'I think that's the difference between them and us. People can be two things together at once.'

Ony looked across at the girl, who was caressing Belka's soft ear between her thumb and finger. His beloved mate was right. It was clear that the girl, like the boy, was excited *and* terrified. They were happy *and* they were sad.

Ball Boy let out a steady stream of air from nostrils caked around the rims with dried blood. 'Do you think they screen World Cup matches in Siberian logging camps?'

'What kind of a question is that?'

'We're criminals now, Narmin. Enemies of the state. We'll be shipped off to the *gulag*.'

The girl inhaled sharply. 'The Party made engineers test an atomic reactor they knew wasn't up to the job. They knew millions could die if it went wrong. Then they acted like it was no big deal when it blew up. *They're* the criminals.'

Splayed out on the rubber mats of the carriage were around a dozen animals, every one as bewildered as Ony and Belka were themselves. In various states of exhaustion, the dogs weren't even attempting to figure out what was happening to them.

Perhaps Ony should find a way to communicate it all. How very close they'd come to facing a beast beyond the worst visions of their most fitful nightmares. How a searing fog lingered in the air, just waiting to sicken anything that drew breath with an infection so strong it would burn them up and corrupt their essence until they were nothing more than shadows. Clever Belka could train them to see it, maybe. At least then they'd have a chance.

With a shocking suddenness, the boy's feet lurched out of their positions and the wheels of the truck began to scream. The vehicle came to a halt.

Up ahead, a row of cars was stretched out across the width of the road. Their lights were flashing blue and red. Soldiers, holding guns, were standing in front of the vehicles.

Wordlessly, Ball Boy and Red Cross Girl pushed open the carriage doors.

'Be free now, little friends,' said the boy.

'As we can only hope to be,' added the girl.

The pair gave each dog a stroke on the head and directed them down from the carriage, then, when every animal was out on the road, the doors slammed shut again.

In every direction, the dogs bolted. Ony, with Belka

close beside him, fixed his eyes ahead. The soldiers were advancing toward the truck.

He wanted to dash away, too. But a different act – one he'd never before performed – was compelling him.

He lifted back his head, high up to Sun.

From the pit of his belly, a call emerged.

'Come to me!' he howled. 'Come to me!'

And all the dogs returned.

~

They ran through the playing fields of a school with no children, and yards of empty cars whose windows were either sooty with dust or white with the droppings of birds. They ran across the bare soil in which people placed their dead, though no fresh flowers adorned the mounds now and no old folk in black cloaks silently sobbed.

They passed shops without shoppers, inns without drinkers. One row of wheeled stalls stood empty; another was blanketed with flies that feasted on produce gone to rot. Never once did the dogs slow until they reached the shelter of the woods, and even then Ony kept pushing further west, not daring to rest for fear the soldiers with their guns had pursued them and an outburst of blasts would bring an end to the good fortune of their escape from Plant.

Everywhere they ran, they ran as one.

When they came to the outskirts of a village, Ony finally stopped. To the confusion of the others, Belka began carefully sniffing at surfaces and objects, as though seeking traces of an old friend. She leaned in close to some railings, then moved across to a tyre laying on its side. From there, she went to a seat fashioned from a tree trunk, then to a post on which markings made by human hand were scribbled. After next looking into the air for several moments, her mysterious business was concluded.

Ony had watched her closely. Belka's gift was the key to their very survival. Since this extra sense was something she'd been born with, others couldn't hope to understand, but they could follow her example just the same. The world had been changed by the dragon: extreme caution was necessary anywhere these animals now chose to roam.

'It's clean here,' she said at last.

Ony gave a grunt of relief, then turned to the dogs who'd collapsed with exhaustion on the grass of a roadside verge.

'Friends,' he said. 'Not one of us needs to be told how lucky we are to be feeling Sun's rays on our fur right now. This is a moment we have to enjoy, because too many of our kind were robbed of the chance. Perhaps, when Moon rises and falls with each new night, we might start to realise just what's happened to us. But we shouldn't trouble ourselves with that question today. Rest now a while. Soon Belka and I will range again to find a home. Any of you who wishes to follow will be made welcome there.'

Nuzzling playfully into Belka's neck, a flash of excitement shone in Ony's eyes before he turned and led her away from the others.

Across a pasture made rough beneath hoof-fall, they came to a barn. Passing through a wooden door frame gone to rot, they found Jayla inside.

The pet began to whine with delight, her tail furiously swishing from side to side. When she stood to approach Ony and Belka, a clutch of pups spilled away from her underside and began yipping, surrounding the trio as they circled each other with joyous greetings. The litter settled and Jayla moved them back into the corner and commanded them to stay, and the three dogs went outside.

'I didn't think I'd see you again,' said Jayla as they ran together along a patch of grass. 'Either of you.' She flicked her head around to face Ony. 'I was right, then.'

'What about?' asked Belka.

'I told Ony that he was going to rescue the princess and defeat the dragon.'

Ony let out a groan. 'The dragon isn't gone. And it was people who opened the cages and set us dogs free. All I managed to do was get myself captured.'

Jayla smiled widely. 'You went to face a beast you knew you couldn't slay. Even though your bones would be burned into twigs.'

'But the dragon still lives!'

'Maybe so,' said Belka. 'But that doesn't take away from what you did. You went there not to claim its turf so you could be top dog. Or to protect only your own brood. You went so that all living things might have a future.'

As they dropped onto the grass in a loose triangle, Ony was suddenly overcome with anguish.

In an odd way, the dragon's awakening was the best thing that could have happened to him. Without its terrible presence, what would he have been? How close he'd come to growing into a devil dog.

It was probable he'd have lived his entire life as a rival to all others, his sole concern the welfare of himself and his own. The wellbeing of his children, were he and Belka able to ever have them, mattered to him more than anything else then, and mattered still to him now. But under the shadow of the dragon's nauseating fog, it suddenly seemed so obvious. The future couldn't be a place where just his own were alright. It had to be somewhere that other dogs' pups could thrive too, or else the world would be just as it was before: dangerous, cruel and filled to the brim with endless fretting.

Cooperation, not competition: that was how he could flourish.

Suddenly emerging from the other side of the field, on

paws that sprang with each tottering step, was Sofiy. She didn't know who to greet first, so simply bounced up at Ony and Belka with a flurry of licks and gentle bites.

Jayla calmed the pup with a paw upon her back. 'She's missed her sister and her uncle Ony.'

Belka's head tilted to the side; observing the youngster's fur – gold like leaves in autumn – and her elegant snout, so like her dear mother's, the confusion soon melted away. 'Little sister. Have you been a good girl for your auntie?'

'Oh yes,' said Jayla. 'You're the best little girl, aren't you? And you just love to listen to stories, don't you?'

Belka grew animated. 'Tell one now!'

Sofiy lay instantly down beside her big sister.

'Right now?' said Jayla, yawning. 'Alright then. Let me see. Once upon a time, there was a bad place ruled by bad men. Everybody was sad and starving and their hands bled from toil. But one day the people of the land joined together and battled their wicked masters and took back the land for themselves, and after that, it was a good place. The best place in the whole word. And the good men of the Party made sure that the people's every wish was granted. The Party put everybody before themselves and cared for the old and the young and the sick, and the people were proud to stand shoulder to shoulder to defend their lands from all the envious enemies across the borders who could only dream of living such wonderful lives. And everything worked, and nobody ever got sick, and the Party never told lies and no atomic reactors ever blew up. And all the people lived happily forevermore.'

Sofiy looked to Belka, then to Ony, then to Jayla.

Belka's head tipped to the side. 'Is that it?'

Jayla smiled proudly. 'Yes.'

'It's not the best one you've ever told.'

Jayla huffed. 'Isn't it? Well that's the way I heard

Narmin tell it to Alek back at Camp. She said it was a fairy story.'

Just the mention of Red Cross Girl made Ony's heart suddenly ache. The soldiers were angry with the pair. Ball Boy even bled where one had struck him. When the boy and girl shooed the dogs out from the truck, the approaching soldiers had faces so fearsome it seemed likely they'd strike him again. Perhaps they would even use their horrid guns on them?

Ony thought back to what Jayla had said about Hero, who always did the right thing, even if it meant they'd suffer for it. Ball Boy and Red Cross Girl had saved the dogs from disappearing in Tunnel forever, and for doing so may now suffer. But then he remembered something else Jayla said, and his sorrow began to lessen. The young people had behaved just like Hero. And since Hero *always* survives, that meant their suffering wouldn't last forever. They'd be alright, in the end.

At a trot, the dogs journeyed together back to the barn where, in the corner, pups were resting in a writhing mass.

Belka looked to Ony. 'What will we do now? We're still too close to the shimmer here.'

Ony kept his eyes on the pups while he spoke, drawing comfort from the soft rising and falling of their tiny bodies. 'We'll go east through the forests.'

'But those are the wolf-wilds, Ony. We won't be safe.'

'I know the wolves. Volya will permit us passage once he hears that the dragon is sleeping again.'

Fretting, Jayla looked between the pair. 'Did you say *sleeping*? You mean, it isn't defeated?'

'It can't be defeated,' said Ony. 'At any time, this awful thing may come awake again. All we can do is get as far away as we can, and hope it stays sealed in its pit until Sun no longer shines in the sky.'

'But Ony,' whined Belka, 'what if there are dragons

sleeping beneath other Plants? How then can we hope to survive?'

But Ony couldn't possibly know about that.

He calmed Belka with some licks to the ear. 'Don't fret about what hasn't happened. Keep your focus on our present task. Once we clear the wolf-wilds, we'll keep going until we find a place where good people still dwell. We'll make a home. And I can finally do something I've been putting off all my life.'

Belka's hazel eyes looked lovingly up at him. 'What, Ony?'

Ony smiled sadly. 'I never seem to have the time to feel my pain. Well, I'm going to make time. I'm going to let myself hurt for a while.'

Jayla nudged Belka playfully with her nose. 'You can make your own litter at last.'

Her neck drooping, Belka looked distantly away. 'No. The shimmer we bore. It may be gone now, but it took something from us.'

'It did,' said Ony. 'I feel that, too. But what does that matter? There are heaps of pups all across these lands who need care. Once we settle into our new home, we'll go ranging together and bring them back to our group.'

Belka shuffled on her forepaws. 'Our *group*?'

Ony's brow furrowed.

'Are you sure that's the word, Ony?' asked Jayla.

'What do you mean?'

Belka moved closer to him. 'Find out, sweet boy. Summon them now.'

He moved to the yard beyond the barn door. He tipped back his neck and, with a voice that belonged to his ancestors as much as it did his own, he howled into the still summer air.

'Come to me!'

Within moments, the first was there. Then, soon after, the full complement was assembled in the yard, their tails high and eyes alert as they awaited the command to set off running together again.

And as those dogs stood before him – dogs of all ages and sizes, some who'd been pampered as pets and some who'd had to fight for every scrap they'd ever eaten, some old, some young, some ailing, some in their prime – Ony's heart was filled with gladness.

Together, they were going to find a better future. They'd make the time to feel their pain, and together, they would heal.

These wounded animals, united by grief and thankful for an opportunity to start over, were placing their trust in him.

He wouldn't let them down.

They were his pack.

23

HURT PEOPLE

KHARKIV, SOVIET UKRAINE
SUNDAY, 15TH JUNE, 1986

PEACEFULLY NAPPING beneath Sun's heat in the nook of an oak's bulging roots, dreams were just beginning to materialise in Ony's mind when a rabble of young males noisily approached.

Ony stretched out his paws and yawned. 'What is it now?'

Vladimir stepped forwards. 'Buka killed Yakov.'

Lurching upright, Ony bristled. Belka had called it correctly, then. She'd seen it the moment they brought Buka back with them on their trek around the fields north of this new city. Since he was nearing the age of independence, they'd decided to take him to Creche to help him learn how to be more sociable, but mere minutes after they left him there, he'd scrapped with Yakov. 'Those two will keep us busy,' Belka had warned.

The youngsters resumed their raucous shouting but when Ony issued a sharp bark, they fell quiet.

'Vladimir! Tell me what happened.'

A young dog looked down at the ground beneath his paws. 'Me and Yakov found a chicken carcass,' he said.

'We were taking it to the dams in the nursery. Buka jumped down on us from the top of the bins. He bit into Yakov's neck and pulled him onto the ground. He'd already won the fight – Yakov was over on his back! But Buka was too rough. He ripped his throat. Yakov was bleeding, then he was dead.'

The others grew excited again. 'He must be banished, Ony! He must be banished! How can we live peacefully like you say when we're threatened by a devil dog like this?'

'Where's Buka now?'

'At Creche.'

While the familiar stream of grief flowed into his heart for the lost Yakov, Ony made his way across the meadow and rounded the corner of the factory shed.

Pups in all stages of development covered Creche's floor. In the corner were the still-blind newborns Ony found abandoned beneath a hedge where the high tenements sprang from the city's southern suburbs. Near a pile of firewood, Belka was tending to the almost-grown girls she'd found, whose mother went into the tunnels of Metro one day and never emerged again.

Belka sprang forward when Ony entered. 'I thought you wanted to nap before we go searching for pups beneath Bridge?' she said.

'That task will have to wait. Buka!'

A blue-eyed pup with a wiry scruff did not hesitate to come before Ony. He stood, his head low and his tail tucked beneath battle-scarred legs, and softly whimpered while Ony issued the order to walk with him and Belka.

As a trio, they wandered from the outskirts where they resided with their pack, and deeper into the city. It was a journey Belka usually insisted they avoid; warier of people now than she'd been in the past, she allowed it only when insufficient food could be scavenged locally. The city folk were generous with their offerings but, as everywhere, their changeable natures made them dangerous. A two-legged stranger could give love and care in one moment, then in the beat of their mysterious heart have only cruelty and bitterness to offer a dog.

They found the wide pavements of the city blocks thronging with activity. Something of interest was happening in the world of peoplekind, and it was charging the atmosphere with a nervous but excited energy. When the dogs came to a busy square, they stopped.

The human folk were seated on rows of chairs before a giant screen. They all wore the same red garment on their top halves, and waved flimsy pieces of paper in their hands. From tall black boxes at its side, ceaseless chatter boomed out enthusiastically. Whatever was so interesting about men running around a field wasn't clear to Ony or Belka, but the people couldn't pull their eyes away from the screen.

On a patch of soft grass to the side of the square, the dogs lay down.

Buka was fascinated by the people. 'What are they doing?'

'Take it from me, little one,' said Belka. 'You could devote your entire life to trying to understand the business of people and you'd still die ignorant. Now,' she added, 'explain yourself.'

The pup launched into his account of the morning's tragedy. 'When I was walking around the shops I found a big bit of chicken underneath the bins so I put it behind the wheel and I was going to bring it to the nursery like you said Ony but there was a dragonfly and I wanted to catch it and when I came back Vladimir and Yakov had the chicken and said they were going to bring it to the nursery but I wanted to be the one to bring it because I was the one that found it. Yakov always says mean things to me and he always makes fun of mama and when I saw him walking off with it I got really cross and then I didn't even know what was happening and then I had Yakov's blood in my mouth and he was dead.'

Ony sighed. 'Talk to me about your mama.'

The pup began crying. He made to reply, but just then a sudden roar sounded among the people. They leapt out of their seats with fury on their faces. Bottles smashed against the hard tiles. The voice from the black boxes was screaming: 'The Belgians have scored again! The Soviets must find two goals in the next ten minutes to have any chance of making it through to the quarter final!'

Buka cowered, but Ony gave him a lick. 'It's alright. Ignore them.'

'A man put food down for her,' whined the pup. 'But when she took it, he grabbed her neck with a hoop and put her in his car and then I never saw her again.'

Belka placed a paw on the pup as he lay whimpering, then glanced sadly over to Ony.

'What did you feel when you saw that happen?' said Ony.

'No dog wants to see their mama suffer. It hurt me more than anything else possibly could.'

Again, the crowd exploded with noise; this time, even Ony and Belka recoiled. But the people weren't furious now – mysterious beings that they were, they were now in ecstasy. 'Belanov scores from a penalty! Can the Soviets do it? Nine minutes to level the score!'

The dogs held themselves with a state of high alertness. Too disturbed by the chaos of the humans, they remained silent a while until they were sure they weren't in harm's way.

Ony put his face close to Buka's. 'I'm not an old dog,' he said. 'This is only my third summer. But I know so much now that I didn't before. And there is one thing, above everything else, that I wish somebody had told me when I was a boy of your own age, and that is that hurt dogs hurt other dogs.'

The pup's head tilted to the side.

'Think about it, little one. It's the dogs who are hurt the most that go on to cause hurt. You've done a bad thing, Buka. A very bad thing. But what happens next is up to you. You can find a way to break this terrible cycle of pain, or you can go on hurting others, and destroy yourself.'

'Were you hurt, Ony?' asked Buka.

'I was.'

'So how did you do it? Break the cycle, I mean.'

Ony brought his snout into Belka's neck. 'I was lucky. I had a very fine girl who refused to give up on me. And through the hurt we suffered together, we learnt something very important: that if we cared about others as we care for ourselves, there would be a lot less pain in our world. Run along back to Jayla now, little one. The angst of the people is about to burst out again.'

Sure enough, just as Buka skipped away a commotion of booing and angry jeers lifted up above the crowd in the square. One man, staggering away on unsteady legs with a bright green bottle in his hands, was weeping. 'It's been stolen from us!'

Everywhere, glass was smashing. Some folk were throwing fruit at the screen, which exploded in violent bursts of red. Looking up at it, Ony and Belka tried to comprehend the images. Some of the men on the field were crying tears of joy, others tears of sorrow. Onto the heads of them all, sparkling particles of coloured paper came raining down from the sky.

'That's it!' the voice from the black boxes was yelling. 'The Belgians have done it! It's all over for the Soviet Union!'

Belka stood and paced away. 'They're such mysterious creatures, aren't they, Ony? Do you think it's the same with them? Do hurt people hurt other people?'

But Ony couldn't possibly know the answer to that.

THE END.

HISTORICAL NOTE

> *"There has been an accident at the Chernobyl Nuclear Power Plant. One of the reactors has been damaged. Measures are being taken to deal with the incident, and help is being given to those affected. The government has formed a commission of inquiry."*

If you were a citizen of Soviet Ukraine in 1986, it's likely the first you officially heard about the world's worst nuclear meltdown was in the above news bulletin. Delivered blankly by a woman with copper-coloured hair almost three days after the accident, her report, which lasted just 14 seconds, was buried deep in the programme, after her colleague had first read out long lists of worker awards and agricultural notices.

Downplaying the crisis was par for the course: as far as Moscow was concerned, it was *business as usual*, and the Workers' Day Parade through the streets of Kyiv – just 70 miles away from the smouldering reactor – went on as planned. But machines in foreign countries were beginning to detect something more serious.

With toxic confetti spreading from Pripyat, Moscow was soon forced to admit the scale of the incident. The alarm now sounded, Soviet leaders wished for a quick end to this embarrassing episode – restoring the Soviet Union's wounded pride was of the utmost importance. The task of safely extinguishing the poisonous inferno was greater than anybody could have imagined, however, so, with firefighters overwhelmed, military and civilian teams were transported to the site to help contain the crisis.

These so-called 'liquidators' were taken from all walks of life, and were assigned a wide variety of duties – from drivers and fence builders to miners and doctors. Numbering somewhere around 800,000 individuals, the average official age of a clean-up worker was 34.3 years old.

The youngest helpers were fifteen.

Accommodating the vast quantity of liquidators was a major operation. The Fairytale Young Pioneer Camp was one of many facilities used for the purpose. Originally intended as a resort for the children of plant workers to learn new skills in their summer holidays, the camp contained a gym, sports courts, an outdoor pool and an open-air stage. Along with everything else within the 1000-mile wide Exclusion Zone, Camp Fairytale – and its three-headed dragon monument – is now abandoned, destined to rot into the poisoned forest floor.

The scale of the damage inflicted upon the natural world by the Chernobyl disaster is staggering, not least in Ukraine, Belarus and Russia, where radioactive particles are forecast to remain in the environment at low levels for thousands of years to come.

The impact of the accident went far beyond the localised region, however. Some 200,000 km2 of Europe was contaminated in the days following the reactor explosion, with radioactive pollution appearing as far away as the lochs of Scotland.

In terms of wildlife, many animals died from radiation poisoning, either by proximity to the power plant or via the food chain; to this day, reports are made of genetic abnormalities in the region's flora and fauna. In addition to these 'natural' causes, many exterminator teams were sent to the region in the aftermath of the accident to prevent the spread of nuclear contamination. Dogs were killed en masse in this extermination drive – and it's safe to say few animals suffered under the wider Soviet regime as much as Man's Best Friend.

When the Red Army classified canines as military equipment in 1924, dogs were assigned supporting tasks including transportation, tracking, and sledding the injured. They were also, however, utilised as weapons of war. To repel invading tanks, dogs were fitted with bomb vests, wired up to explosive devices, and trained to run at oncoming vehicles. Soldiers then fired the detonators.

As a strategy, this proved ineffective. Often, riflemen inside the tanks were able to simply shoot the animals dead from a distance. In other instances, the dogs blew up tanks on the Soviet's own side, having become used to the smell of the specific fuel burned by their masters' training vehicles. This practice was eventually brought to an end – though not until 1966.

Dogs also played a vital role in the Soviet space programme. In 1958, Laika become the first dog to complete an orbit of Earth. She was never returned home, however, and was just one of many canines to lose their lives this way.

What happened at Chernobyl 35 years ago has left a scar upon the human spirit as much as it has upon the physical landscape.

Several major investigations into how the catastrophe could have happened reveal a regrettable truth: that human error played a significant role in the accident. Human pride, however, should not be dismissed in this tragic story; the Chernobyl disaster was not a one-off incident. Great effort was made to cover up several other tragedies throughout the Soviet Union, each resulting in loss of life and grave damage to the natural world.

The concealing of a major accident allows for lessons to go unlearned – and where lessons go unlearned, more, potentially worse, accidents are bound to happen. It's perhaps fitting, then, to consider the political impact of the disaster: some, including the former leader of the Soviet Union, Mikhail Gorbachev, speculate that the disaster at Chernobyl set in motion a chain of events which ultimately led to the collapse of the Soviet Union and the end of communism.

With all this said, it is worth remembering that serious nuclear accidents are extremely rare.

There are currently 440 nuclear reactors in the world. In over six decades, there have been only three major reactor accidents.

Nevertheless, 440 reactors means 440 dragons.

These terrifying creatures are sleeping now.

Let's hope they never wake up.

ACKNOWLEDGMENTS

For their part in bringing this novel to life, I'd like to say thank you to the following:

Firstly, to the street strays of Bangkok, whose morning assemblies provided the initial spark of this story.

To my friends and family, for their ongoing love, support and encouragement.

To John Duffy, Peter Whiten and Gary Stanyard, for assistance and feedback during early drafts of this novel, and to Alasdair McLeod, Kristen Bond, Pamela Whiten, Priya Mandalia, Neil Alexander, Millicent Marriner and Victoria Lane for supporting my other writing.

To Viktorija Čeliković, for her wonderful cover illustration.

Sincere thanks are owed to my fabulous editor, Lisa Edwards, whose unwavering belief in this novel helped make it what it is.

I owe a huge debt to the Duffys (John, Rosie, Lily and Jack) for their endless kindness and support. Running in this pack is always a joy.

Finally, my biggest thanks are reserved for my wife, Charlotte, for everything she continues to do to make my writing better, and for keeping the dream alive.

ABOUT THE AUTHOR

Born in Wales in 1980, Justin Morgan has been a storyteller since he learned to talk.

Justin has studied Creative Writing at undergraduate and masters level, and qualified as a secondary school teacher in 2007. He has taught literature and language to students in eight countries, including three former-Soviet republics.

Living in Gaddafi's Libya, Justin first found a readership as a blogger. A terrifying evacuation at the onset of the civil war, however, inspired him to make the leap into writing novels.

Some of Justin's favourite adventures include tracking big cats in India and Brazil, staying with a remote hill tribe on Borneo, and travelling back to the UK from Indonesia without once boarding a plane. (It took four months, in case you're wondering.)

FOR MORE INFORMATION ABOUT JUSTIN AND HIS BOOKS, VISIT:
justin-morgan.mailchimpsites.com

The "ANIMAL EYES" Trilogy

Man-made disasters, as seen by nature's most defenceless victims.

The Dogs of Chernobyl

(Animal Eyes 1)

Animal Eyes 2

(Spring 2022)

Animal Eyes 3

(Summer 2022)

+

The Road to Chernobyl:

Ball Boy and Red Cross Girl

IF YOU ENJOYED THIS BOOK, KINDLY CONSIDER LEAVING A REVIEW ONLINE.

IT WOULD BE SINCERELY APPRECIATED.

THANK YOU.

Made in the USA
Coppell, TX
28 March 2022

75678936R00152